There is a seagull in my wheelie bin.

Why is there a seagull in my wheelie bin?

Closing and opening the bin is not helping the situation. It's Monday morning, 7.23 am. I am, well, was in the middle of emptying the contents of the bin, all the stuff from the kitchen over the weekend. I am not late for work but I do not have nearly enough time to fully deal with this seagull situation. The bins, usually, are emptied on a Friday and I am fairly confident of the bin usually being empty of a Monday morning. I live on my own. It is my bin. I take full responsibility for the contents of the bin.

This is an outrage.

I am standing in the forecourt of my own house, in pyjamas, burgundy cotton dressing gown and rather nice, if you don't mind me saying so, leather slippers of the kind Noel Coward might be seen wearing whilst playing a ditty at the piano forte. I am hardly dressed for the 'bin run'. Do I normally peer into the bin before putting rubbish inside? Of course I was expecting it to be empty but today? I peered in. What was it? The slight shifting of unexpected weight at the bottom of the bin or the more the subtle fishy nature exuded by the dead bird, the stench clearly had been building since the bird arrived in the bin. I am also not ashamed to say that the very first thought that flit across my mind was that a dead bird should really be in the compostables bin rather than just general rubbish.

At first glance I would classify a dead bird as food waste.

A split second after that, I realised that it was a dead seagull. I spend this precious moment, in my little forecourt outside my little terraced house, genuinely now wondering how on earth a seagull arrived. I keep saying 'arrived' as if it were some passenger on a train and it has....what....disembarked? Into the bin out of choice? A little seagull suitcase under the wing, a stamped ticket in its beak!

First thing I do on slamming the lid shut, is look around. It is nearly 7.30 am. Most of my neighbours, by now, are readying themselves for the drive to work, the great exodus. This is no time for curtain twitching, no time for a stifled laugh at the miserable, befuddled neighbour now contemplating a dead bird in his wheelie bin.

The wrong bin.

I sneak a peek again at the bird. I mean, it is definitely dead. I'm no expert but its neck is at some eccentric, unnatural angle and the smell is so sickly sweet. I don't like the fact that the bird's eye is open, looking back at me, somehow blaming me for its current position. Hmm, It's unlikely that he crashed into the bin itself or that someone trapped the bird in there, still alive. Had that happened there'd be seagull guano at the bottom of the bin and 'signs of a struggle'. Currently there are none.

Hey, look at me, a proper 'Quincy'.

So it must have been already dead when it went into the bin. What I would like to think is that some benevolent soul, just walking along the Avenue, spies a dead seagull and then perhaps this kind soul, alert to the sensibilities of passing small children, would pick up the bird, look for the nearest receptacle and place it inside. A kind deed both for the local children and also according some respect to the dead animal 'One of God's creatures, they might have thought'. Of course, as I peer over the little wall at the edge of my forecourt, I see no evidence of a dying bird. Like? A chalk outline of a dead bird. (surely spread eagled!! is that racist to birds) – or perhaps shell casings? Scarlet pools of blood? Police tape around a cordon? I can only think of a more sinister route for the bird . It is clearly a Mafia warning of some kind. I'm sure they use horses' heads for rich mobsters but perhaps more prosaic, cheaper animals for the little people although now I am thinking how I have so wronged the local Mafia.

(perhaps for posting a poor review on Trustpilot for the local Italian restaurant. I mean I did do that but that tiramisu was just inexcusable, a stodgy clumpy mess of a sweet and not the angelic light sponge that was promised – note to self – in future keep thoughts about local Italian food to myself.)

No! there is a much more likely cause for a dead seagull [arriving] in my bin.

The wrong bin.

It is that ghastly man, the Weasel, the most bigoted man in Christendom who just happens to live three doors down from me! I bet a bird landed in his poisonous garden and he's simply picked it up, no doubt transported, wrapped up in a well-thumbed Daily Mail, and as nonchalantly as you like just dumped it in, being smart enough to take the paper with him. Yes, that'll be it.

Definitely.

I contemplate for a few moments on what to do with the bird. Should I wrap it up? Is it even legal to put a bird in a bin? I do put the carcass of my roasted chicken in the bin but it doesn't feel the same somehow. I start lowering my two full white bags from the kitchen, their plastic ties now leaving a real impression upon my fingers, directly onto the bird. I can feel a slight yield from the bird under the bags and I feel that is as much as I can deal with this morning. I slam the lid shut.

Mrs G walks past. She is a substitute primary teacher. She drags a little wheelie trolley behind her full of marked school books.

-Morning Henry – waving as she passes – lovely morning -

-Oh absolutely, first class – I say just for something to say.

She continues on with her little trolley to her little car. I watch her go but still thinking about the bird in the bin. The street light which is directly outside my bedroom switches itself off. It's had enough. I take that as my cue to scuttle back into the house. I give my hands an extra vigorous wash but this does nothing to get rid of the image of the splayed bird. I rush to get myself ready, now eyeing the sky before deciding to take an umbrella with me, and scoot out of the house.

•

The walk isn't far. I don't know why everyone else doesn't walk. Here's me pounding the pavement and with each confident stride in my Hush Puppies I am walking past streams of cars. More often than not these cars are over-sized, fat, German cars, exhaust fumes spewing from them all. They, in the cars, are stuck in their wheeled cubes. The freedom of the car has enslaved them. Who is driving? Mum….even if it is a Dad. Angry Mums, some barely dressed, barely out of bed and now driving their tiny, tiny embryonic sprogs all belted up in the back, peering out through a rain-streaked window. What experience is that for a new life? Their wriggling tadpole legs starting to atrophy through lack of use. This is the automotive scrum for an available space outside the school.

There are clear guidelines on the road, painted on in great big orange letters and on signs next to the road.
Very clear.
Abundantly clear.
No Parking. No Stopping. No dropping off. But definitely no stopping, ever. Simple simple simple yet outside the school gates these monster trucks will stop. The drivers will do their best to not make eye contact with the poor old traffic monitor who is outside the school gates – some poor benighted soul drinking tea from a thermos, clutching themselves for warmth and definitely not signing up to do this job.
-Oh but, I'm literally stopping for just one second – the little tyke at the back, struggling on their own to get out of the armour plated door whilst the mother stays in her seat, in the warm, revving the engine to keep the heater nice and toasty and not giving two hoots about global warming whilst simultaneously checking her status on Face Arse or

whatever it's called. Once she somehow hears the door click closed, over the ferocious blast of the heater and the throbbing V8 she is straight onto the gas with ne'er a rearward glance to even see if it was safe to drive off. In her wake other little children are committing the heinous crime of walking to school without an armed escort and having to dodge, like ninjas, the off-road tyres of the behemoths, driving as if they are off to invade a small but politically repellent country that happens to produce oil.

I watch this ballet on a fairly regular basis. If ever I am actually involved with it I can only watch through the cracks between my fingers. Although all of the local children who come to the local school have to live locally, very few of the children actually walk to school. The parents often think it too dangerous. The omnipresent threat of paedophiles who are surely the biggest threat around. I mean the whole place is swarming with them, like a paedoapocalypse! There they are on every corner, all dressed like Fagin or Nosferatu simply snatching children and then stuffing them into an already bulging hessian sack.
Surely!
So, in order to avoid this obvious menace, most children are driven the less-than-a-mile to the school. Yes, yes, I know the obvious answer would be that one or other of the parents

could chaperone their own child, this child, the apple of their eye, the object that they hold most dear in all of the world, worth more than diamonds and gold...but no....paedophiles and too much traffic. The walk is too dangerous. -We don't want to walk – they say – Walking, surely, is for losers [see: Poor People] – so they must drive to school, for protection of their own child, that they love so much, in a 4x4 armoured vehicle so their own little mite is safe but these people, these child-loving people clearly have not one care for anyone else's child. They do not think for a nanosecond, not a scintilla of empathy wasted looking out for all children. No! Dear God No! Only MY genes must survive! Mine, you hear! And then, in their giant moon buggies, they all seethe and gnash their collective teeth because? Because everyone else has had the same idea to drive their own sweet youngling to school and so now there is nowhere to park, no space in which to move because the local roads were built to accommodate Morris Oxfords from the 1940's.

So there they sit and clog the roads like a selfish, self aware thrombosis, revving their engines. On top of this there is the additional seething from watching all the people walk by them, getting to school before them. Finally, when their withered progeny make it to school they are either too weak or small or, likely due to eating crisps for breakfast, they arrived puffed up and fat and getting fatter with every car journey and the kindly parents are blind to the real and present dangers of type 2 diabetes and childhood obesity with their children's livers bursting with human foie gras.

Once, when I was young and very much undisillusioned with the world, I tackled a mother who had driven up to the school gates waiting to drop off her dumpling of a child. I helpfully suggested, just suggested mind, that sitting in a car just outside the school gates with the engine on might not be good for the health of all the children waiting in line outside the gates. The look I was given, once she deigned to make eye contact through the bullet proof glass, was withering. She instantly saw me as a man and concluded from this quick assessment that I was fair game, a possible and therefore probable sex offender/paedophile. She pressed the button to lower the window a full two centimetres and I tried to press home the point that although her little mite (I said 'child' of course – had I said 'mite' she would have just run me over) would be safe in the car everyone outside the car would be at increased risk. Could she possibly park the car somewhere?

-No spaces mate – was all she could say before looking back down at her phone.

I was not her 'mate'. I would never want to be her 'mate' in any sense or meaning of the word.

-Erm – I continued – There may be spaces further away?-

The next street, the next town, preferably the next galaxy?

-And you can walk in from there?-

Her look intensified. She mustered up all the hatred that she had within herself.

She said -Walk? – well, actually she screamed -Walk!!!!- as if I had asked her to walk over disease filled glass syringes and I was simultaneously threatening her children with poisoned sweets.

Perhaps I had misjudged the situation. Was this woman disabled? I did have on my school identity/security badge, now the last bastion against terrorism and authority, along with a fluorescent jacket. I, as a teacher had looked after and educated this very child that cowered, in the back of her car. I had taught this child and yet if I suggested that the mother's behaviour might possibly change, be slightly less selfish.....I saw in her eyes that she would gleefully stab me in the heart with a blunt pencil and think nothing of it, in fact should would revel in this action such was her disdain of me and everything I stood for. The social contract in some people is as nothing. They exist only to be as selfish as they can be and any barriers placed in front of them like, say, public laws, social norms and conventions can be run through and not even think for one moment that their behaviour is in any way wrong or, indeed, how it might be viewed by their tiny offspring from the back of an armoured vehicle.

So, today, I watch this ballet and whether I intervene or not, nothing will change and no-one will care and we will all be ground into the dust. I see myself wiser that Canute, in full knowledge that the tide will always come in. In fact I have been called Canute in the past....or something similar.

•

Anyway, today, yes, October and still the lingering hint of summer past but the first day with a little nip in the air. There is the merest hint of the world falling apart, the smell of fallen leaves, of decay, the dry crunch under the feet. A disassembly of nature.

I have my briefcase, hush puppies, a grey woollen tank top, a light striped collarless shirt and a black mac. Briefcase in my right hand, an aluminium stick in my left, for walking. I also sport a black felt fedora with a thick crepe band.

Do I need the stick? I do not. Does my whole ensemble age me? Terribly. But therein lies the point of the exercise. I am at the thicker end of my forties and yet I dress as if I am stumbling at the fag end of a long and hard career. Why would I do this? A number of reasons.

Humour me.

Firstly, older people have the most comfortable clothes, by far. Everything is elasticated or fleece lined. Easy zips and a generous fit. Older people will generally have gone through their lives, victims of fashion either from tight pointy shoes, uncomfortable and man-made fabrics, too many buttons, harsh colours or fashionable 'fads'. So I have grasped the old person's fit, comfortable shoes, layers, trousers with a bit of give. I am no longer a butterfly, no need to attract and yet I still have to fly. I see myself as one of those end-of-season raggedy moths you see, still flying, still getting the job done.

Secondly, if my clothes are no longer fashionable then they are no longer expensive. If I want colours then I'll wear a scarf or a badge. Colours are an extravagance.

Thirdly, and this is the main reason but I'll put it third so as not to draw attention to it. If I dress smartly but 'old' then in my position I have a little more dignity, a little more 'gravit ars' (thank you Mr Frankie Howerd!). It doesn't change what I say but those who listen take me just a little bit more seriously. They may also be less inclined to talk to me, to badger me.

-Didn't want to interrupt- they might say.

Yes, that's right. At my time of life, time is a scarce commodity and I don't want to waste a second of it talking to dullards. Less people approach me because I appear less approachable. A fabulous outcome for all.

The hat? Well, people barely make eye contact with hat wearers, unless of course it is a baseball cap – we'll save them for later – but a decent fedora. No-one else wears proper hats so I am thought of as a benign eccentric, meeting no-one's eye.

The stick – genius – I felt that if I used a wooden stick, perhaps with a little silver handle then I would straight out of central casting, a Gestapo spy or an old billionaire from the deep south of the USA perhaps with an empire of Fried Chicken to keep up. But the aluminium cane, a modern cane suggests that it is used purely for medical reasons. Oh yes, unspecified disabilities, the king of all disabilities. A symptom of an ageing and diseased frame. Two sticks might engender sympathy from people, opening doors and the like. No. Too much. One stick is enough for people to look and then look away, lest it be contagious. Oh yes, let's play to our basest of instincts. People, seeing disease, even difference from themselves will stay a healthy distance away. There is a clear, evolutionary reason for this. If you stay away from anything where there might be even a hint of it being dangerous and then you survive, well....there you are....you can now pass on your genes and your behaviour allows you and your descendants to survive and prosper. Does this explain racism?*

Well, not excuse it but explain it.

[*Foot note – This is really a side note and perhaps explains racism but does little to move the story forward. I mean, by all means read it but, you know, just a foot note - so Country A and Country B. In Country A you have humans, pure breed and bright green skin. Country B you have pure bred humans with bright blue skin. The two countries are separated by a huge mountain range or a giant mass of ice or an ocean but something pretty insurmountable. One day though, after millennia, a valiant group of strong males from the land of the Greenskins make it to Country B (Bluedesia? Yes, let's call it Bluedesia), climbing a mountain or a building ocean going rafts. What happens? The Blue skinned citizens of Bluedesia are different from the green skinned humans in that they have blue skin. The Greenites do not see those with blue skin them as 99.99999% the same, they just see the very different skin colour. A glaring difference. Evolution has shown us that if you distance yourself from anything different from yourself, you will survive. So, there is a rift. The Greenites are warrior explorers but they are treated badly by the Bludesians. The Greenites exert some force (They are the strong males from the land of the Green after all) and there is a self-fulfilling prophecy. The Bluedesians were right to fear these new people and shun the Greenites as they are seen as dangerous. More Greenites arrive though, strong Greenites and, in small places, start to colonise Bluedesia. Bluedesians are treated like second class citizens by the new and stronger Greenites and so the much larger population of Bluedesians start to riot and rebel against the Greenites. The Greenites see this rioting as merely evidence of dangerous behaviour, behaviour from the Bluedesians who must be subjugated.

Laws are made in Bluedesia but mainly by Greenites, and the nation becomes civilized. Then, hundreds of years later, there is a 'struggle' and the Bluedesians finally, with the help of some benevolent Greenites, gain equal rights. And yet, in Bluedesia (renamed 'Republic of Greater Greenia many years ago) people with blue skin are treated less favourably than people with green skin – there is much rejection of people born with purple skin! – In our bones, in our DNA there is a distrust, there is an abhorrence of anyone who is different. You stick with what you know to survive. The laws that rule everyone in the Republic of Greater Greenia (RGG) were written by Greenites who had not long been in the country of Bluedesia, as was. These laws unconciously favour people formerly known as Greenites and have Green skin. So what do we do? You could, as a Green person, calculate in monetary or land terms by how much the Blue People (Actually the term 'blue people' has been outlawed and it is now more acceptable to say 'people with blue or blueish colouring) – have been damaged, slighted etc but this would be outrageous to the Greens (interestingly not called 'people with green or greenish colouring but still 'Green') as these Greens have been born into the Republic of Greater Greenia (RGG) and it was not these people's fault that their distant forefathers, this land, formerly known as Bluedesia subjugated the 'people with blue colouring' – So, do you get a person from country C, who is unbiased and has no interest in country A nor B?

Country C, known as the Kingdom of Rubidia, with all of its Ruby red skinned inhabitants. But neither the Greens not the People of Blue or Bluish colour completely trust the Rubidians to be completely unbiased – No – perhaps science could provide an answer? It would be important that it is the Green scientists who do the research which will show that despite many years of false and inaccurate suggestions, allowing the Greens to justify their overbearing behaviour against the Blues, historic behaviour saying that Blues were less intelligent, scheming, lazy. Science, the truth, would finally show that the only difference between people with green skin and people with blue skin is that one set of people has green skin and the other set have blue skin. What should then happen is the law makers, mainly green, should tear up all the laws. All monies, all lands should be redistributed in a completely fair and transparent way and there should be a day zero.

Yet, all the time one type of person has the upper hand on another type of person, why would they do that? This would be akin to the Nazis, themselves, in the spirit of fairness, having all of their scientists genetically testing all of their citizens and then ending up with results to say that no citizen is really different from any other and all citizens should be treated the same. However, what with trying to take over the world, the Nazis were too busy in the 1930's and 1940's to explore equality legislation.

So, there are only two ways to solve the Green/Blue problem. One, all blue and green people must intermix leading to a homogenized race of cyan (purple??) coloured people ranging from aqua to teal. Yes, there would be moaners for diversity and both blue and green peoples would be losing their distinct cultural identities. Well, yah boo sucks because as soon as the first Green explorers came ashore in Bluedesia, everyone's cultural identity was changed forever.

Two, aliens from another world would arrive in RGG. The Aliens – Dark Grey in colour, if that is a colour, called Grayns, and terrify Green and Blue people. But these Grayns only recognise light in the infra red and ultraviolet spectra and are therefore unable to distinguish between green and blue. Both the green and blue people are enslaved by the Grayns and they are finally treated as equals.

Three, All people in all countries poke each others' eyes out and as their species (they are all the same species!!!) dies out, another will take over, thank you again Mr Charles Darwin.]

●

The stick is also very good for fending off 'friendly' dogs.

-Oh, he's very friendly. He won't bite- as the uncontrolled little bastard jumps up on my clean trousers with his dirty paws. Yes, a short jab in the side'll sort them out. A little yelp and the owner soon takes them away accompanied with a disapproving glance at me. Good, excellent. It's also good for poking away small, round children should they get too close. Little bastards.

I'm in early at the school. I like being in early. It means I look keen but also I get to avoid a lot of the tedious people. I have brought with me a flask of coffee. Coffee that was freshly ground and which has been pressed this morning using a cafetiere. Nothing fancy but certainly not poisonous instant muck that is provided by the school. Sometimes, if I am in early, sitting in the staffroom, drinking my fresh coffee from my flask, one of the tedious people will come up to me. Today, sadly, is not an exception.

-Oh, fresh coffee. Smells fabulous. I so wish I had the time to make one of those-

So, let's describe the situation here. I am in the staffroom, minding my own business. This young teacher, early twenties, addressing me (there is no-one else in the room) but their focus is on making a coffee with the granules provided by the school. He is clearly not a teacher of English because, I assume, of the superfluous "So" in his sentence.

Unless he has been transported directly here from California where I believe this superfluous "so" is part of the common vernacular, what he is saying here, however clumsy his grammar may be, is that 'I am lazy and I haven't got enough to do, or they actually do not have enough time. If I did answer (I will not) but if I did, here are my options.

1)I got here an hour ago

2) Be more fucking organised! Michaelangelo painted the Sistine Chapel with the same number of hours in the day that you have at your disposal.

I mean, what is it with teachers? Yes, it is a busy and hard job, it may even sometimes be called stressful but some of them, not all, not nearly all, but some are just so disorganised as to make their own jobs, their lives even, more stressful than they need them to be. Some teachers scrape into the profession, not necessarily the brightest of bulbs but they try so very hard. They find the job difficult. It is difficult and hard. Teaching is also, or at least was, a very difficult job to be sacked from. In those dark days you had to be seen buggering the bursar on the headmaster's desk to even get suspended. Nowadays, if a student even suggests you might have touched them inappropriately, you're out. Even if you didn't, everything is over and you'll be swinging by that strong light fitting in your hallway within six months.

No.

If it's just a case of not being able to do it, a teaching job is very difficult to be sacked from. If a poor teacher, and I mean poor in the sense of not being able to teach, is ever challenged about how bad they really are, I mean about how they actually cannot teach, then after many, many classroom 'visits' and 'teaching observations', out come the waterworks, out comes the 'stress' card. – OK, OK, just carry on for now, we'll review your performance in 3 months – but of course this never happens and another year passes by. People go off with stress and then it is their whole career….and the other teachers that have to cover colleagues who are off for stress, go off with stress themselves with the stress of doing two jobs instead of one and so it goes on.

Or you get out, like me.

I sip my coffee. I continue to read my paper. Another one of the dullards comes in. He seems to take up 95% of the space around me. He is young but with thinning hair which he tries to contrive into something fashionable. He is on a hiding to nothing there. There is an unnecessary Terry Nutkins ratio when the thinner the hair is on top the longer it has to be at the back. To my untrained eye he resembles a Grateful Dead roadie. And he is wearing a T-shirt. Jesus, he's a teacher, a professional teacher.

-God, a flask. That's brilliant. Why didn't I think of that?-

Here we go.

You didn't think of it because you're an idiot. I continue holding up my paper, as widely as possible in front of my face. Clearly his proximity indicates that he wishes to engage in a conversation. Why? I can feel him standing there, in front of me. Doesn't he know that in the Universal Declaration of Human Rights if someone has a newspaper, especially a broadsheet, in front of their face then this person clearly has the right not to be disturbed.

He is young. He knows not the etiquette of attracting someone's attention. As far as I am aware he has made a declarative statement and a rhetorical question which hardly merits a response from me.

And yet he still stands there like Ozymandias.

He huffs. This 'huff' is, I have no doubt, to communicate to me that One - he is still there. Two - trying to attract my attention without actually having the wherewithal to do such a thing, on which I am very much relying. But no, he lingers still.

-What?! What is it?!- I have folded down my broadsheet so only my face peeps out over the paper, a nosy neighbour over a fence, a war time Chad or, indeed, an irate visitor to a school wanting very much to be left alone.

-Yeah um it's just that I think... -

He thinks, alleluia, spit it out man!

-...That there might actually be a staff meeting soon but I was just reminding everyone as you know, one of my tasks-

Then he actually did little air quotes with his sausagey fingers in the air around "one of my tasks" as if his entire job was crammed full of little tasks and he barely has time to stop, when in fact no-one had told him to do this clearly self-appointed little task and for him, this sausage fingered Cro-Magnon, the staff meeting was one of the highlights of his week, possibly his life. In fact I imagine someone else in the school, busy, clearly fed up with this ingrate in their face, has come up with this little task and the dimwit is out of their space but now annoying me.

-Great, fantastic thanks.- I gnash, just about able to spit out single words without releasing a whole torrent of vitriol, a torrent which would no doubt aggravate my ulcer. I flicked the paper back up, shields to maximum and continue to try to solve nine across.

•

Staff meetings, in fact any meeting of any kind in any organisation are universally needless. There is always a better and cleverer way to communicate a message. The person leading the meeting wants to put over a message. They have no interest in what the listeners (not active participants) have to say. It may look like they have interest, but they don't. The attendees must attend but usually they know what is going to be in the meeting, it is after all *a fait accomplis* and so they listen. The meeting minutes are sent around 5 minutes after the meeting is finished on some dreary e-mail just in case people didn't understand what was said or, sin of sins, did not attend the meeting. Meetings do however serve a more sociological purpose.

My guilt, such as it is, means that I have to thrust my partially consumed paper into my briefcase and trundle along to the hall where the meeting is held. Fortunately as it is a meeting before school there is the hard deadline of the school bell limiting the length of the meeting. Meetings after school? Don't get me started. They're just there to chew up acres of time and are all, without exception, utterly pointless. Dare I not attend?

My actions are as slow as possible. I drained my cup before replacing it back on my flask but I really don't feel as if I have the energy to even get up out of the chair. The dullard has gone, flicking his long hair in his wake and now in the staff room it is just me. I mean, I'm not even here to teach just to bloody assess. I don't even need to go to this meeting.

Actually, looking around, I see I'm not alone in the staff room. In the little alcove there is a woman. I can only see the back of her, at the perpetually active photocopier. This is the modern day equivalent of a donkey in a wheel drawing water from a well. Goodness where would we all be without photocopiers? Oh yes, much less paperwork, more actual study and far less waste. My heart always sinks a little just hearing that worn old machine on the verge of a breakdown, but then aren't we all on the verge of a breakdown but at least, for the copier, there's an engineer on call. There it is, just churning out reams of Maths worksheets for year eight. A geography quiz for year 9 just to be stuck in a book and completely forgotten about until tomorrow when it all starts again. The tottering towers of virgin paper shoved into the drawers of the machine like dough into an oven. In it goes, press copy times thirty. I mean there used to be such things as textbooks where the whole syllabus for a course would be laid out for a student. The teacher might write notes on a board, notes that the student might write down. There would be a discussion even, lively repartee...but now, we need a worksheet because someone in government has deemed it so. Textbooks gone, irrelevant, dated and surely much more expensive than copying out three thousand random worksheets of dubious quality everyday(!) Some children can't even fill in or read worksheets... but then that is where I come in.

In fact the woman, girl, lady who was at the photocopier was purposely not attending the staff meeting either and yet her body language, as much as I could see of it, was very much not hurrying, not rushing. It might even be that if she finishes off the copying, she might not even go to the meeting at all.

This is an outrage.

Non-attendance of the meeting is a capital offence. The judge dons the black handkerchief. But there she was, perhaps blissfully unaware of her crime, but surely she heard the dullard when he came in with his little task to remind everyone. No, she must be admin, must be. In fact when she turns around she'll have little pods in her ears I bet she's doing photocopying for the head. Yes. Must be….

Finally, with a great wheeze and expiration, the machine churns out the last of its copies. The woman grabs her pleasingly warm output from the machine and, I look, no pods in the ears, and then she comes and sits down next to me. Not near me, not opposite me, next to. I retreat back to my paper, my defence mechanism, crossing my legs. I sense imminent interaction.

-Are you skipping the staff meeting as well?- she said as she leaned in, lending a conspiratorial air to what she was saying.
-Erm, well-
-Ah, now – She parried- You can't say 'erm, well' because that's exactly what our mutual friend said just now when you skewered him, and you're certainly not a dullard now, are you?-

I felt as if I was being railroaded here. She picked up her photocopying in both hands, tidying the pile up around the edges, as a news reader might do at the end of the news when the lights go down.- shuffle shuffle- and she sat back down.

-I've seen you here before- she said.

-That is possible. I have been here before- I stared onwards at the crossword, clinging to it like wreckage at sea.

-Well yes but, you're not a teacher-

This was puzzling. Was I being grilled or at the very least lightly toasted?

-Erm, I was a teacher, I might have the air of a teacher perhaps?-

-Oh no- she said. She seemed very certain about this - You are clearly dressing up like a teacher or at least the perceived stereotype of a teacher. No, if anything, you are wearing a costume but I'm not sure why-

If I had feathers to spit I would have spat them all out. But OK, I'll raise the ante.

-If we're talking about costumes, what's with your costume them, black and red jumper, black woollen mini skirt set off with red and white trainers. Dennis the Menace!-

-Oooh, so close! And there was me thinking you were a little cleverer and a little brighter than these other... dullards-

Did she say dullards? Is she reading my mind?

-I was thinking there about introducing myself – she said - but come on, Dennis the Menace!?-

I found myself scrabbling in the water; mind games. Blank. Was I being challenged by this woman? Why was I trying to think not of Dennis but...

-Minnie the Minx! The beret! Sorry-

-You see, that's better, but really it's the fact that you noticed it was a costume! – And quick as a flash she asked - And who you supposed to be, Doctor Doom? The Gestapo officer in 'Raiders of the Lost Ark?' If I saw your palm would it have one side of the headpiece for the staff of Ra?-

-What!? I'm not wearing a costume, Miss... er... - But she didn't get the hint and she didn't introduce herself.

-Yes, but I can see, the black mac, the proper leather shoes, the grey... what is that...a sort of a tank top? Grey! These clothes age you terribly... I'd say, if I didn't know you better, that by wearing old clothes you were trying to disappear, yes, that's it. If we taped up your face with stretchy bandages, stuck on a pair of sunglasses, you be a dead ringer for the Invisible Man!-

For once I lifted my eyes from my crossword and looked at my interrogator. I was actually speechless, I mean, I could get this abuse at home. Actually I couldn't because there was no-one at home apart from me.

She had a sparkle though. Her face was closer than any face I've encountered recently apart from my own which doesn't count. And yes, I am really quite short-sighted and if I see anything out of the corner of my eye there is quite the prisming effect in that anything in the corner of my vision starts small but should they get closer, moving in to my central vision, then they get much larger very quickly. I then react by moving away, feeling under attack and then people then move away from me thinking I'm a madman flinching at shadows and spectres. But to look at this woman. There was.....something.

I remember, as child, at Christmas, a table, usually backed into a corner and on the table would be a jigsaw puzzle. It was left there as soon as school broke up for Christmas. A thousand pieces was usually the maximum size. It was my mum who loved them. She went out especially to buy a new one and they were often jigsaws of great works of art. 'The Kiss' by Klimt or 'The Sunflowers' by Van Gogh. I remember one year we had the 'A Bar at the Folies Bergère' by Manet, the girl surrounded by everyone drinking, having fun but all we saw in the picture was the mournful girl and we saw everything in the mirrors.

There was Mum, a crooked paper hat atop her head with a sherry in hand. The edge pieces would be done whilst cooking Christmas lunch. That was usually just a matter of pulling the pieces out of the bag and assembling the two piles. There was much heralding when the corner pieces were found. But then she might stand up for a bit, look down on the puzzle, concentrate on one area, hold a piece in her hand, hold it up to her eye and look at the picture on the box. She would then look at the colours and then scan the pieces for similar colours. She would then have a group of similar coloured pieces which she would then put together. If she got two or three pieces together she would put the sherry down and, never taking her eyes off the group of pieces, carry on. She might be there for hours.

When I was very young I really didn't have the patience but as I grew, and if I wanted to spend time with Mum, I just had to get into it. I had a different strategy. I tended to look for the details on each piece and so I would often find faces or hands, pieces with writing on. This particular jigsaw, the girl at the bar, I remember that I found parts of her face on different pieces, five or six pieces. There was an ear but her ear seemed too large. One eye or one piece was different from another. The hairline on its own seemed far too high. The teeth or lips were far too small and so I just didn't make the connexion between the pieces but, with other pieces in place it became obvious they were the only ones that would fit and of course they clicked together. Of course the ear was there and yes the lips were full, yes the eyes were different but they worked and when I looked at my own eyes in a mirror… I could see that they were different. Different shape from each other, one higher than the other. Of course. How did I not see that before? I clicked the five or six pieces into the space with confidence.

-Oh lovely, well done- and she would often pat the new pieces down as if to welcome them back together or just in lieu of patting me on the head for a job well done. Then, a decent bit done, we put a cloth over the pieces and come back to it, with fresh eyes tomorrow.

The first Christmas after Mum died Dad didn't buy a new puzzle.

-Load of old nonsense- he'd say- You just put the pieces together. And then take them apart. Utterly pointless.

So I took out one of the puzzles we'd done before, out of the sideboard. It was the 'Great wave off Kanagawa by Hokusai. I somehow managed to shuffle the table to the edge of the room by myself. I tipped the pieces out, separating out the edge pieces from the others. I then constructed the edge and then wept for what felt like hours. The outside was complete but the inside was all jumbled up.

So, I look at this young woman, her orange hair in those red bowed bunches with a black beret. Her face unfairly curved but at the edge of my glasses and if we took each individual element, yes, her over pink ears stuck out a little.

She put a few strands of her hair over the ears, consciously or subconsciously to put the ears in the shade.

Her mouth was certainly big, too big, underneath a deep philtrum but behind the lips stayed those teeth which were big and white with a definite overbite.

Her nose, dainty but long and when she spoke certain words I could see the very tip of her nose move downwards, words like -OR, BOAR, SAW - elongated vowel sounds. Her eyes bulged ever so slightly and we're certainly big and bright, not quite light bulbs but they had a look of slight panic. Her chin was...not small, not quite Mr Punch like but not a rounded point either. But, now turning my head a little more and then noticing one ear had an attached lobe and one was not. She was suddenly the girl at the bar at the Folies Bergère. All the different pieces. That enigmatic girl on her own in a world of people, all the elements seem to fit together perfectly. I felt slightly giddy. Who was this?? I had glanced down to look at her name badge, as is the modern day trend to find out someone's name. But this was not without its dangers.

-Are you looking at my chest?- she said, knowing full well that I was.

-Er, um —

- And you had the temerity to skewer that young man for an 'er, um'-

- Actually (Get a grip man, it's a woman and a very ballsy, confident woman at that but she is not the Gestapo), -I was just trying to look at your name badge-

-Or you could actually ask my name instead of using that as a flimsy pretence at ogling-

-Miss Fields, Lillian-

-Ah, okay, and you work in what, admin?-

I regretted saying this the instant the words left my mouth and saw the look on her face.

-Would you like me to get you a spade perhaps so you can dig yourself a deeper hole?-

-But...-

-So, 7 out of 10 for recognising that I was in costume but you guessed wrong and minus a gazillion points for assuming that because I'm a woman using a photocopier but not in the staff meeting I am a ditzy admin bird-

-I never said 'ditzy'. Your word, not mine!-

-Indeed- she said - but still-

I said nothing. I froze.

Oh for God's sake man say something intelligent, witty, even erudite but say something! This is the most interesting conversation you've had for years.

- I'm sorry but I was just distracted by your.... ear lobes-

She squashed her eyes into the shape of almonds with her smile.

-Okay...- she said slowly, not quite sure where this was going... - Yes, you noticed that one is attached and one is not. So you noticed the costume and the ears. Mmm... this is good... Potentially-

Good for what? But I couldn't ask that.

-It's asymmetry you know. We all have it in our bodies to a certain extent. They do say that men and women who have very symmetrical faces are much more beautiful but anodyne and not really very interesting, but our hearts are on one side, liver on the other but then some people have organs where they shouldn't. For instance I have three kidneys. The spare one is floating about-

What? I thought. Where is that going? Is that even a thing? I must have looked puzzled. A quiet moment passed and she moved to get up and grab her photocopying.

-Gullible- she finally said.

-Oh yeah, right, okay, hahaha. Of course, I mean who has three kidneys. You got me-

-No, I do have three kidneys- she said - but look, nine across, 'Seagull! I bleated, inside those who can be taken in' Gullible-

She was right. She was absolutely right. Who was this woman? I took the pen and wrote it in, finished.

-Thank you-

-You're welcome- she said.

She was about to go. Time was pressing. Do I tell her? If you don't tell her then this moment will be nothing but a cherished memory, nothing more.

-I think the seagull bit put me off-

-Seagull?- She cocked her head slightly, one orange bunch hanging down.

-Well, this morning, I went out to put my rubbish in the bin and... there was a seagull in there....-

I waited. Did she now think that I was actually a lunatic and she should slowly back away now. Her head stayed tilted.

-That is probably the most interesting thing I've heard for some time. Tell me more...

She sat back down and I told her what there was of this story. My theories, the wrong bin and so on. And, yes, I might have embellished the story for comic effect and, yes, she was kind enough to listen, not interrupt and whether it was the subject of the story or just how it was told, she listened and probably noticed that I rarely told stories to anyone.

The bell rang and from nowhere people streamed into the room, breaking the spell. Lillian quickly gathered up her copying and went to go.

Act man, act!

-Oh, erm…..Lillian, will I see you again?- I was still sitting but now facing her, she with her sheaf of copying clutched to her chest.

-Well, of course- she said and I smiled uncontrollably.

-But you don't know my…

-You are Mr H Green… I'm guessing Henry?-

Again, I was slightly lost for words, indicated thus by my cod fish mouth…

-There is an H Green signed in as the only visitor at Reception-

Oh. She's good.

-And also, Henry, if you are pretending to use a stick, at least keep using the same hand. Not very convincing otherwise- And with that she strode out of the room, Minnie the Minx. I looked up at the big clock. I had just two minutes to find the inimitable Mrs Croxford!

•

I'm not late, of course I am not late. She needs me more than I need her. As the staff room clears out I may as well stay sat down. It's easier for her to find me. If I go off and try to find her, well don't I look needy. I learned all this from my predecessors, older women (Over fifty, always over fifty) with the cardigan, always wool, and the scarf. Women who do my job always wear scarves. The age and size of the scarf very much depends on the age and size of the woman. My direct predecessor was on the larger size, big cardigan and the scarf would hide, if hide is the right word, camouflage perhaps, the wattle of an older lady.

When I was younger and keen I would go up to London each year. There, at the start of term in September is the National Conference where all the assessors would turn up. The array, the sheer variety of scarves was astonishing. It must be similar to the feeling an explorer gets, hacking through a previously unknown part of the Amazon forest and there, one last hack with the machete and happening on a natural clearing and seeing just the dizzying amounts of birds and colours on display. It would blind the eyes and dazzle the brain.

Of course there are the elegant women, and all of them are women except me, with couture fitted dresses and the lightest of Hermes scarves, lightly knotted around the neck. Then to the older and dare I say shabbier end, a big old grizzly brown cardigan and a self knitted frilly scarf out of yellow mohair. But there is always a scarf. I am an outcast there anyway, being the only man doing this job. Shunned; appalling sexism and so I thought I was suffering because I did not wear a scarf. So one year I tried. I thought that I couldn't wear a big winter scarf as I might look like Rupert the Bear. Also I might overheat. So I went with a sort of thin knitted cravat which I thought was OK, relatively smart, with it just loose around my neck, a sort of teal colour. When I was there and they looked at me I definitely heard braying. Some women wiping tears from their eyes whilst one in particular, in a stage whisper said... -Looks like Albert Steptoe!-

The whole sociological art of wearing of scarves is a complete mystery to me. Perhaps a subject for a PhD?

Perhaps.

I no longer wear the scarf nor do I attend the conference. Still, because my predecessor was an old school battle-axe (she expected her room to be ready, all the equipment ready, students to be prompt, tea and biscuits to be provided regularly and still, deigning to turn up at all, she charged a huge amount for her services) Mrs Croxton knew that I was much less trouble and so I really could get away with anything. But I didn't, I am a professional. Of course. And here comes la Croxton!

-Oh, Mr. Green, I am so sorry there, hope you haven't been waiting long, really-

You see, really she's doing me a favour. She could get anyone in to do this, she could but... it's as if I'm the Prodigal Son returned home, the fatted calf slain for my mere presence. Oh Frabjous day, Calloo Callay!

-It's your usual room today. Hope that's okay?-

I've only ever been in one room

-Fine fine fine-

Poor old Mrs Croxton. Yes, a little frilly scarf, of course and, dare I say, a little frumpy dress and always with the strange shoes. Today it's ballerina pumps. She must be in her late 50s, face always flushed but she's been saddled with the job of having Additional Support as part of her role. As if ordinary support wasn't enough. No, it must be Additional. Really, these two words are 'special code' for all staff.

Students 40 or 50 years ago... and actually in my lifetime, I remember it at school, did not have 'additional support'. I suppose this is allied to the Victorians not believing in having a 'care in the community' policy for the mentally ill and seeing fit just to lock up anyone in Bedlam who was in any way 'psychiatrically troubled'. No, 'additional support' is a relatively new phenomena. It used to be quite acceptable to put all the 'thick' kids in the bottom set and essentially have a policy of benign neglect without the care to find out if any of the 'thick' children may actually have a disability or even some sort of learning need. I think this policy came in when the word 'handicapped' was not outlawed *per se* but now it was only your old Mum or Gran who used it in a benevolent manner describing disabled people. If the kids were described as 'touched' then that will definitely be your old nan. She might also describe them as 'off with the fairies' but this means something wholly different now and perhaps a time to move away from specific descriptors.

In the late 1980's, early 1990's there was different legislation coming in covering Special education. The word 'special' would be mouthed by inappropriate parents not wishing to offend. Of course the irony of using the word 'special' euphemistically clearly labelling students as anything but 'special'. Like most adult language, used with good intention, will be jumped on and misused. 'Special' is merely used as another epithet for the playground bully, whilst pushing a kid to the ground into a dirty puddle. It gets added to Paki, Epi and Spazmo. Special education of course, a super irony much like what a super injunction is to normal injunction. The bully himself, unbeknownst to him, and it is usually a him, will also be on the special educational needs register.

No doubt for euphemistic emotionally disturbed reasons or being emotionally challenged.

All children know it is never good to be on any sort of register. The only other one they know about is the Sex Offenders register. If a student has any sort of learning needs, usually out of their own making, there is an instant stigma of being different which means less good and the school has a legal obligation to support a students with Special Needs.

To put measures in place to... well, what? That's the problem. Do you put things in place to bring the student up to just the average level of student? Can't we do better than that for them? You might put enough support in place so that they do better than average but might then your average student, through no fault of their own just being average say...

-Well, if I got a load of extra support who's to say that I wouldn't do better-

So maybe the support that goes in shouldn't have any measurable outcome. It doesn't make anyone better but a lot of money has been spent, measures have been put in place and we all get to feel very good about ourselves.

I have certainly helped out in classes of students who are really quite physically and severely educationally disabled. Yes, here is where your mum might say 'handicapped'. Once, when, yes, I was keen and the scales of cynicism had yet to fall over my eyes, I taught a young group of students aged between 16 and 25. It was over a summer as I recall. I was to teach them all Maths. Maths! There were twenty or so students in the class and in my keenness I had produced a huge range of worksheets (oh bless that overworked photocopier) and there were practical lessons with cubes, counters, cards and beads. I was going to teach Maths and I was armed! I also had three teaching assistants all of whom were keen, all young. Oh yes, we would be a success.

All of the students had their own technical terms to describe their disabilities. Moderate to Severe to Profound learning disabilities. In essence this means students who have difficulty communicating, difficulty learning, difficulty holding on to one or two pieces of information of any kind. I was going to teach them Maths.

Yes I was.

I may have produced more materials than I strictly needed.

First day, First lesson. 3 hours. Parents bring in students. 100% attendance. Everyone is early to class. Why is this? Wheelchairs, self-propelled and electric. Walkers and frames. Students rocking rhythmically in corners. Students bringing me a sticker book that I had to look at. One young man, keen to show his genitals to all who wanted to see them. It took half an hour to get everyone settled down, to get them to give me some sort attention and then I wrote my name on the board.

-Do we have to copy that down? - said one keen individual.

-No- I said. -You just had to know it-

-How will we know it if we don't write it down? - he said back to me.

I looked at my three helpers on their tables, stifling laughter but offering no help.

I was going to teach them all Maths.

And then as we got started -Everyone OK, you know what you are doing?- then stupidly I said -Any questions?-

-Yes. What did you have for breakfast?-

-Er, ok, not really to do with what we're doing but I had porridge with a bit of jam-

-Oh, lovely- he replied - And what jam was it?-

-Erm, raspberry-

-Ooh, raspberry. I love raspberry jam, I do, but I don't like the seeds. Did it have seeds in it, in the jam?-

-Erm... Can we just start getting...-

-But did it have seeds in it? -He was quite insistent as if the answer held the meaning to life itself.

-No seeds, no- I said - Now if we can just…-

-What are you having for lunch? – He said.

Now, this young man clearly had a moderate learning difficulty and by asking these questions he wasn't being wilful or purposely annoying but he needed to know. -I'll just come over and tell you OK? – I said to him.

I went over to his table.

The rest of the lesson was 1% maths 10% people needing the toilet or setting up the equipment and 89% a talk about what everyone was having for lunch. I was frustrated but I was determined to teach Maths.

Determined.

I used worksheets with written questions on before finding out that very few of the students had any sort of reading capacity. I took to using cards with dots on to represent the numbers. They could add the values on the cards. Or they could use beads or at least see if one pile of beads was bigger than the one next to it.

By the end of the lesson I thought I'd made a breakthrough. Yes, slow progress and lots of students moving at different speeds but I was, no, I am teaching them Maths!

The next day, in they came, 100% attendance, early, early, early, and yet again I was asked what I had for breakfast, what I am having for lunch and also, variety, what did I have for dinner last night! I was so excited. We used the cards, the beads, the counters but it was as if yesterday hadn't happened. I put beads and counters in piles, which one was bigger. Yesterday they all gave such a wonderful impression of learning, such joy on their faces as if they had made progress and yet, today, the same joy of learning the very same thing that we had done the day before and so it was as if they hadn't learned anything at all. And again, the next day and then the day after that they all came in, they all loved being in the class but everyday I taught them the same lesson. And they learned nothing. I was teaching them Maths. But no one was learning Maths.

At one of the many breaks whilst teaching this class I spoke to one of the learning assistants. An older lady, scarf (you know that by now) and I asked her how she thought the lessons were going.

-Oh wonderful- she said - you are such a wonderful teacher and they all clearly love you-

Such flattery.

-Yes- I said -but surely you've noticed that we're doing the same thing everyday. Nobody is really learning anything-

-Well of course, how can they learn anything? You must have read their files-

I hadn't.

I didn't even know they had files let alone what was in them. At the end of the week I went to see my supervisor, just to let her know how things were going. I remember her very clearly. Genevieve her name was, great hulk of a woman, always seemingly hunched over a computer keyboard, always pushing her forever sliding glasses back up her nose. She had to peer over them to see the screen but with her fingers always on the lenses and so the lenses were always smeared with finger marks, something I cannot abide. I'm surprised she saw anything through them.

I always find myself cleaning my own glasses with a precision lens cloth.

But she was a benevolent soul. The tiny little office only made her seem bigger. Every square inch of the walls were covered in lever arch box files with goodness knows what inside each one. Her desk was like the Wreck of the Hesperus. She seemed constantly to be looking for something on or under her desk. There was a perpetual cigarette burning in an overflowing ashtray on top of the desk, always surrounded by paper. How there hadn't been some sort of dreadful accident I do not know. But there she was, doing her absent talking to you whilst also looking for something on the desk, more often than not a cigarette lighter.

-But Genevieve, I just don't understand, I've essentially been teaching the same lesson everyday this week-

-Ah yes, one of the learning assistants came to see me, tells me you've been doing a fabulous job, fabulous. Very patient, very kind-

-Well, that's all very nice but, I'm trying to teach them Maths and...-

-But you are teaching them Maths dear boy, - (I was very young and she was really quite a lot older so the 'dear boy' was noted but justified)

-Yes but they're not really learning any Maths- I said.

-And that's a problem is it?-

I didn't think she was going to say that at all.

-Well, isn't the whole point of a student coming onto a course to learn and then move on, to a higher course, to build on what they have learned?-

-Oh dear Henry, really, I do admire your fresh faced principles. Hmm, let me just get one of the files- and she pushed herself up to standing using the desk, a few folders slithered to the floor as she did so. I motioned to pick them up but she said not to bother. She reached up onto one of the shelves and pulled down an oft opened box file, the adhesive tape on the hinge worn from the constant opening.

-Here, here's one for Michael, in your Maths class. Electric wheelchair, needs hoisting and support for toileting. 19 years of age but I'm afraid his fate was sealed on the day of his birth. Let me read to you.....- and Genevieve pulled out the first thick wad of paper from the box file, flipped over the page and then with a flat palm pushed her glasses up her nose with her fingers. -So let me see, OK, this is part of the medical paperwork we have, so so so- she says, scanning down the close typed page -Okay, so here, Michael, born at such and such hospital was found to be born in the breech position, a contusion was upon his neck and the umbilical cord is very likely to have restricted his airway for some minutes. The resulting lack of oxygen to the brain for between three to four minutes has resulted in a number of insults to Michael's brain. This is likely to lead to some profound physical and mental disabilities. It is likely that Michael will need to receive one to one care for the rest of his life. Michael is otherwise fit and healthy... and so on... The rest of the report goes on to record every single hospital appointment, brain scan, medical intervention that Michael has had to date but, very sadly, his card was marked from day one. And Michael, indeed, is one of the lucky ones- She placed the file on to her desk with a definite thud.

-Lucky? I said just thinking how one or two minutes can have such a profound effect on someone's life.

-Well, Michael is one of two children. He has loving parents who fight tooth and nail to look after him and get the support that he needs. Having a child with profound needs is no picnic- Genevieve stared back up at the row of files - I mean, some parents cannot cope. That child, that poor benighted soul might have been fostered or placed in a children's home. Who wants to adopt a child with profound difficulties? I mean, people do, God bless them but there aren't many who would volunteer. And now, the students turn up to your class, just for three hours. My goodness, wouldn't you want three hours respite?-

Yes, yes of course. 100% attendance. Respite care.

-So young Henry, you teach them Maths and you treat them all with care. My job, such as it is- there was more peering over the glasses for some sort of spreadsheet on the computer -I just have to make sure the money keeps coming in from the council and the students enjoy their time here-

-And the teaching?- I asked, the main reason why I was there.

She paused, closing the file and just leaving it on her desk. She tapped the lid twice.

-You do what you can-

Over the next few weeks I was in and out of that smoke-filled office and spent time breathing in a lot of second-hand smoke in order to read through the rest of the files. I'm not ashamed to say that sometimes, at home, just preparing dinner I would then think about what I'd read and I'd weep.

A number of them had had traumatic births and a minute or two without oxygen. Some had severe infections; meningitis and swelling of the brain. Some even had mothers who picked up an infection which crossed the Rubicon of the placenta, brains failing to fully develop.

None of them had stood a chance.

But that summer I did my best. We went out in the grounds, we looked at trees and grass. Everything was a learning experience and who knows, some of it may have been absorbed by osmosis. I did teach them Maths but they ended up teaching me a lot more. I tried not to think about them aged 25.

At the age of 25 their funding stops.

So I decided to get trained in dyslexia. Here were some students, not 'thick' as used to be described but tarred with the same brush and finding it just as difficult to escape the clutches of the bottom set at school. At least here I could make a difference, however small.

I just do what I can.

Mrs Croxton will always provide biscuits. It's not that I don't eat biscuits but I know if I get into the habit then, sitting down all day, I will just expand to fill the space. Besides, on the same little duck egg blue plate, Mrs Croxton will always produce five little biscuits. I don't even know what these biscuits are called. They have the same consistency as Rich Tea biscuits but somehow thinner. They are in the shape of a running track, to my mind anyway and have tiny holes like pinpricks through them.

They are completely bereft of any flavour or taste.

At the end of every day Mrs Croxton will bustle in, get my feedback and then take a quick glance at the full complement of the five biscuits still fanned out on the plate. I mean not even a custard cream or a bourbon or even a HobNob. Who doesn't like HobNob's? Never have we even been close to a HobNob. But I will say to Mrs Croxton, as I do every time....

-Well- patting my stomach for dramatic effect, -I really must look after my figure- and then say -and I really didn't want to spoil my dinner.

Thankfully Mrs Croxton doesn't ask what I'm having for my tea.

-OK- she'll say and take the biscuits away but when I return, whenever I return, be it the next day or next month, there the biscuits will be, fanned out in exactly the same way, five insipid finger biscuits. I can only assume that they are the same biscuits. In fact perhaps they are the school biscuits, like waxed fruit in a bowl.

Look but don't touch.

I settled down in the little office, quiet, lots of light, big translucent windows. I turn on my laptop, open up a Word document and I then set out two copies of paperwork.

All testing has to be done on the same pre-printed papers, purchased from the same company meaning that someone somewhere is making a fortune. If I don't use their paperwork, the tests are null and void and I'd be defrocked, possibly de-scarfed, as an assessor. Mrs Croxton totters in bringing with her my first willing victim. He already seems frightened to death. He is clearly aware of the subtext of 'additional support' and 'special education'.

What really attracts me about doing this job is the little bit of maths, the little bit of writing and the fact that all of it is analogue. Yes, there is an awful lot of theory behind it but in practise all I do is use a stopwatch to measure how fast or how slow a student completes a particular test whether it be reading, writing or just how quick the brain can work out little puzzles. That's it! I like the fact that I could have been doing exactly the same thing with a student maybe fifty or seventy years ago. Yes, a lot has changed but then not much at all. It's just me and the stopwatch.

The boy in front of me is tiny. A year seven swallowed up by his new blazer. His hair, even at this early part of the day, is relatively untamed, suggesting a little bit of spirit. Mrs Croxton closes the door behind him with a click. The boy is standing in the middle of the room where he was placed. I do always wonder what Mrs Croxton tells them before she wheels students in to see me. I always try being myself with students coming in, especially tiny, frightened ones. I fiddle with the stopwatch or leaf through the paperwork. All unnecessary but it allows them to come into a room where they're not instantly the focus of attention. Only when I finish fiddling about do I then look up and say -Oh, please take a seat, I'll be with you in a mo- and then it's not so formal.

-Okay, so, you must be...- I dramatically peer over my glasses. I already know his name, -Charlie Cross, is that right?-

He nods. He's got the first answer right. Confidence. -And you're in year seven is that right Charlie?-
Another nod. Fabulous.
-So, Charlie, do you know exactly why you are here, sitting in front of me?-

His eyes scan around the room, his teeth bit his bottom lip and his hands on his lap, were quickly thrust under his legs - I think it's something to do with reading?- he said.

-Okay and, Charlie, this is a very important question... -I paused again for dramatic effect -by being in here this morning.....what lesson are you missing?-

His eyes suddenly lit up. Suddenly he was part of a small conspiracy.

-Double Maths- he said as quick as a flash.

I clap my hands -Oh dear Charlie, I'm so sorry about that I really am. Look, perhaps we could do this another time if you wanted to...-

-Oh no no, it's fine. I don't mind missing Maths, certainly not on a Monday morning-

-Well that's okay then, as long as you don't mind- I smiled and then, thankfully, so did he.

I organised the oblong desk so I'm sitting at one end, at a right angle to Charlie. I explained to him that we're just going to do a few tests that involve him reading, a bit of writing and a couple of puzzles. I certainly don't promise that they will be fun because the 'F' word is enough to kill off any game. How many times have I heard 'Maths is fun', because it is the kiss of death. To be honest, usually because this is a one to one interaction, everyone who does the tests just wants to do their best. There is no-one to show off to as in a classroom and the egos are left at the door. I also try and maintain a slight air of mystery about myself. I certainly want them to feel comfortable but ever so slightly on edge, just so they concentrate. So I place pieces of paper in front of him, little plastic booklets and, by example, show him what to do.

-If you could just read this string of letters like this- and I use my index finger to show him the path of letters I want him to read. I then check to see if he understands what I need him to do. I zero the stopwatch and tell him to read it as fast as he can and then press the button, listening carefully for any mistakes which I mark off on my own copy of the sheet.

In giving instructions I hear myself say exactly the same thing in every test, saying it in the same manner, the same cadence. You'd think I'd change it occasionally but then, I think, my conscious mind would recognise this and perhaps think I'd made a mistake. Then I'd get flustered and the confidence in the room would vanish.

The first time in my life I remember coming across this sort of vocal automation I suppose you would call it, was having my eyes tested as a little boy. Obviously I was one of these very bright young boys, off the chart with intellect but then, working through primary school my grades started to slip down to average and then, goodness, remedial classes were suggested. I remember clearly being taught, just to catch up, with a lovely young teacher. Her hair was the fuzziness as her mohair cardigan. She would write things down in my book. I would read them and then she would be astonished by how well and how quickly I completed the questions.

She was clearly very patient and was just used to teaching very slow 'special-needs' (there is that word again) students. -Have you had your eyes tested?- she asked. Where do you sit in the room? Can you see the blackboard?- Questions questions (and yes, the board was black and I am that old), good questions all. The next week I was taken to the local optician, Mr Raglan, in the Arcade but actually he hired an ophthalmologist whom I never saw outside the consulting room. I could only have been eight or so. I was in this dark room. I sat in the big black chair, not dissimilar to a barber's chair as it was pumped up with a big chrome lever by the foot. Then the contraption, placed on the face, a pair of glasses, the sides and width and height all fully adjustable. It was a Mr Lauder, I think, wearing a bright white sort of smock which certainly gave him the air of a medical professional. His hair was slicked back with some sort of brilliantine. Then, with me looking forward to a big coloured box at the end of the room, rows of letters, black on white in tapering sizes, he would slip different lenses into the frames and then..... and this is the vocal automaton, once I had this lens in he would pull out another lens and this time, one with a thin brass spindle handle on it so he could rotate it in front of the lens. I was asked to look at the red targets.

-Are the red targets clearer with lens one or lens two?-

When he said 'one' his voice, became relatively deep, certainly in my 8 year old experience, and then 'two' would be much higher. Not falsetto but a lot higher so it was impossible not to distinguish between the two options. Once you got going with the tests he simply said 'one' plunging down down down and 'two' racing back upwards. But the tone, the pitch of each one never changed. There was something comforting in that, exactly the same sounds and afterwards you just don't even register that there was a difference. I suppose it's like listening to the football results on the radio, just hearing the intonation of the number tells you instantly if it was a win or a loss or a draw. And so now I keep what I say and the intonation the same. It may not comfort the student but it certainly comforts me. Needless to say they found out that I was blind as a bat and after I started wearing my very thick NHS tortoiseshell glasses my grades took a dramatic upswing. There was also an equal upswing in the number of times I was now pushed into puddles in the playground with the words 'specky four eyes' ringing in my ears as I got up. At least now I could clearly see who the bullies were, you know, so.....every cloud.

Little Charlie plugged away at the tests I was giving him. He was on the home straight now. I was getting him to write out a piece of free writing. He just had to write for exactly 10 minutes and so I could sit there, one eye on Charlie, his awkward spidery hand certainly not helping him write legibly, but I could also take a peek out of the window which looked onto the playground. I was mulling over everything I needed to do today. I would have two of these assessments to write up but that was fairly easy to do. I would have to go shopping which was always a nausea. I don't mind it but shopping for one and cooking for one and eating for one is all a bit soulless. I might pop over to Waitrose but if I go I'll end up getting a ready meal and then there will be a meal deal with the pudding and I really don't need pudding and I'll get a bottle of white and that'll be that. Really I should go to Tesco, get some proper ingredients and make something and it'll be a damn sight cheaper. Then I'll have to speak to the bloody builder, see how slow their progress has been today. My God, these bloody builders, if they'd been in charge of building the Pyramids at Giza, well, they'd still have scaffolding up around them now.

-Yeah yeah yeah, another 2000 years to finish mate, just can't get the right materials!-

And then, yes I'll have to go around and see Dad. That's a whole other level of nausea. The stopwatch ticked over the 10 minute mark.

-Stop. Stop writing please- I put the stopwatch down.

There is usually now a conversation about the stopwatch. Again I am purposely playing up to stereotype and having the tools that a stereotypical assessor might have. The younger ones aged ten or so are always fascinated as often they won't have seen anything like it. I know now that most people just use a mobile phone if they need a stopwatch or timer. Disappointing. There must be a bit of theatre I feel, a bit of magic.

The stopwatch is silver...in colour. It has one large black hand which measures seconds to an accuracy of plus or minus half a second. There is also an inset hand, much smaller, at the top of the white face measuring minutes passed. There is a very pleasing knurled top which, when depressed, starts the watch and then when depressed again, stops the watch. There is a ring surrounding the top, no doubt to loop a ribbon through it so the stopwatch can be worn around the neck. There is also a smaller little button at two o'clock. When it's pressed the second hand goes back to zero.

At the back of the watch there is a swirled pattern in the metal and, on one side only the silvering has been worn through revealing the brass underneath. The most pleasing aspect though is the tick. In my hand, in which it fits perfectly, the tick although not loud can be heard throughout the small, quiet room, an audible reminder to the person taking the test that time, quite literally, is ticking. The watch never leaves my hand. If they are interested then I point out to them small letters at the bottom which say 'Made in USSR', and tell them this was a huge country which ceased to exist a long time before you were born. I then might tell them that my Grandfather took the watch out of the pocket of a dead Nazi in Berlin at the end of the Second World War. Or my father, whilst on a scientific expedition to Borneo, had the watch given to him by famous professor who was dying from malaria. My father was to take the watch back to his wife, but when my father got back to England he couldn't find her and he kept trying but is still looking after the watch. Or my father, during a rare moment of quiet whilst helping Fidel Castro and Che Guevara take control of Cuba in the early 1950's, he won the watch in an ill-fated card game of Bezique. Three men died at the card table that night and my father was lucky to survive with the shirt on his back and the watch.

Of course none of these stories are true.

I bought the watch on eBay in 2005, but where is the magic and romance in such tedious truth.

I quickly mark Charlie's tests, who seems a lot happier for the ordeal to be over and also having checked his phone to see he's missed all of double Maths but he is still as nervous as regards to what I'm about to tell him.

-Okay, so, Charlie thank you so much for doing such a good job with these tests. Now I have to write up all of the results into a big report and this will only go to Mrs Croxton and your parents. No one else. But it does look like you have dyslexia.

Charlie shifted in his seat, looked down at his shoes.

-Now, you did really well with all the tests especially the ones with shapes and dots and all of those ones without words which means you're a bright boy. But when we did the tests with the words, that's when you sort of slowed up a bit. But I think you know all this already don't you?-

Charlie nodded and finally looked me in the eye.

-Ok, so- I continued -it does mean that reading is always going to be difficult for you, I cannot lie but, and this is important, it's not your fault at all. Your wiring in your brain might be a bit scrambled but there's not much you can do about that either. Nowadays though, you have phones and computers that can read everything for you and you can also speak into a phone and it turns into text. Now I think that is proper magic!-

There was a little smile appearing on his face.

-So I'll write all this up and all hopefully your life might just get a bit easier and as a bonus you got to miss double Maths. That gave the biggest smile of all.

-Right, off you go now, OK?- The smile was enough for me.

So, there we are, that is all I do. A tiny cog but by doing that I'm improving someone's life even if it is only by the merest sliver.

I do what I can.

So, obviously I do need to speak to Mrs Croxton but before she appears and bores me to death about the ailments of her Persian bloody cat (what was his name? Mr Snookums or something tedious like that) I'm just going for a quick walk, get the circulation going.

There was something very interesting in walking around a school when all the children are in class. There was a definite hubbub but muffled behind closed doors. Different lessons at different stages. Somewhere teachers were squealing pens on boards, urging bored students to copy it down. Sometimes interaction, all up at the front to see the teacher do a demonstration or a single student reading out loud to the rest of the class in halting tones. Learning at all sorts of speeds. However, walking through the school whilst all the pupils were in class was a much easier task then after the bell goes. I had about 5 minutes to do what I was up to.

First, a wee, then next the teachers' lounge and then, well, I'll just go into the playground, walk down the little passage just outside the very bustling kitchen. I see smoke.

-Well well well, Minnie the Minx. Caught you smoking behind the metaphysical bike shed!-
-Jesus Christ Mr. Green, I thought you were the Head or someone important for a moment- she said, the cigarette now hidden behind her but the treacherous blue smoke curled up and around the black and red mohair top.
-Oh, I see, so I'm not important, charming that is- I say.
-Anyway, you haven't caught me smoking you have in fact caught me holding a lit cigarette. I am merely holding this for a friend-
I looked around dramatically, the large and overflowing wheelie bins, an unsightly oil stain on the tarmac but little evidence of any other person.

-A friend? Have they gone far? Is it Beryl the Peril perhaps or Dennis the Menace?-

-Oh...fuck you! – in a hugely sarcastic tone much like a sarky year 11. She brought the cigarette from behind her, dragged in an impossible amount of smoke before stubbing it out on the tarmac. I wondered, just a little, as to the flammability of the oil on the ground. -If you must know, I have had a very trying day so far. Not only was I subjected to what felt like an interrogation this morning about my clothes, my job, my very womanhood, I have had to endure 3 hours of 11 F, the dullest class in the year, for very basic maths. I mean, bless them all but dimmer bulbs I rarely teach. More spoon feeding than teaching and so the time just stretches to such an extent that I feel I am in a time loop, never to escape-

I smile, remembering my own summer Maths class.

-And now I am being harassed in my very own, very private 'I don't really smoke' smoking time-

-Actually Minnie, can I call you Minnie?-

She nodded, quite seriously.

-If you must know, I was off for my lunch and spotted smoke and thought it might be my duty as a responsible adult to activate the fire alarm-

-Well, how very public spirited of you. And now you can see it wasn't a fire...-

-I did think if you could stand the abuse, you might want to have lunch. It's either you or Mrs Croxton and despite your abrasive manner and the fact you may be a fictional cartoon character I'd still take my chances with you than her- She hesitated. Was I being serious, was I flirting? Was her abrasive nature just a defence mechanism?

-What do you have for lunch?- was her considered response.

Again I smiled, thinking back to that summer.

-Erm, mature cheddar cheese with pickle...-

-Hmm,- She was wavering.

....On fresh sourdough and a slice of Gala pie-

-You're on. I'll see you in the staff room in 5 minutes.

She seemed to spin on the spot, still with her red bows on her orange bunches. It was a ballsy look. And clearly, whatever names the students might call her she clearly cared not.

If I'm honest I'm a little uncomfortable about eating in public. Don't get me wrong, I like to eat out at restaurants, sit up at a proper table but I can't do communal dining, all sitting at benches, I'm not a monk nor am I a schoolboy. No. I need proper covetable cutlery with some heft, linen napkins, that sort of thing. That is when eating out becomes an occasion. Eating out of a sandwich box, sitting on a low chair balancing everything on your knee so you are just one movement away from the whole lunch all over your shirt. No, but that seems to be the current fashion, unless you have to eat at your own desk. Why don't they just bring round a nose bag and have done with it. You can eat whilst you work.

If I do bring in a packed lunch it will be in a tin, not some insipid Tupperware box. There is likely to be a sandwich but made with proper bread. Today, as aforementioned, cheddar and pickle on 'homemade if you please' sourdough bread. I want bread with substance. Didn't all bread used to be earnest, chewy, a little bit of a workout to eat? Bread today, just pap. You squeeze it and it's gone and you can barely butter it for fear of ripping a hole right through it. Anyway, I spy Minnie the Minx who peers into the staffroom without coming in and beckons to me from the door, her eyes darting around as if this was suddenly not a suitable place for lunch. I quickly gather up my lunch and launch myself out of my chair trying not to look too old. I'm barely out of the chair when a teacher dives onto it, as a chair in the teachers' lounge at lunchtime is prime real estate indeed.

-Where are we going then?- I say, juggling my paper, lunch box and flask in a now bustling corridor. I look at some of the students, year 11, towering above me. One of them clearly needs a shave. He looks 30 not 16! Frightening. Both of us swim upstream, up the stairs through shouldered rucksacks, satchels. We try to avoid shrieking girls with so much mascara on their eyelashes that they look like human Venus flytraps. Finally we duck into a classroom, Maths by the look of it, the array of technical words up on the wall, all neatly thumbtacked onto a notice board. Circumference, ratio and tangents. There is also a long string of a numbers, on a strip of paper around the room like numeracy architrave.

-Pi?- I say.

-Oh yes please- she says, eyeing the generous slice of Gala pie I place on the napkin which I've lain down like a miniature picnic spread.

-Yes, very good, of course. Have some. I always bring too much.

I don't. This is a relatively small lunch today seeing as I was getting home early but still it is always interesting to watch someone eat. I place half of my sandwich down on the mini picnic blanket, in anticipation, but tuck into mine, trying to eat over the tin, and avoid a crumb avalanche (crumbvalanche?).

I venture a question, after a bite of my sandwich is swallowed and I've also drunk a little of my barley tea that looks suspiciously like whiskey.

-So, is this a date?-

-At work?- She laughs, mid-sandwich bite! -Goodness, no. You might call it an application process though. I mean I used to sign up to those dating websites but very quickly it seemed that men were only on there for one thing and that meant cutting to the chase. Have you done anything like that, dating sites?-

-Ah, you're assuming I'm not married or with someone already-

She took a healthy bite out of the sandwich, a small bubble of pickle was caught in the corner of her mouth and as she chewed, the liquid sort of tracked along her lip until her tongue peeped out and dealt with it.

I cannot remember the last time I watched someone eating so close up, let alone to eat with such relish. She pondered on her answer but not for too long, unfortunately.

-Oh no! I mean no offence, but you certainly exude an air of a single man-

-None taken I'm sure (!), please continue eating my lunch!-

And yet strangely I wasn't the least annoyed. She didn't seem to have any sort of editing facility on what she was saying.

-Well, I only ask if it was a date as you've agreed to have lunch....and you are eating it-

-Yes, but you don't know me from Adam...or Eve – she said. - If you were married, well, you'd be all furtive like some woodland creature, looking about to see if anyone you know is watching, about to grass you up. Also, if you were married and happy to cheat on a woman then you'd be addicted to it and you be making all the moves, being a bit more savvy and all schmoozy. But mainly, no wife is going to let her man, her relatively young man out of the house dressing like, I don't know, Harold Shipman?-

-What?! I didn't dress like Harold Shipman!... Do I?-
Do I??

-Well, just a tiny bit. Shiny shoes, Fair Isle grey jumper, brown cords maybe? That can only be a single man's idea of, I don't know, professionalism? Safety? Trust? But am I right, are you single?-

I paused, considering another bite of the sandwich -Whether I am or not is neither here nor there.

-Ha! Knew it. But it's fine. It just means that I have used too many dating apps and have become jaded with the process–
She took another large bite.

She carried on.

-Oh but the cutting to the chase! What is wrong with men?! I put my picture online, trying to convey I don't know, vivaciousness, fun, but also seriousness, culture, looking for romance and possibly marriage material. All that in a photograph which took all of 10 seconds on my phone....-

I did think just for a second which cartoon character was she dressed up as in the photo to convey all of these emotions simultaneously.

-...and then within 24 hours my inbox is crammed full of potential Prince Charmings which I then have to go through.

-And how does one edit such a list?- I ventured, eyeing what was left in my sandwich tin and not wishing to volunteer anymore food.

-Well, three main categories. The first is an obvious NO. This could be the picture and here the clues are a young man, late 30s, but the picture was obviously taken 10 years ago and even then, fattening around the gills and, in its infancy, a thinning thatch. He lists his characteristics as 'absolutely crazy' or 'great fun to be with' and this really means 'plays games with elves and hawks' and 'clearly still lives at home with his parents'. NO no no. Sorry, I should have asked, do you live at home with your parents?- she dropped in as another unedited side note.

-NO! No I do NOT! - Which is true although partly not true-

-Sorry sorry, anyway, second category- and now she was becoming very animated, using her alarmingly long fingers, I mean not E.T. fingers but they were still employed to count off issues with this second category -Very good photos, almost too good. Some headshots, some of them after working out, towel over the shoulders- do you workout?-

Work out what? I genuinely said which answered a lot of questions.

-Right OK anyway, you know these guys seem OK and then you message them, say 'hi' and then they send you a message which is just a long list of all the things they are going to do to me, not with me. And I'm not talking buying ice cream either. If it's not that then they send me a picture of their dick. I mean I wouldn't mind but as a Maths teacher I need some sort of scale next to it, just for comparison. No offence, but, well, male anatomy... it's all a bit 'Last Turkey in the Shop' isn't it?-

None taken, again- I thought.

-And the last group are the weirdest of the lot. The pictures, seem OK, seemed perfectly normal. Likes 'world cinema', whatever that means, 'reading books', 'Italian food,' 'long walks'. You message them, all very pleasant...-

As she said this she grabbed a handful of chilled South African seedless grapes from my tin -and you meet up with them and they turn out to be so crushingly dull. I mean just no conversation, no spark. They'll have a hobby but it will be so mundane that it's not technically a hobby just a way of avoiding the yawning chasm of life before death. One of them said, as if thinking of something, anything to say,

"Oh, I do like cycling"- "ok" I said "what sort, mountain biking? Speed cycling, Tour de France!" Desperate for some excitement, "Oh no just a three speed, sit up and beg. It's a Raleigh Chiltern. In fact it's how I got here tonight as it happens", and as if to prove it he pulled his reflective cycle clips out of his pocket. Who wears cycle clips!? Out of his pocket! As if this was akin to revealing a Yellow jersey from under his tweed jacket-

She crushed a large grape in between her back molars like a car being crushed. I heard the squelch. Through fixed gritted teeth she said -Do I talk too much?-

Erm.

-Don't answer that...-

Which was an answer in and of itself.

There is a pause. We listen to the bustle of the school surrounding us.

-So tell me about yourself?- she asks as if she actually wants to know.

So, I go to answer, one eye on the very last thing, nestling in the corner of my lunch tin, covered over with a bit of kitchen tissue. She was taking a big and final bite of her sandwich, stopping herself voluntarily from speaking.

What to say? Can I sum myself up with just a few words as so many young people seem able to do on dating apps? I thought maybe I was too sophisticated for that. I thought I was at least worthy of the small paragraph you get written on the back of a decent bottle of wine like "a heavy, full bodied merlot, dark, brooding with vanilla and peach top notes along with a warm cherry and oakey finish. Good with meat and fish." Or "a light and airy Pinot Grigio, with a crisp apple finish and citrus tart acidity." I would be mellow, warming but with a bitter aftertaste, burnt walnut shells and sweaty leather.

I open my mouth to speak and the bell goes and takes away any words that may have escaped.

-Never mind - says Minnie the Minx -but you can tell me on Sunday night. She hopped down from the table, bouncing on her toes with far too much energy. She notes, with her darting eyes, that there is something left in the tin. Her first recourse is not 'thank you dear stranger for sharing your lunch' no, she has the temerity to covet what is left.

Dramatically I whisk away the paper tissue to reveal a tart, but not just any old tart, oh no. Thin, crisp, sweet pastry filled with a vanilla infused set custard with ½ a strawberry, sliced longitudinally, on top, all glazed in a thin layer of caramel. It is certainly the most beautiful looking tart in the room.

I am desperate to eat this.

My sandwich was greatly diminished. My grapes, all lovely and chilled, still had 'TV advert worthy condensation' still beading upon their chilled skin. My precious slice of Gala pie, gone. Was this woman interesting or was she just an out and out scrounger? Perhaps I was just a feeder?! Was I enabling her behaviour or was she just nervous, sheesh, she can talk if she's nervous. But do I even want to be with someone who just takes? What happened to equality here? Just because I spend more than tuppence ha'penny on my lunch and I don't just buy a plastic pot of congealed pasta from the nearest discount supermarket. But, you know, how often do you meet people who dress up in a costume and then chat and see if anyone notices that it's a costume? I noticed. Is that the test? I've a feeling that if I let this woman into my life then things are not going to be the same again. And if she eats my tart... Then that is it.

Ok, I can always buy another tart. There were always more tarts.

By the time the bell had finished ringing I had lifted up the tin, offered it up to her, as if it were nothing.

I'm glad, from her, that there was just a little bit of decency in the form of a hesitation, a look at me as if to check if I was serious and were we just a boy and girl at school swapping and sharing a lunch and it being the most natural thing in the world. She gently lifted up the tart out of the tin and, still knowing the bell had already rung, took a hearty bite. The instant sugar rush made her eyes glisten as much as the glaze on the strawberry and this was enough to confirm my decision was correct.

-Thank you- she mouthed, crumbs scattered everywhere.

I quickly gathered up the shattered remains of my lunch into the tin, the little branches of grape stalks like a skeletal lung. The few little grey globules of aspic from the gala pie and some butter absorbed into the napkin, little grease spot, stuffed, all stuffed into the tin; shut with a click.

-Sunday- I said, leaving the room, assuming I had to go. I mean I could have stayed all afternoon but we both had lives to lead, jobs to do, curse them.

-Yes, Wine Vaults, before nine though, and you need to wear just a tiny splash of colour. We don't want you becoming a curmudgeon.

I closed the door behind me. Becoming a curmudgeon. Becoming a curmudgeon. I said these words ten times in my head before it lost all meaning.

The afternoon passed peacefully enough. Another lonely boy struggling with words. His head down, wrestling with his pen, I observed a small fight outside in the playground. It seemed spontaneous enough, like two drunks taking swings. It was over as soon as it began, but I certainly hadn't felt suitably qualified to intervene had it gone on. One boy wiped his cut lip with the back of his hand, tasting the blood with his tongue. A smile spread on his face.

Real blood.

Sometimes there is no substitute for relieving this pressure for boys.

Having left the five fingered biscuits on the plate from Mrs Croxton I got off early and got the Number 2 bus down to Southsea.

•

My goodness, what would Mr Dickens think of Portsmouth today? Gone is the squalor of urchins up chimneys and the hordes of beggars and gin soaked mothers. But has it been replaced by anything better? The rain had been threatening and I wanted to go down to Southsea. I could have walked, of course, I could but time was pressing a little. I didn't get the bus often and when I did I realised, at an instant why I often don't.

First task, looking for a seat which isn't peppered with chewing gum or has a delightful grease spot on the window or some other unidentifiable fragment of human detritus on it. I am surprised people don't feel compelled to wear one of those 'scenes of crimes' all over romper suits. A biohazard suit. Then, moving to the seat, the bus driver clearly looking in his mirror and accelerating off just before you take your seat and watches you lurch backwards into your place. I become a person of ridicule and hilarity in equal measure to everyone else on the bus. I sit down, trying hard to avoid the stare of the morose, diseased, infirm and disenfranchised but this is when the coughers' chorus starts. I swear that people only go onto the bus just to give voice to their cough. All manner of coughs, from the dry, wheezing death rattles, that go on and on and sort of then fizzle out in a muted crackle to that of the good old wet barking cough often heard in the company of phlegm which is sometimes hawked into some crusty tissue, you hope. I try to lift my mood by staring out of the window watching the rapid decay of Portsmouth through the grease covered window of the number 2 to Southsea however, the passing vista usually has me determined to scurry home and hide or at least vow to never take the bus again, ever.

The number 2 snakes down Copnor Road, lurching out past inconveniently parked cars, young people darting about on electric scooters on and off the road like unswottable gnats. But this road, a main artery into the city, is sclerotic, tiled as it is with a great rash of Turkish barber shops, takeaways, burger bars all of questionable provenance.

Corners of the little tributary roads where once there were thriving little corner shops, all long gone. No need for them as the double whammy of car ownership and supermarkets killed them off. Grim choices are made if you want a pint of milk. Some dismal Co-op or Tesco Metro.

The erstwhile cornershops along the route, long boarded up and then shoddily converted to a house or flats, their past betrayed only by a bleak UPVC door front at 45 degrees to the pavement. It's the same for pubs. Long gone Tap rooms, bars, gentlemen's clubs all sold off for more pokey flats. sometimes the shiny enamel bricks remaining on the outside, the only evidence that the pub ever existed.

The pubs themselves, killed off by the smoking ban and the demonization of the drink. But the space replaced by tiny boxes with no consideration to any great aesthetic. Just stick a front door on it, a lick of paint and rent it out quick smart.

The bus crowns the ridge of Copnor bridge, across the railway line and heads down South, skirting home and Baffins, past St Mary's Hospital, a hospital which was hollowed out in the late 1990's, most of its lands sold off for urgent Urban Development where there was built many more poor quality, small homes for poor, quality, small lives. Now, if you need any sort of hospital service you have to slip right off the island and up the hill.

Left turns then rights, traffic traffic traffic before reaching the top of Victoria Road North. The theatre which was then cinema which was then a bingo hall which is now a mosque and that just tells you something about social change over the last 100 years. All the houses along the road, all grand

Victorian houses, set back from the road giving... gave... the area part of its charm.

And I suppose, like tooth decay, there is this unnoticed creep. I can only imagine that when these houses, two to three storey Victorian town houses, beautiful stone double fronts, built in the 1880's the 1890's when the city was on the march the place would have been wonderful. The rising tide of gentrification and also the middle classes, disposable income, large families and each room in such a house would be necessary. Rooms for children, a nursery, and annexe for a nanny, later on a room for a governess. Rooms for an old faithful retainer perhaps. A scullery, a larder, parlours, and the respectable forecourt for a little garden, flowers, raised wall for a gentleman's.... Englishman's castle. This was the city of a young H.G. Wells, Arthur Conan Doyle. Elm Grove was called Elm Grove because it was a wide boulevard lined with mature elm trees. A Horse-drawn omnibus trundling down the Grove with boys lighting lamps of gas and streets kept swept.

Then all was swept away by the First World War.

The masters of those houses gone, maids, boys gone to war and after the turmoil, when the waters had stilled, the houses were suddenly too big. Smaller families, more expense. New houses to suit were now built on the fringes of the city and these Victorian houses were themselves no longer kept up. Then another upset tide, upset now falling from the sky. A Victorian terrace, built for 50 years and now the terrace had holes punched into them, unable to resist the persistent punch of mechanical warfare.

Families shrank, families arrived but with no suitable homes and so the slicing began. Like a cake, an ironic layered Victorian sponge, these large houses are filleted, sliced and patched like an etherised patient, always uncomplaining. Each floor now with a kitchenette, a small boiler and bathroom. A bed sitter is born and each little cell is compartmentalised like honeycombs for bees. Enough space and no more than that. Each floor sliced up for flats. The beautiful stone façade of the house pierced with pipes for drainage, coaxial cable for TVs, the digital optic fibre, those little disappointing boxes drilled into the century old brick so occupants can watch inane game shows on their screens. The houses, unkempt, unfeeling, paint peeling, beautiful wooden doors with stained glass once painted and brass once buffed and now replaced by all white PVC doors, blocking all that glorious light and two to three years is all it takes for dust from the traffic to show on the white, brittle 'uncared for' plastic. The house resembles some unvisited coma patient wheezing their last on a bed with all the tubes coming in and out. The little forecourt garden, with a tile patterned path, individual tessera once painstakingly placed by long dead artisans. The little brick walls, the small lawn or well tended rhododendron all stripped out, to be replaced with a slab of cracked concrete on which to park a series 5 BMW. The weeds pierce through the concrete.

When it rains the water simply washes into the overwhelmed drains and as the bus snakes down the road I cannot bear to look at those weeping houses. How poorly we treat our heritage, everything that surrounds us. Private landlords, greedy for profit and no real care for those who put such effort into aesthetics. We are all just waiting for the houses to fall down one after another once an extra room is squeezed into an already straining ageing house. Soon they will fall and then like those houses built after the bombs came, just simple soulless boxes, thrown up with just a cheap need to accommodate. No aesthetic, no style and so continues the blandening of this place.

Some buildings are kept though, whole but converted out of need into dentists' surgeries and children's nurseries but the glory days of this place are long past and the evidence is etched into the buildings.

As the lurching bus pulls into Palmerston Road, the diseased and shambling stay on the bus, I suspect just to stay warm. A mobile TB clinic if you will.

I disembark.

Southsea itself, the road, the shops are no better.

In the late 1990's the place was buzzing. There was a great clamour and ballyhoo about independent shops which needed to be kept 'above all else' but only certain shops. I was never quite sure which shops were chosen, a sort of cabal at the parish council perhaps where I could only guess at the sort of age and race profile and please prove me wrong but probably mainly old mainly white and 'let's keep the status quo'... but at what cost? They just keep rising the rental prices and then there were little independent restaurants, a handful of coffee shops, bars but also newsagents, a little fishmongers, banks, a baker even a market on some days and if you couldn't find what you wanted, there were not one but two department stores and one was John Lewis in a purpose built space, all green with round corners, a beautiful art deco store which everyone took for granted.

And so it went on.

Why would anyone leave this place? There is everything you could possibly want. House prices were zooming upwards because this is where people wanted to be.

But, like decay, things didn't happen all in one go. If 300 people die in an airliner crash there is a huge investigation, millions spent on this to find out just how these people died. In a small city, how many people walking across the road or cycling, are killed or injured by cars in two years; 50, 100? Is there a huge investigation? Is there an office in the council furiously searching for the answer? Is each death seen as an accident which could have been avoided but really no one wants to consider the fact that all of these deaths are avoidable if cars were slowed to 10 miles an hour or pedestrians are separated from giant cars.... don't get me started on those again.

And so, one lovely independent shop selling sausages. It is closed for a while, boarded up. Oh that doesn't look nice at all. A little infection which might then go on to infect the shops next to it. You might need to put the rents up, just a bit, just to recoup your losses. And then a charity shop goes in where the sausage shop was. Ok, just one charity shop, Ok, but, well, doesn't really do for the all round aesthetic but, there we are. And then another shop closes, rents going up just a little bit, boarded up, just a coffee shop going in, and a national chain coffee shop. No heart or soul. Same as shops everywhere else in the country... but they do pay the rent. More closures, more charity shops and before you know it, no department stores, just faceless coffee shops and charity shops and no real point of coming to Southsea at all especially if I just want a loaf of bread or some buttons for a shirt. And in each doorway of each closed shop... a sleeping bag, some cardboard and what you once had, what you took for granted is no more and exists only in the wistful minds of those who remember.

But I am only here as Waitrose is still here. That is the real glue holding the place together but I imagine, soon, that will close as well and all the dominos will collapse. Everything will be built on but there will be nothing to see.

Of course I forget all this doom and gloom when I am in there, basket in the crook of my arm, I am sold. I pick up the wine, my meal for one, a lemon curd tart (only because I didn't have one this afternoon) and a sourdough loaf. Lovely and completely unnecessary. It's a slog home, at least 40 minutes walk but the sky above is lightening and I would rather the walk than risk the bus.

•

I managed to get back just before the schools got out, avoiding the jostling of the older kids, all buoyant and boisterous along the pavement, as well as the giant cars picking up their tiny tots, a complete reversal of this morning. I closed the door, make sure it clicks shut and stand, sort of slump, against the door. Feel safe. Inside.

The instant I feel safe, the slight sagging and destressing, a drill from next door starts up which sounds like they are drilling directly into my skull. I tense up and stand straight. I had forgotten to speak to the builders. I hadn't of course. It was impossible to forget. The amount of drilling they had done I felt the house should be completely perforated like Swiss cheese. The house must be considerably lighter now. I'll have to speak to them today, soon, but not now. I should also check the phone for a message. There will be one. But if I don't look there isn't one.

I flicked the kettle on. A green tea will have to suffice for now. I wait until it cools on the side, putting off the builder conversation and the message for a few moments more.

It's cold when I drink it, a little scum on top from the hard water, like a slick of petrol.

So, it's a little complicated but I now own the house next door. In fact it wasn't complicated at all. I've been living in my house for some time and got to know the old boy next door quite well. He kept himself to himself, university lecturer and a little eccentric, even more so than myself. Spoke a lot of languages and studied a lot of Eastern European languages, the Slavic tongue, Hungarian, Czech, Serbo-Croat, if that even exists! Of course I only found all of this out after he'd died. He drank himself to death. Eventually falling over in the little conservatory in the cold winter a few years back.

We'd had some odd chats over the fence but after he'd retired I see him trotting out down to the off licence, getting his 'tea' and he would return with a clinking bag. That would be a daily occurrence. The garden, usually overgrown, had just one small mown patch of grass where he'd set up his deck chair and he'd sit there for most of the day just drinking his tins of lager. A man of environmental principles, the big recycling bin at the front of the house would be chock full of cans by the end of the week. He was always perfectly polite, chatting about the state of the country, politics but by the evening I would hear through the wall endless wailing and sobbing. I would hear it for a while, wonder if I should just pop over, see if he was alright but often, to my shame, I just turned up the volume of the television.

I'd often do the odd job around the house for him which was in as bad a state as he was. He'd be grateful, overly so, often wanting me to stay, have a drink, a Scotch, which I did occasionally. Anyway, as I say, he was polite enough. Except when it came to talking about his family.

Although the story was patchy and told as it was through the haze of drink over a few years, he had no direct family, no wife or children of his own. He had only his brother who himself was wealthy but greedy. Apparently.

The brother had two idiot sons of his own. The house that my neighbour lived in was the house that he and his brother had been brought up in. My neighbour never really went into it and when I asked he would often just stare into the distance. Anyway, as is so often the way, the brothers fell in love with the same girl. And if this story is to be believed then my neighbour fell in love with her first and then she was stolen away by the brother. The brothers then never spoke again...despite the girl going off with yet another man not long afterwards.

Once my neighbour retired, his brother was in a position to allow him to live in the family home after their elderly mother had died. The brother could see he was an alcoholic and the brother was the only relative and saw no harm in it. My neighbour however still smarted from the loss of his only love. He knew himself that he was an alcoholic and all he wanted was to commit a lot of pain upon his brother, glee from beyond the grave if you like.

So, in spite, my neighbour offered to sell me his house. I said no, certainly after hearing the story which I did not want to get involved with. However, I did not say 'no' without the slight hesitation which was seized upon by the drunk and addled old soul who realised there was a way to persuade me.

-Look- he said, during one of those times where I just popped around to fix something. Essentially a light bulb needed replacing so it was just a ruse. He wanted to know if he could trust me with his plan.

-I'm certainly not long for this world- he said mournfully - and have no great need for worldly things. We'll go to the solicitors, you and I, I'll just need an amount that would see me fine for the next few years but you let me live in the house for as long as I'm alive. That's all I ask. I just don't want the house to go to my ghastly brother-

And I said no again and again but every time I said so he said he trusted me. He said I was a good man. So, yes, if only to stop being browbeaten, we went to the solicitors.

The house, the deeds, foolishly for the brother, were solely in my neighbour's name. His drunkenness had been falsely assumed as foolishness by the brother. The solicitor, knowing the circumstances, made the sale watertight and was kind enough to put on the deeds a name of a trust so although the brother would know the house was sold he wouldn't know to whom.

I was true to my word. My neighbour, seemingly happy that he had got one over on his brother seemed freer than he had been before. I kept an eye on the house, my house, but also kept an eye on him. But I was often shooed away. I might have, once or twice, told him off about his drinking but certainly if he carried on at the rate he was drinking he would find an early death. All he ever had to say was "yes, I know and what a ride it will be!" But to watch someone actively, gleefully even, going about their self destruction was difficult. He was often bruised around the face or had cuts on his hands and face from falling and yet he was resolute. For those few months before Christmas I barely saw him, just hearing the odd ping of the microwave in the kitchen, a tiny sonic reminder that he was still there...until he wasn't. He lasted just two years after he sold the house to me and for a sum much smaller than most people's deposits nowadays.

He was right though, the brother was furious. The brother paid for the cheapest possible cremation but did not even attend himself. He came around to tell me, to ask if I knew anything about the house. He'd already been to the solicitors and was furious to find out that the house had been sold and his brother had been living there all this time as a tenant for peppercorn rent. I don't quite know why he was telling me all of this. Perhaps he just had to tell someone who knew his brother. I certainly didn't volunteer any information. I did just ask the once whether he'd ever visited his brother, perhaps he might have mentioned what he'd done but then all the anger went out of him, a deflating souffle, perhaps reflecting on mistakes made.
Perhaps.

I left a decent amount of time before I even entered the house.

The brother never returned.

It seemed a little strange then, a house I had been into a number of times but now there is no one living there. You could feel that no one was there. Even if he had just stepped out for shopping and the house was technically empty it still felt as if it was occupied but now, whether the house was taking a breath when empty, I don't know. The house though had been in a state. Nothing that couldn't be fixed but even the thought of doing it all myself overwhelmed me. The first thought I had was knocking my house and his together but I was on my own anyway and had no real need to live in a six bedroom terraced house. I mean it would be nice to have more space to put in books and... well, just books really but that hardly justified the cost. I could do it up and sell it but then somehow I'd feel bad, making a profit from the sale. I knew my neighbour, former neighbour, really wouldn't have cared but I would. I could give any profits to charity... but perhaps I didn't care that much. So, a number of days thinking and I decided to do up the place and rent it out. Yes, I could choose who my neighbour was at least and I could also sell it if I wanted to. It would also take off the pressure from me having to work all the time. So, yes, a good idea but then the realisation of dealing with letting agents and builders. I left the house locked up for three months more.

It is just a little hop over the tiny front wall to the next door. I have a key, of course I have a key, I own the house and yet because the builders are in I need to knock. Not for them to let me in you understand, no, but to give them fair warning that I, the owner, the person paying through the nose for their work they're doing, am coming in but if you are just sitting about having tea then you have these 10 seconds to pick up a tool and at least pretend that you are doing something useful. I let myself in after a good 20 seconds and still, still as I get through to see them they are drinking tea in the kitchen. Oh and I thank my lucky stars that they are here at all! I mean, what other occupation or industry gets away with such shocking practice. If I just didn't turn up and do my job even once and then I were to give some very flimsy excuse such as "parts, materials etc" but all knowing that I was doing another job, I would be fired and understandably so. They get away with it because we let them get away with it. We give them money, deposits, because they are so desperate for the work and then they seem to do the work as and when, only turning up again when they want paying. Also, how do you replace builders if they leave halfway through the job. I hate it! And apparently because my job is, "so small, almost not worth doing really" you know, as if they are doing me a favour! They turn up sometimes and then turn up late, go home early and I seem to be powerless to stop it. They know that and I know that so we all get along in this great corrupt pretence. Hate it! Anyway I have stopped buying biscuits and tea, because they were just taking the piss. There's only the two of them if they turn up at all and it was a packet of chocolate digestive or hobnobs a day and the vast lakes of tea! No more. They said they've got a week left and, fool that I am, I have taken them at their word.

-Ah, Mr G- says builder one, the older one, 'Andy, mate' with his unnecessary bulging tool belt, his colourful legs (the profits of any job must all go on tattoos) and his overly tight T-shirt. -Nice to see you. Just lettin' you know both the electricians been, signed off all the works and the gas boilers have been certificated-

Is "certificated" a word. I'm not questioning it.

-Actually mate, looks like we'll be finished by the end of the week after all-

This was obviously a shock to him even though last week he'd said it was a solid gold promise!

-Don't touch the walls though, wet plaster-

If there's one thing I loved about the building process it was the smell of new, fresh plaster on the walls. Something so earthy and primal about it. Maybe that's why these builders are so primal themselves.

-Yes, good good, so...- And here I had to gird myself for the big list of things that were promised to be done, -the tiling in the bathroom? I did get the tiles a few weeks ago and...-

-All in 'and mate, definitely tomorrow for the tiling. Just need to let the plaster in the bathroom dry out first but matey boy here,- and 'Andy mate' motions to Darren, the skinny scrawny deputy builder, with his mug full of my tea, a bit of it slopping onto the lino as he raises his mug in some sort of sarcastic salute to me.

I try so hard to ignore it as I am also ignoring the sugar all over the kitchen surfaces that were only put in last week despite a promise of months ago. 'Andy, Mate' sees me looking at the spilt tea -sorry mate, yeah, no probs, done by the end of the week, definitely. –

And it is the word 'definitely' that scares me, so indefinite, and the word 'mate' was used three times in one sentence and I thought I would blow my top. When exactly did the word 'mate' become acceptable to use by tradesmen or in fact anyone doing a job for you. Not once, in my entire life have I called anyone 'mate'. People have names or they have titles and 'mate' is neither. I'm not his 'mate'. I have no inclination of becoming this man's 'mate' and therefore have no wish to be called 'mate'. I think, as any act of deference has simply melted away, the use of 'Sir' in a servile capacity is no longer used by the working class, mainly because there is no longer a working class to use it. This builder calls me 'mate' because he doesn't want to be seen in anyway beneath me despite the fact that I am paying his wages for the service he is providing. I don't want him to doff a cap towards me, or bow but he sees himself as my equal on some social level? Hence the qualifying 'mate'. He is also aware that every time he uses the word 'mate' the little muscles in my jaw clench and so he uses it more and more just to wind me up. He clearly thinks me a snob... which I clearly AM.

Of course had I hired a different firm of builders, one with a history, perhaps older gentleman who did not dress as if they were on a set of a porn movie, may have that deference, they may well call me 'sir' and probably charge me twice as much for the same work. I clenched my teeth and swallow down the bile.

-Okay, so tiling this week and then, bathroom working by the end of the week?- I find myself in supplication mode, 'oh please please pretty please finish the bathroom that I am paying you to finish'. 'Andy mate' takes an enormous swig of tea. He then makes that 'ahhhh' noise to tell everyone that his thirst is eventually quenched and that it was indeed a great cup of tea and then...

-Definitely mate-

I say nothing more, after thanking him obsequiously just for turning up, the pathetic little toady that I am. As I pull the front door to leave I just wait there, listening. I shouldn't and I know I'll hear something I don't want to hear. I hear laughter, dirty Sid James Carry On mocking laughter, obviously at my expense.

I wait, OK, I cower in my own house just listening to next door. The drilling has stopped and it isn't long until I hear the front door go. They both get into the van. The van is always outside, that dusty, rusty pile of shit van. Yes, go on, slam the door. No, surely that wasn't hard enough, slam it again, then make sure the radio is on, nice and loud, local radio station playing. That's it. Dance music from 30 years ago. No, louder! They both spark up in parallel. Deep drag, tap the ash out of the window and the idling diesel engine disappears for another day carrying their equally idling builders.

And relax.

•

The little green light on the answer phone is flashing. It was flashing when I came in and still it continues to flash. It will be the same message as the one before and the one before that.

I have an analogue answer phone. Actually I should say I still have and use an analogue answer phone. I have a Wi-Fi box thing in the front room, I have Internet access and I'm sure that I have some sort of digital answer phone on the main telephone in the house. Two reasons why I still use my actual analogue answer phone is that if I receive a message it is recorded on a tape. There is actual physical evidence of the message existing. On some sort of digital platform I probably need to scroll through 150 options until I play the message and I can hear the message but... does it actually exist? Is it somewhere in the ether, ungraspable. If it is deleted there is no record of it having existed at all! But the tapes, the analogue C90 tapes, with all my answer phone messages... are all stored away. They exist and they are evidence of my own existence. I steal myself by the telephone table and press the button.

-You have... One... New message...- says the digital female.

-Hi Son, just Dad here, just phoning up to see how you are...- pause... noise of rustling, possibly the unfolding of a piece of paper by the telephone... -Also I've got that dry cleaning that needs picking up. And I could do with a shave. Anytime,

anytime-....pause.....-but I could do with that shave tonight. Anyway, hope to see you soon- -Beep. -You have no new messages- she metallically concludes.

You see, you see! He phones almost everyday but he still has to say Dad! He phones up just to see how I am, but it isn't just that is it? There is always something to do. Dry cleaning. He can send out the dry cleaning but I have to pick it up. It's not urgent, Oh no, not urgent... well it is urgent but anytime....but actually now. Bloody now.

I'm now shouting at a machine.

I put the oven on. 180 degrees C fan. I don't even have to check the cooking instructions on the packet anymore. It seems that every meal for one is 180 degrees C fan. They must think that people who eat meals for one are real 'go-getters', literally no time to prepare real food, too busy doing deals on the Stock Exchange, phoning brokers, BUY! BUY! SELL! Not the reality of people who, if there was more than just one cooking instruction aside from 'pierce then remove plastic covering and place on oven shelf' then such would be their depression that they would place their own head on the oven shelf instead; Chicken a la Plath.

My electric oven puts a stop to all of that. I dutifully pierce the top of the two plastic containers and place them in the oven and set the timer for 25 minutes. I put the burgundy in the freezer just for the same time. This is just enough time to set up the laptop at the other end of the table, scraping other work, bills, into the middle of the table where a paper mountain thrusts ever upwards. The tectonic pressures of lethargy and 'can't be botheredism'. Once the paper mountain reaches a critical mass, the sides get to a certain angle, then everything comes sliding apart. Only then will I deal with the paperwork.

I take today's work out and place it next to the laptop. There is an e-mail. In fact there are lots of emails offering exciting opportunities of penis extensions, double glazing, walk-in baths, conservatory curtains and cruises to Scandinavia. There is also an urgent e-mail wanting me to activate my dating app. Just one click and then you'll click!

Click!? Really, a bit 1970s!? But there is just one e-mail that is not spam but not necessarily as welcome.

My sister, K. My younger, much more talented, famous photographer sister. Younger but clearly more responsible sister. Sister with husband #3. I think. I mean, she is with him, I just can't remember which husband she is up to. And the e-mail will be 99% about her, what she has been doing, all the fabulous places she has been, name drop name drop, and then 0.9% about asking about Dad, if he's OK and essentially was I looking after him and then the 0.1% was about me, perhaps even as a postscript. She's always threatening to come back home, it's her turn to look after

Dad. But, oh, so difficult to tear oneself away from the glittering lights of LA or the virgin forests in Borneo. A-list celebrities, media moguls. It must be so tiresome, so fed up with taking on photographic assignments in the most beautiful parts of the world with the most beautiful people. Of course she'd much rather give all of that up to collect dry cleaning, to sort through laundry and sit watching 'Countdown' with an old man and his wandering memory... Wait, what's that? Another assignment to do? Photo documentary of the new Asian movement in downtown Melbourne? Just can't say no? Definitely be back after that. Definitely.

Hmm, there's that word again. At the moment she is in rural Peru documenting the Aztec temples new and old, juxtaposing this and that, blah blah blah.

The alarm goes off on the oven. I set the table which takes all of 10 seconds. Knife. Fork. Place mat, featuring scenes of Dublin. Pastry fork. Napkin in ring. Very large glass. And yes, my sister may be jet setting around, a carbon footprint larger than that of the Iron Giant, and last year, ironically, documenting melting glaciers, flooded plains in Bangladesh and forest fires in Australia. Perhaps if everyone who is so bent out of shape about the environment just stops flying, we might actually stop having to worry about it!

The cardboard sleeve says that my dinner is a 'Carolina Smoked BBQ pulled pork with roasted yams and Black Eyed Peas'. This is my own adventure into the Deep South, as I spoon the meal from the plastic dish onto my warmed plate. A red and brown slurry oozes out of the dish and the meal, on the plate, sort of sags, like a sighing jellyfish. I am careful that it doesn't ooze over the edges like some volcanic pyroclastic flow. Despite the poetic description, the meal looks like every other meal for one, a distinct disappointment. It is indistinct from lasagne or 'basil infused shepherds' pie' as they all end up in some sort of splat. But the disappointment is then reflected in the one who eats it, on their own, leading to contemplation of the life choices they made leading to having to eat identikit meals for one.

Christ! Meals for one, a modern phrase that is almost but not quite as ghastly as rail replacement bus service! It is all I can do to stop myself pushing my face into the meal and drowning. I visualise the scenes of crimes officers leaning over my dead body….

-Death by drowning in….what's that? Lasagne? Carbonara? Just put down meat based meal-says the pathologist.

At least the burgundy is good. I could quite easily become an alcoholic. How much easier is that made with the screw top lids! But every sip is tempered with thoughts of the neighbour dying, no doubts alcohol poisoning in the conservatory and if I did become a lush, who's going to look after Dad? Essentially there would be no-one who'd even miss me. At some point after three years, the door will be broken down and they find my mummified body in the chair, glass raised and remnants of an (unidentifiable) meal for one nearby.

So I just have the one glass with the delightful lemon curd tart. The tart is so citrusy and sweet with that sharp flavour running through it. I should of course have cut it in half. It serves 2 but I can eat both. On the box it says 'serves two' but two what? Children under three?? Two cats? It's all going in.

Plates in the dishwasher which needs to go on. I just about muster the energy needed for the escape velocity to do what must be done.

•

I put the key in the door and keep it there for at least five seconds before turning it. I take a deep breath but, standing in an overly hot landing of a sheltered accommodation block, thin blue carpets, insipid watercolours screwed onto the wall, Constable miniatures and given the fairly failing eyesight of most of the residents, the miniatures seem more like an eye test than art.

All the doors have safety glass in them, full of wire for no real reason that I could ever work out. In each room, certainly on this floor, I could hear televisions blaring through the walls and doors and the smell of over-cooked vegetables and gravy. Good old gravy, the emulsion to cover up any culinary disaster.

I turn the key, push the door open and hear the familiar tick of the Countdown clock and try to make my way through the fierce wall of heat. I swear that one day I'll come in to see clay pots hardening on the windowsills whilst glass turns back to liquid.

And there he is, in the same old wing back chair, a little table to the side with a mug of tea, cardigan on top of a checked shirt. Grey slippers and he is leaning forward to see every letter chosen on the giant screen.

-Hi Dad- I shout over the television, waiting for a space between a contestant saying "consonant and vowel please Rachel".

-Oh, Hi Hux- he said, not turning away from the screen for one second -be with you in a second. Last letters round, the numbers then the conundrum. This guy's got no chance. Just getting fives and sixes but the woman got a nine just now. A Nine! Can you believe it... Campanile!-

Anything I might say in the next ten minutes will be completely unheeded so I resign myself to sitting in the other wing back chair trying to deal with the extreme dry heat and the volume from the TV.

Many times in the past I've tried to address both of these issues. The heat; I turned down the thermostat and I mean down to 21 degrees from 26 degrees but I was told off for messing with the electronics. My contorted face and my bleeding ears were not enough evidence for the volume to be moderated on the TV so I waited for him just to go to the toilet or get another tea and then turned it down just so my fillings didn't get vibrated out of my head. And then he sits down, swears he can't hear it and whacks the volume up again. I mentioned at the time that some armies around the world used sonic beams as weapons. Large pulses of noise to disorientate the enemy. But they found out that the elderly were impervious to it. Of course he didn't hear what I said.

-Yeah, campanile- he said -I didn't get it. But they went over to dictionary corner and that gay guy was there with the pen cam. Campanile…and then he makes some off colour joke about being camp-

-Dad, I don't think you can say that 'gay guy'-

-What? But he is gay…- he says, now concentrating harder on what he is saying.

-Well I know he's gay, yes but... I think you're using it in quite a negative way. You don't refer to the other people as 'not gay' do you?- And as I said this I felt all the energy drain from me. Why did I even start this?

-Of course not....If he wants to be gay well that's his business and I have no problem with him being a bit gay-

A bit gay?- Where does that come from?

-So why can't I call him gay?- He had started climbing on to that high horse.

- I mean, goodness- he continued, whether I was listening or not - they make such a song and dance about it 'oh the gays,' 'being gay' and now it's all legal and they can do what they want, get married, have kids... but I can't call a gay man 'gay'?-

Here it comes....ready....

-I mean what's the world coming to?!-

And there it is, touchdown, rant over.

-Look, you just watch the letters. I'll make you a tea, OK?-

-Oh, lovely. Here's the mug- which he handed to me without turning away from the screen-

I take the mug to the little kitchenette. I see the remnants of dinner in the sink, no doubt for me to wash up. I boil the kettle. I mean, if I was the parent and he was the child you would say that his behaviour was disgraceful, unacceptable and I really should switch off the TV, smack his legs for being so rude and send him to bed. But of course, I can't do that. Despite his behaviour he is still the parent and I am the child despite the balance shifting so I am now the adult. I have the responsibilities and the headaches and he's the one who needs the help, the guidance. But unlike a child, he is fully formed, certainly in his mind and regardless of my guidance from the modern world he will never change.

I suppose it is a bit like the odd moment you might meet your old primary school teacher but with you now as an adult and them retired. You still call them Mrs or Mr X and would never dream of using their first name even if you knew it. Suddenly you are reverted back to being a child.

The conversation here is because parents get older over time and you age over time, there is not one single moment when they become infirm. Infirmity creeps along like a gathering fog until the father knows he is reliant on his son's help but still cannot bring himself to say 'I love you' and 'thank you' because that would just confirm his infirmity.

I can hear the television as clearly in the kitchen as if I were in the front room. I pour the water in, squeeze the bag and add a splash of milk. I put the squeezed bag in the tiny bin in the corner. The kitchen is completely nondescript and yet it is perfectly appointed as long as you are not hoping to turnout Michelin starred nosh. A simple oven, a toaster and kettle. A few drawers filled with fewer ingredients. Black top, white tiles, stainless sink. It would win no design awards but it had everything that was needed, certainly more than what dad needed. His laundry was part of his sheltered accommodation (but not dry cleaning obviously). He could cook his own meals if he wanted to but there was a supper club downstairs which he often went to. There was also Bridge club on Mondays and Wednesdays, Cribbage on Friday mornings and some sort of tournament at the weekends, usually Backgammon. Tuesdays were Scrabble but Dad had been banned from all Scrabble until further notice due to an 'incident'.

'They were both perfectly good and acceptable words' he'd told me and words that had they been allowed to stand would have seen him get to the top of the Scrabble leader board.

He did tell me what the words were and, yes, whilst they are legal words they are perhaps not words to be used in polite and genteel company in sheltered accommodation. "Do not go gentle into the night" came to mind. There was much raging and hence he was yet to be returned into the Scrabble fold.

I placed the tea back down on the same ring on the side table next to him. The conundrum was coming up and soon the noise of the TV could be silenced.

NEEPHOTEL – were the letters that rotated on to the screen.

If I were very mean, which I am, then I could, through the noise of the urgent tick of the countdown clock, just ask him where the ticket for the dry cleaning was or whether he wanted his shave in the kitchen or the bathroom. Obviously he couldn't scream or shout because I was here doing him a favour but he knew that I would know I had specifically chosen that precise 30 seconds of time to annoy him intensely. Only slightly worse would be me blurting out the word....

TELEPHONE

....which I did.

I mean, you either see them or you don't. I saw his vein twitch at the side of his head and his hand gripped the arm of the chair a little tighter. He had heard me. He said nothing. He didn't need to. There was a buzz from the television. The young man said...

-Is it 'telephone'?-

The crumbly and anodyne presenter says -let's see if it is...- and the answer is revealed.

A smattering of elderly applause from the audience. Dad finally turns around from the chair to look at me.

-I told you he'd win. That young lad's doing really well. Champion material-

He makes absolutely no reference to my getting the answer correct before him. I make no reference to the fact I got it right. And so it goes on...

Fortunately the TV, by remote, was silenced and the room was deafeningly still. Dad pushed himself up out of his chair, with a little huff and puff but soon got to standing. I am guilty of watching but not interacting with this micro pantomime every day. My dad never used to struggle getting out of a chair yet now he does or at least it seems effort is exerted. I can see the arms tense a little, pushing up and there is that little 'ech' noise from the chest and maybe blowing out some air, and then exhale loudly and congratulations at, once again, escaping the earthly clutch of the chair. But every time I see him I notice it gets that bit harder until, I suppose, one day where he doesn't get out of the chair at all. I say nothing and look away before he sees me looking.

He shuffles a little in his slippers. My dad never used to shuffle. He was always out walking, striding up and downhills, an OS map in hand, a compass dangling around the neck and off we would all go. Ham sandwiches and a flask of tea were deemed adequate weapons in the teeth of a gale and horizontal rain. He would stride back then, but now, barely shuffling.

-So, you said something about a shave, Dad- I said when he was finally closer to me and the residue of sound from the TV had finally decayed away -Don't you shave yourself?-

-You know I've only ever shaved one person in my life – he said thinking the answer obvious -Of course I shaved myself, but, well, these last couple of weeks I've been going to one of those Turkish barbers, just down the road-

There seemed to be one down every road nowadays, and they only took cash. What was going on there I wonder.

-OK, but why? – I asked.

-You'll think this silly but, this sort of tremor that I've got in my hand, just makes me a little uneasy with it all. And also, my glasses. I've got to look so close in the mirror now and so if I've got my glasses on I can see but they just steam up and...-

I could see he was getting a little distressed even by telling me this, a weakness shown, a chink in the armour. He didn't want to be infirm or rely on others and yet he'd only ask if he really wanted it done. Of course this meant me having to shave him. I was not relishing this prospect.

-Can't you get, is it Rochelle, your community helper to come in and do it for you?-

-Christ no! She's hardly off her phone anyway so she wouldn't be able to concentrate but also, have you seen her nails? Like painted talons! She'd have my eyes out, those things so close to my eyes. like scimitars they are! I don't know how she does anything with them, picking her nose or wiping her arse. Lucky she's so bloody lazy!-

More unnecessary images scarred into my visual cortex.

-And why do you not want the Turkish barbers doing it?- I was now grasping at any particular avenue for avoidance.

-Gangsters in there, all of them. I mean they do a lovely job don't get me wrong but when I was done the other day they tried to use a lit taper to burn away my ear hair. The smell! And it cost £15 a pop-

Oh I see, so essentially I am able to do it because 1) I won't burn your ears and 2) I'm free.

His face crinkled into a smile as he knew it to be true.

I wheeled one of the black stools in from the breakfast bar into the bathroom. I'd actually not seen Dad use any of these stools so had no idea if he could even sit up on it. The stool had a sort of pneumatic pump mechanism underneath so it could be raised up and down.

The bathroom was as austere and also as well appointed as the kitchen, no doubt a job lot for the black and white tiles. In fact, if it wasn't for the walk-in shower cubicle I'd be hard pressed to see a difference. In he shuffled and with a bit of help I got him up onto the stool. At least he could hold on to the edge of the sink for balance.

-So Dad, you must have some shaving kit about? Cupboard? Up here? No, down here? Maybe...- although there just seemed to be towels in every cupboard. He pointed to the little cabinet just above the sink.

-Of course, how silly of me, the tiny cupboard which is just out of reach-

-Well, I didn't want that girl rooting about in my stuff. Nosey cow she is-

-Now, come on Dad, I'm sure she's very nice and she thinks the world of you and I hardly think there's much on the second hand market for....- and here's me looking in the cupboard above and trying to dodge it all as it comes tumbling out into the sink. I avoid a minor concussion - ....what, ten year old half bottles of Brut and Old Spice and... what's this?- I look at an old aerosol can, the rust from the bottom had etched away at the label. -I mean, can you even get Old Spice anymore? And, Dad come, on this can, how old is it? Pre war?-

-Cheeky bugger – he said.

-And what's in it? Agent Orange? Sarin?-

-If you must know, and if you can stop being so cheeky for one second, I got it at Christmas - He could see I was going to say something, probably about which Christmas!

-....but not this Christmas but I didn't feel the need for throwing it away as I still use it-

Now I am intrigued. I tried to hold the can and press the nozzle without coating my hands in rust which is flaking off and also in danger of eating through the can itself. It was a disappointment to both of us. After an initial 'fffftt' which coated the sink with some sort of white cream, the gas, if there was anything left in there, escaped and there was then, despite my finger firmly holding down the nozzle, a thin white liquid dribbling out over my fingers and in white and rusty splats on the floor tiles.

-Oh- We both said.

-Well it was my emergency can of shaving foam. Christmas, what, 1983?- he said, his eyes looking upwards as if to capture the very moment in his mind.

-83?! So this is, what, 40 years old??

-Oh, it was just one of those Christmas packs your mother- and he went quiet just for the skipped beat of a heart- I lowered my eyes a little at her memory.

When a memory has been locked away for so long and you feel you've lost the key and then the key appears from nowhere, the box bursts open...

-Yes... your mother used to buy me those Christmas packs which had shaving foam, aftershave, talc! I mean for God's sake, talc! Does anyone use talc anymore?- he said, half smiling, glad of revisiting the past if only for a moment. I hoped he was asking this rhetorically! Anyway, that was the last of the foam.

-And emergency foam, an emergency because?- I thought I'd ask.

-Well, for all those times when I didn't have any proper foam or I'd lost my proper soap or run out or misplaced the brush. I must have used it ten or so times-

-I'll put it in the bin – I shouted back to him from the kitchen, the creamy liquid starting to calcify on my fingers.

-You know this can probably has proper CFC's in them. Just by pressing the button probably tore another hole in the ozone layer-

-Oh I shouldn't worry about that – he said to me as I came back into the bathroom - Well, me, at my age, I won't worry about that.

-I see- I say, restarting the hunt for any sort of shaving material before finding a little basket in the very small cupboard under the sink next to the bleach.

-Oh, sorry, yes- said dad, possibly picking up on my exasperation- the girl did say she tidied up a bit but, as I say, I've been to the Turkish barbers and haven't used it often.

I pulled out the little plastic basket which held very little. There was a navy blue sponge bag with little anchors on it under a thin layer of dust. I unzipped it and placed everything that was in there onto the place next to the sink.

1) A small, clear but amber bar of soap. Cellophane still wrapped. Unused Body Shop.

2) shaving brush- used- ebonite handle with slight residue of shaving foam. Bristles black with a white tip. A number of bristles are missing. The bristles are stiff as iron nails.

-Ah there's the old brush- Dad pipes up - Real badger hair that is-

-Very balding badger by the looks of it- I say as I place it down on the side, not wishing to touch it ever again.

3) One safety razor. It looks like it is stainless steel with a very pleasing to the touch knurled pattern on the handle, no doubt for grip. Inside the top of the razor is the actual razor blade which is corroded to the point of

crumbling. The edges are ragged, oranged by rust but also, if I'm not mistaken, flecked and speckled with blood. I place it down as if it is exhibit A, m'lud.

4) One packet of three safety razor blades in a foil packet- opened- all blades similarly rusted like their fallen brother.

-Might need a bit of work that razor- said Dad, whereas I had merely contemplated throwing the whole lot in the bin.

5) One disc of a plastic material, not unlike the size and construction of a tin of shoe polish. The words 'shaving cream' in bright blue writing are emblazoned on the top. I picked it up with just finger and thumb. The contents of the container rattled as I shook it. I placed it down without opening it. I was yet to find any objects that might have been used to shave and even now I was mentally making a shopping list that I would no doubt be tasked with.

6) One toothbrush. Although brush is a very loose descriptive term for the item I held in my hand.

-Do you use this?- I held the toothbrush up to Dad's face who immediately moved his head away from it.

- Too close too close!- So I moved it away and hopefully into focus for him.

-What's wrong with that?-He said, genuinely shocked that I was questioning him about the brush but he knew where I was coming from.

-It's covered in toothpaste which I can only assume has been in and in out of your mouth but that is not the worrying thing, no, because this brush or the 50% or so of the bristles remaining have the stiffness of mush!-
He looked down at the floor, suitably scolded. I mentally put toothbrush onto the growing list.

7) Toothpaste tube- used.

8, 9, 10) Three square foil packets, use by date 1984 December. The foil is coming away from the plastic backing. I do not even take these out of the bag. Replacements are not going on the shopping list.

11) A long thin leather zipped pouch, not unlike a pencil case but you'd only fit two or three long pencils inside it. This I had not seen for a long time. I placed it on the side and unzipped it. Dad looked at it but said nothing. I lifted it out of its case. The little sheath was made of something like green malachite, striped like a shimmering mackerel with fat green stripes. I grabbed the blade from the sheath and there was a slight stiffness in the hinge before it eased out. This, I assume, was also stainless steel but here although the straight blade did not shine, you could see the potential for it to do so, this almost surgical blade.

-German steel, that- said Dad -you can just tell by feeling the weight of it, the balance of it... quality-
But I was barely listening.

I was suddenly transported back to a time when I was so small that I couldn't see over a sink in a long forgotten bathroom.

The door to that bathroom was wooden like all the others in the house but the square pane of glass was mullioned and etched into the glass were tiny shells.

I still have no idea how this is achieved.

Normally there would be the sounds of the shower hitting the ceramic bath, the swish of the shower curtain, the flapping of the drying towel but with my father there was also the quietude. There was still the warm moist air in the room, the window cracked open to let out at least some of the steam. The door would be ajar and I would peep around, trying not to make the door creak as it so often did. There was Dad in our small, black and white tiled bathroom. A towel over his shoulder with which to wipe the blade and another towel around his waist. Broad shoulders but strangely hairless backs of his legs. He used to cycle an awful lot and I suppose that's what kept him so spry but his legs were naturally hairless. Sneaking in and there he was, staring hard into the little shaving mirror which was attached to the wooden frame of the window and moved back and forth by a concertina joint like a garden trellis. The little mirror with a slight magnification. There was Dad, constantly battling the condensation on the mirror from misting up, a squeak from the threadbare flannel on the side. On the little window sill stood the shaving brush, slick with white foam and there was Dad, contorting his face this way and that, lifting up his chin as high as it would go as if trying to keep his face above the water like a drowning man and then there it was, the flash of the blade, a glint of silver under the relatively dim bulb. The cut throat razor almost at the throat, the skin under the chin drawn tight from the stretching and then the blade seemed to glide through the foam in one easy stroke right up to the underneath of his chin. Then without even looking, swishing the blade in the hot water in the basin and then pulling it out, a little flick to get rid of excess water and then a little wipe on the towel draped over his shoulder while simultaneously tilting the head, stretching the skin under his neck at a slightly different angle then another swift glide the blade, up then wash then wipe.

In that corner of the bathroom I could have just stayed for the whole spectacle, holding my breath to avoid detection but then, inevitably, my father would be stood, perhaps shifting his weight from one leg to another and he would flip the hovering mirror so, without turning he put his face as close to the mirror, just one swollen eye and a monstrous magnified nose and I would see him looking at me through the reflection. I knew he was going to do it as he did it always. And always it would make me jump out of my skin.

It was probably around this time of my life, Saturday afternoon TV and 'Clash of the Titans' was always on, Larry Olivier, Harry Hamlin as Perseus and there is the moment in the film (thank you Ray Harryhausen) when a mirrored shield is used to see Medusa for the first time. A direct look from her would be enough to turn a man to stone yet just seeing her reflection... but I cannot watch this film to this day without thinking of my father staring into the mirror and turning me to stone.

If I did stay longer in the bathroom, my presence was accepted if a little grudgingly. I would listen to the sound of the razor, harvesting hairs to the sound of sandpaper, the little splash of water and also the echoing drip of the leaky tap that seemed always to be in want of a washer. The gurgle of the water away down the plughole, the rush of the cold water and a splash of aftershave usually of sandalwood or resinous cedarwood. But the blade would be wiped clean and dried before it was folded back into its sheath.

Sometimes though Dad would take out the thin leather strop that was folded just once in the mirrored medicine cabinet.

He would attach one end to the metal hook that was screwed into the wall. Usually a flannel or a bag of spare toilet rolls was hung from there and no female in the house knew of the alternative use of the hook. He pulled the leather tight and very gently, without any ceremony, simply placed the blade on the leather and passed it back and forth before closing the blade and putting both blade and strop back into the cabinet. If I were lucky enough to witness all of this male activity there would be the warning. His hand would be on the cabinet but not letting go of the little glass handle. He would look at me, this time using the reflection in the mirrored cabinet door.

-I never want to see you use that. Do you understand?-

I nodded. I wanted so much to touch the blade.

-It's very sharp. It will cut you. Do you understand?

I nodded again but said nothing.

And of course, later, I get a chair and climbed up to the cabinet and opened it and cut myself with the blade.

Idiot. I still have the scar on my finger.

After that incident the razor was never seen again. It certainly wasn't in the cabinet. I never again crept in to see that piece of theatre, yet now I hold the same razor in my hands.

The first shave, by all accounts and by this I mean my father's account, was a disaster. OK, so no one died but blood was spilt. I learned a valuable lesson though. The water was not hot enough. The plastic razor was rubbish. The flannels were too rough. Old people have very thin skin and are sensitive to temperatures that are too hot or too cold. Yet they are unable to articulate whether the temperature is just right. A sort of anti Goldilocks syndrome. I used a new plastic razor, I used soap and tried to get some sort of foam from it but the foam just wasn't thick enough, just not right.

The main problem was I was shaving him like I shave myself, by looking in a mirror. It just didn't occur to me just to look at his actual face and shave it. I'd be a lot closer to the action to start with and I wouldn't be guessing where the blade was.

But I did what I could.

There wasn't a lot of blood but there was a need for little squares of absorbent tissue paper to be applied. Despite the moans, the squeals and the protests I was asked if I could do it again, sometime perhaps at the weekend. And there was me thinking that if I purposely did a bad job then I'd never be asked to do it again. I mean, the plates I broke when washing-up at home and still I was asked to do it again. I threw away the shaving brush, much to Dad's disdain but it really was a balding badger. All the other bits of rust were equally dispatched. I made a mental note of things to buy and, before the booming TV was reactivated, I bade my farewell.

-Oh la la, ma tete, J'ai gueule de bois!- It must have been that wine, or perhaps, more likely, the amount of it. My father, as I remember never had hangovers at all. There was always something wrong with the wine. It had spoilt or it was corked. But it was the wine, definitely.

What does worry me is that I drank most (all, who am I kidding, I live on my own and have no one else to blame or share the blame... or the wine) and yet I remain reasonably functional this morning. I am sure, that this is a mixture of still being relatively young but also, the number of times I've done this before. My liver must be skilled at processing it all but I'm sure scars will be left. Oh God, I can't even get blotto without the middle class guilt of the fact that my semi pampered life will mean that I live relatively long so I therefore have to look after all my organs especially my currently rock solid liver. Can't I just become a functioning alcoholic, oh I know so many! I devoutly promise, did dib dib that I won't become one of these awful, awful preachy recovering alcoholics that have been through it and they want to help. Oh they are so so smug! Such bores at parties. But perhaps, today, I might just give the sauce a swerve, give the liver a bit of a rest.

So, coffee machine and double espresso.

More toxins. A paracetamol and caffeine chaser.

As I pop out the last two paracetamol from their little foil covered plastic coffins I consider a trip to Tesco. The list. But I'll just sit a bit as the coffee and let the drugs work their magic.

As I think I mentioned, Dad was a keen cyclist. Of course he's coming from a time where there were far less cars on the roads, although the cars that were on the roads were still belching out a partial digestion of leaded petrol and a car was an expensive purchase. I suppose he was swayed by his own father who never owned a car and didn't see a need to do so. If you bought a car back in the days of my grandfather it would no doubt be second hand. There would be rust, of course, that was inevitable and the car would not be reliable. My Dad certainly did not need a car but we did end up buying one at some point. A bottle green Morris Minor, second hand of course, which constantly needed fixing but it did allow us, as a family, to go on little expeditions. At the weekends and school holidays. But there was always tinkering, oil leaks, alternator problems, the ever present threat of damp which meant it hardly ever started in the cold. And so dad cycled. Like his father, he just didn't need a car. And now, I don't need a car. See that word 'need'. Now all cars are made in about 20 minutes, never rust, I mean rust is unheard of. They never break and always start. I mean, they are miracles of a technological age. These young people, buy a car that is so much cheaper, relatively, than they were and so much better that now everyone can buy a car because they 'want' one instead of 'needing' one. This of course then allows you to live your life at a much larger radius. Instead of walking or cycling to a local shop, NO, you drive 10 or 20 miles away because you can. You then get a job which instead of near where you live, NO, you now have to drive 20 to 30 miles to work and then 20 to 30 miles back again. Now you are shackled to the car. You need it. And it wouldn't be so bad if it was just you but it isn't. Everyone else wants a taste of this new found freedom. And everyone is happy to queue up on the same motorways at the same time everyday for this wonderful experience.

And so I cycle.

Portsmouth should be a superb city in which to cycle. It is flat, most of the land I believe, wasn't land at all before the 1500's and a lot of it was reclaimed from the sea. I should know more about this but, you know, I'm really not that interested. The land is just flat, that's the main thing, no tortuous hills, so a bit like the Dutch cities. In the 1920's and 1930's even 40's most of the men in Portsmouth worked in the dockyard and most of these men would gain access through Unicorn gate and most of these men would get there by bicycle. Inexpensive yet individual transport because it was a cycling city and yet, and yet... what happened? The city is on an island and there is no space to expand into. After the war, more money and so car ownership went up but the roads got no bigger so cars and bikes shared the roads. It became much more dangerous to cycle so more and more people bought cars, for safety, until everyone is in a car, and there is no room for both.

Yet I still cycle.

I am clearly an absurdist. I am a contrarian. It seems faintly ridiculous that I should use a vehicle that costs nothing to run, no costs for parking, keeps me fit but does have the slight downside of (and Portsmouth has the highest cycling accident rate for any city in the UK) of risking imminent death when riding at 10 mph from A to B being side swiped by a 10 tonne truck or being slammed in to by some clumsy moron with a heavy right foot who spends more time looking up his Tick Tock big buck hip hop whatever it is on a screen rather then paying any heed to a man on a bicycle.

-Yeah well, I didn't see him- (Correction - you didn't look. If you'd have looked you'd have seen him).

There are the seven ages of man but there are also the ages of a cyclist.

Yes, you might start with a balance bike or stabilisers and then either you go down the BMX or 'proper' bikes of MTB's or racers and then, you get older, realise the call for the Olympics isn't coming and you either try and extend your racing career by encasing yourself in lycra like some overstuffed haggis, spend part of your pension on a bike that weighs little more than the credit card that was used to buy it, then spend every weekend going out for 7 to 8 hours and therefore avoiding any contact with your no doubt loving family. It's either that or golf.

OR you buy a proper bike, probably three gears, that's easy and comfortable to ride and you don't have to dress up like a botched sausage. If you have to buy new clothes for a mode of transport it becomes a sport and no longer has a point.

I, you'll be unsurprised to know, favour the second option. I have two miles to cover. I could walk but today I am in a hurry. I could get the bus but have no wish to contract scrofula or any other communicable disease today. I could drive but it is better for me, and better for the entire planet that I cycle. Also I don't have a car.

As a younger man I used to wear everything to keep me safe on a bike. A huge array of flashing lights, a reflective vest, fluorescent orange and yellows. Reflective lozenges slotted into the spokes like glittering peacock feathers and the obligatory helmet strapped on tight and painted bright. What would astound me were the old codgers on their three speed Raleigh Chilterns, Sturmey Archer hubs, sit up and beg with their corduroy trousers, flat caps and black anoraks without so much as a reflective sticker between them all them. Goodness me I often thought, well they're just asking for trouble, they'll be killed in an instant, almost invisible. But what never occurred to me at the time was they had already cycled for most of their lives. They had survived. They had evolved. But I thought them all fools. And yet for all of my lights, my reflectors, my fluorescence and my reflective qualities, my pure scintillation, it seemed not to make the slightest bit of difference as to whether someone would screech their brakes in front of me, or cut me right up on a junction or essentially act as if I were completely invisible. In fact it was quite clear that wearing all this reflective cycling garb was merely an invitation to be hit. In fact it simply made it easier to be hit as I was more visible. Yes, that was it! I was making myself an easier target.

So, once, after a particularly unpleasant coming together between myself on my 1/3 of a horse power Raleigh Chiltern and a 300 horse power BMW M3

- Sorry mate- he said as he at least got out of his car but only to survey the damage to his bonnet and although he was saying to me…

-Sorry mate, didn't see you- you alright?- he not once looked away from the dent my bike that I had made on his precious motor car. It was nothing that couldn't be buffed out…..

I make very little impact in anyone's life and this was the physical evidence.

…and he didn't look because he didn't care. And he didn't care because even though my day had been completely ruined, bike ruined, he would receive no penalty and was simply annoyed because he would have to fix his bonnet. Police don't care. Not even called. I was injured but as I was walking wounded, I was suddenly a statistic. A cycling incident. Chalk it up. No one made any notes as to how I was hit.

1) I was decked out like a fucking Christmas tree.
2) He was texting while driving and his music was on so loud that African elephants in the Serengeti could feel each tremor through the subwoofer.

3) His glasses were so dark that it looked like Ray Charles had been driving and he may well have done a better job!

So I ride my bike. I don't wear anything that I wouldn't wear whilst walking. I cycle in the style of someone sitting upright on a chair and just as comfortable and the only extra item that I don is a fatalistic view of cycling in that if I do get hit then they better make a decent job of it.
I've not been hit since.

I mean, look it's, what, 10:30 ish. What are all these people doing in Tesco's at this time of the morning? Is this just an indication of how fragmented the working patterns are in this country now? However there does seem to be an awful lot of old people just pottering about, spending their gold plated pensions. Retired at 60 and then they realise because of the fabulous health system that has been there all their lives, they've got another 30 years of interminable boredom, Countdown, walk-in baths and Saga cruises to endure.
Today though they are making it their business just to get in my way. It's the out and out dithering that gets to me.
There's always two of them. Hubby must come as well, dressed up, tie, jacket, high waisted trousers all the way up to the nipples and I mean where do you buy trousers that

high? And both of them, let's call them 'Agnes and Gerald' standing by their trolley, have a discussion in the fresh meat aisle. This is a discussion they could have had whilst eating their supermarket own brand bran flakes at 4am when they got up.

-Well, of course, we have to keep an eye on Gerald's cholesterol now he's past 65. He's on statins as well, yes, but it's all down to diet. No more fry ups of a morning for Gerald- Poor Gerald- and he's on these, whaddya call them, these plant yoghurts, supposed to bring down your levels. He says they taste of flour water although how he knows what that tastes like I just don't know and he could murder a fried slice. Well, I said, he can have his fried slice, I told him that but I shan't be visiting him in hospital after his quadruple bypass, absolutely not!- Agnes adjusts her imaginary glasses. They could have discussed all of this over their Daily Mail crossword. Of course they read the Daily Mail. But no, they are discussing it now, in front of the chicken where I just want to pick up some chicken, legs, thighs, don't care really. Instead of me doing this though I am now the only audience member for a short play about chicken. It is an urban, gritty, domestic drama harking back to those plays from the late 1950s written by those angsty, angry young men. Writing about gritty issues at the time, giving a voice to those previously unheard by society.

Setting- the fresh meat section in a contemporary supermarket in Portsmouth. A shopping trolley partially filled with vegetables and fruit, is in front of the chicken, currently blocking access to any other customers who might wish to peruse the chicken.

Characters

Gerald, (played by Jim Broadbent) a retired gentleman wearing very high waisted trousers. White shirt, blue knitted tie, sky blue flat cap, glasses with metal frames.

He wears comfortable shoes which slip onto his feet.

Agnes, (played by Meryl Streep) slightly smaller in stature than Gerald- a stout woman, large bust, wearing a shapeless shift of a dress that does little to disguise her obese and waddling frame. Grey hair, recently permed, thick stockings under the dark flowered dress and costume jewellery necklace that clacks every time she moves, much to Gerald's annoyance. Agnes is wearing tight fitting shoes that make her feet look like risen loaves fresh from the oven. They are clearly uncomfortable to wear.

Scene 1 Act 1

Curtain Rises

Harsh spotlight on both characters.

Agnes holds two pre-packaged packs of prepared chicken, one in each hand. Agnes is staring over her pink framed glasses that are attached on a chain around her neck and she looks back and forth between each packet. To the audience the packs look identical.

Agnes- We didn't talk about what we wanted for tea tonight, did we Gerald?

Gerald- No, we didn't.

A pause as Agnes continues to look back and forth between the two seemingly identical packets of chicken.

Agnes- (still looking at the chicken)- We could do a chicken pie. What would you say to a chicken pie, Gerald?

Gerald- Well, I…

Agnes (continues talking as if she hasn't heard Gerald) - But then if we have pie what sort of meat do we want. I mean the price of this chicken, just astronomical.

Gerald- Oh I know.

Agnes- (again seemingly ignoring Gerald's brief interjection)- One of these is a bit cheaper but it's in a different colour packet. This one says it's 'Halal'.

(she says this with the emphasis on the start of the word instead of the correct way at the end of the word.)

-Oh, I don't like that. Isn't it just for Muslims? I didn't think they ate chicken?

-Gerald- I think everyone eats…

Agnes- Oh no, I don't want that. I want proper chicken.

Gerald- It is proper chicken dear, I think it's just been blessed or something.

Agnes- (finally looking up at Gerald, aghast, lifting her head up so she can look at Gerald but without moving her glasses as both hands are employed holding prepacked chicken)- What?! Blessed? By a priest?

Gerald- No, I think by a… you know…- (Gerald does know but he doesn't want to say as he knows what the likely reaction will be…)- one of those Holy men.

Agnes- Oh no Gerald, I can't have that in my pie! (Agnes deposits the Halal chicken back in the chiller section, now just holding it by one finger and thumb as if it is somehow contaminated,)- but we could get some thigh pieces Gerald, we could do a nice stew.

Gerald- Yes, we could do that.- (Gerald makes a slight move to raise the cuff of his jacket perhaps to look at the time on his watch, and then catches himself doing it and pulls the cuff down in the full knowledge that the last time they were shopping Gerald checked his watch and he was instantly accused of- oh sorry Gerald am I boring you? Is there somewhere else you'd rather be?)

Agnes- (Agnes is now looking between two pieces of seemingly identical packs of pre packaged chicken thighs. She is peering over her glasses again)
- I mean, one pack has got thighs and drumsticks but this other pack has just drumsticks……but you've got less meat on a drumstick… but it is cheaper. Gerald what do you think?

Gerald- (Gerald looks out towards the audience with a look that perfectly communicates that he retired at the age of 60 and he is now in his late 60's and he could have another 20 years of this purgatory and if he felt the cold metal of the barrel of a loaded shotgun in his mouth and he pulled the trigger it will be a merciful

release. In his last dying moments on earth he would
hear the echoing boom from the report of the gun. There
would be the metallic voice " In-store cleaner to
aisle 8 for wet spill"- alongside the perpetual
wittering about chicken.)
Lights fade to black.
Curtain down.
Rapturous applause
Oscars all around.

Finally, now they've gone I can have a look at the chicken. It
takes me one, maybe two seconds to choose.

In the basket.

Another thing, and it is very much a thing, when did it
become acceptable to eat your way around a supermarket? I
remember, not so long ago, that you would go into a
supermarket with a trolley or a basket. You would then
browse the shelves in a no doubt glorious hedonistic
experience of consumerism before taking your chosen items
to the till and then buying them. You could then take the
items home. You might unpack them and then you might
consume them. Call me an old 'stick in the mud', dyed-in-the-
wool traditionalist.

You want something, you find it, you buy it, you eat it. In
that order.

And now? At some point, and I cannot put my finger on
exactly when... it became acceptable to eat in the

supermarket. Yes, of course, if loose grapes were on sale of course you would try the odd one, of course you would, just to taste. You wouldn't buy car without road testing it would you? No.

This is not what I mean.

So, children in shopping trolleys are given bags of sweets from the shelf to eat. You haven't paid for them. They do not belong to you until you have paid for them. This is in flagrant disregard of my choose-buy-eat system.

This is choose-eat-buy!

I mean, call me a traditionalist (oh, you did!) but why don't parents just tell their children- "you can have something when we get outside"- or even- just shouting at children! That used to work. But now, adults, I mean, really?! If they don't eat a Scotch egg and a pork pie whilst walking around a shop, they're going to lapse into a diabetic coma in minutes, is that right? And you never see anyone sneakily eating an apple, banana or mixed salad, no, it's always a Scotch egg, a pastie or pork pie. And then what do you do, do people then take the empty packet to the checkout? Do people have the effrontery to do this, the brass neck? Unlikely because whenever I am looking for something like washing liquid or dishwasher tablets...whoa...there we are, the half eaten remnants of a Scotch egg, hollowed out, a trail of orange breadcrumbs. How long has that been there? How did we sink so low as a society? How did it come to this where society somehow accepts people eating pasties in a supermarket.

We are all complicit.

Perhaps we should all be weighed coming into the store and on the way out. Anyone who has put weight on can be tasered…or at least pay a fine. Needless to say I found a half drunk orange juice open in the detergent aisle and the remnants of a Mars bar near the curry cooking sauces.

It's all making me a bit sick. And the power of the paracetamol is running out. I gather what I need and take it to the checkout in record time in the full knowledge I've forgotten most of what I came in for. I just have to get to some fresh air.

One of the benefits of the pandemic was personal space. In the sharp hindsight optics of hundreds of thousands of people dying perhaps personal space is not the glinting jewel that one immediately refers to but, for me it was quite the salve. You may have picked up that perhaps, I am on Jean Paul Sartre's side when it comes to other people, especially real people in my vicinity. I know that in different societies there are different distances which constitute personal space. In Spain, certainly, people seem quite happy being close enough to see latent food in each other's teeth. In

France they move further apart and further still in jolly old England. In Italy they are quite happy in each other's trousers.

If it were allowed, and I wouldn't be stoned to death a result, I would wear a large Elizabethan hoop dress which would enforce a distance of at least a metre from any other person. Of course it may have the added benefit of keeping people 50 metres away as they can see a man wearing a hoop dress.

Is the circus in town?

But my fantasies had been realised. There was paint on concrete. Warnings. Stay two metres apart. Arrows showing you which way to queue. And when you got to the checkout you had all the time in the world. Only your items are on the conveyor belt and, yes, they were conveyed. You had time to put your items in your bag. Of course there might not have been anything to buy, certainly no toilet rolls but still I was fairly confident that people had relatively clean hands. I saw quiet where most people saw sombre. I felt space where most people felt distance. It was sheer luxury. It couldn't continue. I mean I thought that people would see that giving everyone space, giving everyone a bit of time would make society relaxed and just altogether better. There was the scarce belief, just for a few moments that this was going to happen. When the barriers started to be taken down people were still wary and timid, little woodland creatures sticking their noses out of burrows to see if spring had arrived.

In Portsmouth it certainly didn't take long for elbows to be sharpened, barging to begin and queues to be concertinaed once more.

Yet somehow it was worse.

It was worse because we, all of us, knew that we were better than this. The space was luxury and yet we will cram together because we just want to get out as fast as possible and if that means treading on heads then so be it. Often, when I have packed my bags at the far end and now I need to pay, the person behind me has already barged through with their trolley actually barring my way to pay. It takes a lot for me not to grab their trolley and push it hard back at them, hoping they fall and by falling they understand that just because someone has left a space it doesn't necessarily mean that it has to be filled in an instant. But of course nature abhors a vacuum and I abhor space hogging cretins at checkouts. I may say something to them, looking at where their trolley is....

-Oh, sorry, are you paying for me?- In the most sarcastic tone but this is usually met by furrowed brows. I'll only say this to someone who wouldn't instantly punch me to death, perhaps a woman over eighty.

For now I have my own goods on the conveyor belt shuddering their way up to the checkout. You see, I leave a space for the person in front. I give them time but what that does mean is the man behind me gets as close as possible. I don't have to look but I can feel his presence. He is so close that, because we are not married I feel I should have a chaperone. We are so close that in some societies we would be married. We are so close that I might have been made pregnant. I have to keep mumbling under my breath. This too shall pass.

The woman ahead -COME ON!!- is fumbling with the change in her purse, little coins individually counted out. COME ON!! Please! I almost offer to pay for her just to get her and my new stalker gone.

Finally I say a cursory hello to (I peer at 'happy to help-Suzanne's badge) and stand at the other end of the checkout. My headache is back and it has joined forces with another headache, one that presses and pounds across my forehead, brought on by this whole stressful situation whilst the deep engine room throb of the hangover provides delightful base notes. Piccolos and timpani, together at last. I hold out my bag, pleading for the young Suzanne to get cracking and send it all down. But I only see the jumbo bottle of Domestos bleach slide down towards me.

My eyes are closed. My mouth is dry and I find I'm hanging on to the edge of the checkout. I see that instead of the rest of the items coming down, the paracetamol, the whisky, the ibuprofen, the razor blades, shaving foam and brush, Suzanne has activated the little red light above her till. What? What! Oh, yes, of course, to sell the whiskey she needs an adult's permission. Why did I choose this till? I exhale the sort of exhalation you do to stop yourself being violently sick. I try to breathe away the pain.

Appearing at Suzanne's side are now two women. One, the older and smaller of the two but wearing a tailored jacket but of the cheapest nylon so she must be a supervisor. Next to her, a younger woman in one of those awful fleeces that seems to constitute a uniform nowadays. Who is she? They all come together in whispers, occasionally looking at me. What have I done? Am I the millionth customer? Am I to receive one of those giant cheques? Or am I the millionth customer who is going to complain? Much more likely.

The older lady, giving a final and definite nod at Suzanne, comes around to speak to me. The pain across my eyes is more than I can bear and I can just about bring her face into focus.

-Hello Sir, I just wondered if we could have a brief chat?- as I see the rest of my shopping being hived off into a separate bag- perhaps we could go to my office?- She grabs at my upper arm and suddenly I am focused and back in the room.

A line has been crossed.

-Could you please let go of my arm- which I say with more menace than I intended. She lets go of my arm but does not move away- what is this?- I am panicking a little but strangely this allows clear thinking -you don't have a security guard so clearly you don't think I'm shoplifting so....-

-Yes we could go into my office, sir, it might be for the best...-

-Or perhaps we could stay right here and you tell me what this is all about- I could hear someone shouting... before realising that it was me... The two women exchange a look, agreeing a pre-made plan and I am moved just to the side. Their voices are lowered now realising I didn't wish to be escorted anywhere.

-Look sir, I'm sorry, but it's just that we have a number of items that we sell in the shop that, if sold together with other items, well, they raise a red flag and...- The old woman tailed off and the younger woman, with an altogether brighter voice carried on...

-We have a duty of care to intervene-

I felt hot and dizzy. Fortunately there was a chair behind me. I sat down but to my annoyance I was bookended by these two women, one sitting next to me, the other, the younger, kneeling in front of me. She carried on talking.

You have bleach, 5 packets of paracetamol, a litre of whiskey, and two types of razorblade. I am a trained in-store counsellor.

My heart shuddered.

-You're a what, sorry?-

-I've been on the course-

-What, to be an in-store counsellor...?- I couldn't help but laugh but stopped quickly as my laughed made me look more like a lunatic.

-Yes, sir, but we have a duty of care, but...-

-Yes, you mentioned that. But you don't have enough tills open because you want everyone to use those silly, ghastly self-service checkouts. The shelves are littered, positively brimming with half-eaten Scotch eggs and yet you have an in-store counsellor?

-Er, yes!- said the young woman, clearly trained to miss any point that I was trying to make.

-And you were hoping to sell me all of this stuff, at a premium, I might add, but when you think that I might use any of it to top myself, I assume, then the red flag goes up because, what? You care about me? Or you care about the fact that you might lose a customer?-

-Oh no sir, we have a duty of care...-

-Yes- I paused, -you said-

-So- my thoughts now gathering and clarifying -if I say that the bleach is for my father's bathroom, the paracetamol is for my thumping headache which in part has been brought on by shopping at this soulless excuse of an enterprise and the razor blades are for me having to shave my father because any social care that he was entitled to has now evaporated in this heartless society, The whiskey is for me so I can drink it in one single draught and hope all my problems simply melt away. And if I wanted to rid myself of the abject pain and suffering of modern life I would simply put myself forward for a full frontal lobotomy, grab myself a ghastly polyester fleece and work here for 40 hours a week, perhaps in the hope of being fast tracked to the heady position of in-store counsellor! Now, can I buy my shopping?!!

•

-So, did they sell you everything you wanted?- asked Dad.
I pulled a chair in from the dining room into the bathroom. This meant that he'd be more comfortable, no teetering on a stool but I would be inversely less comfortable having to bend over all the time. Never mind. I told him of my shopping exploits, with some embellishments of course.

What is a saga if not a piece of tapestry on which one embroiders your particular version of the truth.

-Well, for a store that had a 'duty of care' they still needed to make a profit so as long as I told them I had no desire to top myself they were quite happy. I bought everything but could only buy one packet of paracetamol. I could go back 10 times or more, buy one packet each time. I suppose this deters the casual suicidist.

Dad was now sat up in the chair. There was now another three days of growth on his face since my last effort. There were still a few little nicks (Stevie Nicks!!!) from the hacking job I did last time but they had healed up to a thin red line, barely visible to any other eye save for mine. We exhausted our small arsenal of chit chat and now Dad was looking squarely into the mirror and looking back up at me. This time I was much better prepared. I had taken the safety razor apart, at home, and most of the rust had been from the crumbling razor blade. Any tiny dots of corrosion on the razor itself were easily erased by a piece of sandpaper judiciously rubbed.

I used the razor myself at home, just to give it a test drive. I was surprised at how pleasing the weight of the razor was, how the weight made such a difference to the quality of the shave. It wasn't perfect, rubbing the mirror and bending over the sink but it was… pleasing.

I was prepared.

Sleeves rolled up and folded over themselves, tie tucked inside the shirt. Dad was quiet. He'd seen me lay out everything new at the side of the sink. As new and shining, as everything I'd taken out was dull. The safety razor affixed with a new blade. Two different types of shaving foam to choose from. One of them with the pleasant scent of bergamot whilst there was also a small roundel of black soap which needed just a splash of water and the new brush to agitate it all into a thick lather. That one had a more oriental green tea and lemongrass aroma. I'd also done just little research of how to do hot towels at home and it doesn't take a huge leap of the imagination to think it would involve a sealed bag and a boiling kettle. I gave it a whirl. Fortunately the dining chair had arms so dad could steal himself if the whole performance was overwhelming for him. I ran the hot water into the stopped sink, rubbed a hot damp flannel over Dad's face which was now tipped upwards, his chin held in my hands. Suddenly there was trust as if from nowhere. Was it that I was exhibiting confidence in what I was doing, certainly more so than last time. Confidence is everything, but was it more that he'd resigned himself to this being it. If he moaned or criticised then I'd do it no more. He was past the point of doing it himself. Still holding his head up, I put on the fluffy hot towel. I wasn't quite sure how to arrange it. I should have watched the rest of the youtube video but, anyway, I sort of cupped his chin with the middle of it and then twisted the ends of it up and then over the top of his head like tying a plum pudding or a Victorian gentleman's toothache. I cradled his chin and his neck and I couldn't help but feel the texture of his skin and compare it to my own. It was certainly warm but surely that was the towel and the hot water. It was the thinness of it. It did hang slightly loose but not overly so. Elastic up to a point, but still soft and thin. I suddenly felt nervous as if this skin would tear as soon as I started shaving. I took away the towel after a good minute or so, pleased to see that he was still under there, his face not having dissolved away through the steam.

-Right then- hearing my own voice at least trying to be confident which did much to dispel my worry -do you want this spray foam or the brush?- I spoke to him through the mirror. It was difficult looking at your own father so close but the mirror, the reflection, gave a natural distance.

-Oh, I think the brush, don't you?- he said, almost enjoying this performance. And that is what it was. I was merely an actor, acting the shave. I put a little towel around his shoulders and unscrewed the pot. I moistened the brush in the hot water and then shook the water out. Droplets clung to the bristles like misty branches in a predawn forest. I dipped the brush onto the cake of soap and lathered up the brush.

-Right, close your mouth- and he did so. He was watching what I was doing in the mirror but I was now watching the actual face. The bristles, although new, although full of lather still felt stiff and I felt his skin move over the bones of his cheek. He didn't complain. I then brushed around the jaw line, from the back to the front. Subconsciously Dad pushed his jaw out a little just to make it a little easier to brush. Under the chin I could feel the three day old growth of hair against the brush. I lather it up again until half of dad's face was foam and smelling of crisp lemongrass.

-So, Dad, last chance to back out. Happy for me to go ahead?-
A small but perceptible nod from the man in the mirror.

I reached for the razor which was on its side but not resting on the actual blade. I placed it in the foamy water. Gave it a good shake, to warm up the metal and then pulled it out, shaking off a few drips which plinked in the sink. I caught my father's eye in the mirror.

The tiny little flat we were in was quiet but that didn't mean it was quiet. The paper thin walls next door, above, below meant that all sorts of noise percolated through. Radios on. I heard big band music from one side and something with a beat from another. People talking into telephones but shouting into them as if not comprehending the amplifying nature of a telephone at the other end, every syllable was heard. Yet I was buoyed by this hubbub. Almost like a noisy barber shop and I was just shaving someone, anyone.

I can't say that I have ever killed an animal myself let alone skin one however I've seen enough TV to know that skinning animals is all about keeping the flesh taught. If you shave yourself you instinctively know what parts of the face you're going to run the razor across but shaving someone else, I'm sure, there has to be a constant conversation.

-I'm just going to do underneath first, okay- and Dad stuck out his chin pulling all of that loose skin under his chin quite taut. With my fingers I pulled the skin around his Adam's apple and here goes nothing.

I put the blade to the bottom of his throat and pull it upwards towards his jutting chin. The foam is gone and to my astonishment so are the hairs which I see on the razor. Such a sharp razor requires very little in the way of pressure. I breathe out hard realising that I've been holding my breath. Keeping the skin taut again I ran the blade upwards, nearby and again I feel the hairs being cut. There is a distinct possibility that I could do this! It is one thing theorising, doing all the research in the world but it all comes to nought if you can't pony up and do the do.

Once underneath the chin is shaved I can then press my fingers onto the pink clean nude skin and pull tight the skin that goes up the jaw line to his ear. A few swipes of the blade and across the stretched hollows of his cheek.

The only bits left now are the more technical areas. To do the point of his chin I hold his head to the side, mainly because it afforded me a better angle but also he cannot see exactly what I'm doing in the mirror. I twist his head the other way so I can access the other side and then the only remaining foam on his face is that on his upper lip. He does his best to stretch this part of his face, his philtrum, over his teeth and, standing in front of him, I shave downwards as closely as I dare. And then rinse any foam off with the flannel. Not one nick. I breathe normally again.

Whilst rinsing out the brush and the razor, Dad pushes himself up from his chair, moves as close as he can to the mirror and scrutinises my handiwork, tautening and flexing his raw skin, running his fingers over it, feeling for stragglers. Only when I finish washing everything and rinse the hairs down the plug hole does he finally pass judgement.

-Hmm, it'll have to do-

High praise indeed.

•

Friday means a deadline, all be it one that is self-imposed. Any outstanding dyslexia reports are written before the weekend. I feel that if I didn't adhere by this strict brick wall then I'd never get them done. I could do them at the weekend as weekends seem very similar to other days of the week. People still work, places are open and I wonder if we didn't just lose something by not treating at least one day a special. It used to be Sunday but it needn't be Sunday. I remember very clearly a time when shops were shut on Sundays. People had to plan buying food the day before. Oh heavens, the planning needed, but of course if nothing is open on a day this means that everyone gets a break, whether they like it or not.

People used different clothes, Sunday best. People walked out and you could measure all other days by Sunday. But if shops are open on Sunday, people have to work because people want to shop. People want, or need to shop because they have no time to shop in the week. And so we are in a constant shopping society. I mean there's no more money, it's just spread a bit more thinly.

I switch on the computer, leave the cursor blinking and just pop next door, just to see how they are doing with the bathroom. I can already hear them crashing about in there. It's supposed to be finished today. Why is there still crashing about? Unless it's noisily packing everything up and I say that without much belief aloud.

Tidying up! HA!

-Hello, anyone in?- I shout upstairs knowing exactly where they are. The crashing suddenly stops. Is it burglars? There's nothing to steal.

I start walking up the stairs. They still creak.

-Hello?-

Now I can hear muffled voices and much shuffling in the bathroom but as I make it to the top of the stairs old 'matey boy' greets me in his tight white T-shirt with his unnecessarily large tool belt and dirty boots.

-Hey, mate, just coming over to see you in a minute-

Was he my arse! Why do people lie so?

-Oh yes, well I thought I'd come over, save you the bother. You did promise that the bathroom would be absolutely finished today, did you not? Shall we see?-

I don't know what got into me. Maybe just the power of avoiding doing one job has to be channelled into something else. The energy has to go somewhere.

-Oh yeah yeah yeah, all done, tiling, shower, shelves all done as requested but we can't go in there just yet cause the erm...- and it was this 'erm' accompanied with a furtive look at the closed bathroom door... -plumber's just finishing off, a few odd joints that needed sorting but, you know, brazing an' that and today was the only day he could come so......-

I'd never heard him talk so fast. Did he appear nervous? Should I be nervous?

-Anyway mate- he went on -can we just pop downstairs, we need to show you a few changes in the...... downstairs toilet. Just a few changes because of the pipe work in the bathroom.

And now his ushering me downstairs was really quite insistent. As I started down the stairs I heard him behind me, not even going in the bathroom but tapping on the glass and saying -just popping downstairs mate. You're gonna be long in there?- A pause.

-'bout 15 to 20 minutes mate!-

Do they all call each other 'mate'! Is it some sort of conspiracy, a special code!? But without actually seeing my own finished bathroom it does at least appear to be all finished and these builders I will never see again. Even if the house falls down and they are the last builders on earth, I would rather fashion bricks out of mud with my bare hands and fix it myself.

I know what it is, he's just being nice, buttering me up because he and his little chimp want their money. He's showing me what he's done but, actually he's showing my what I have paid for. Yes, he can be proud but he wouldn't even be here save for my money, money which is not from an inexhaustible supply.

-There's a little hairline crack, look, in the plaster, just there. Which I point out to him just so I get some sort of conversation going. Of course, he has an answer. He has an answer for everything.

-Well, yeah, of course there'll be cracks. That's the drying out of the plaster but also the movement of the house-

He says this in a way so it feels as if I, personally, am being blamed for the movement of the house.

-Oh yeah, all these old houses move about. Once you slap a few coats of paint. Bosh! It'll be fine!-

What does he mean by 'bosh'? It is the same sound as 'slap dash'. I don't like it. The walls have been freshly skimmed with plaster, that glorious earthy smell. Still a little damp in patches. Still unpainted and yet there are cracks. The wall, however small, is breaking. I contemplate this for one second as I'm bending over, spying the crack, as small as it is, with one beady eye. As I close in, all around me disappears, I am a satellite zooming in from space and the crack is suddenly a dried river bed snaking through a parched landscape. The fresh plaster, the dying planet. Even in new life there is the always the spectre of death. Each newborn baby, born in the knowledge that it too will die. I think, momentarily, of telling him this but I then imagine the back and forth eye rolling between him and his little chimp thinking me to be a complete moron, ripe for the ripping off! I merely say- hmm- and he completely ignores it.

There is a deep grunting noise coming from upstairs as if, briefly, someone is in pain.

-Erm, shouldn't we go up there, check they're ok?-

-Nah, he's alright, just doing a bit of......pipe work... tight fitting joints...... that sort of thing-

He is disguising a smile and it is there, just for a moment before it disappears and we are looking at some skirting board joints in the conservatory which he seems especially proud of.

-I mean, we're very happy to come in and paint it for you. I've got some great guys who could come in, they be done in a few days-

And for 'a few days' read 'a few weeks' for what will be a botched job using the cheapest possible materials.

-I mean, the joints in these skirts really are good but they could do with a specialist team to paint them, get the best out of them-

-Very kind of you to offer but I already have my own team coming in next week to start painting-

Obviously I have no such team organised at all but the idea of having anything to do with this man again brings me out in a cold sweat. The conservatory though, I like. A simple shape, two doors with a tiled floor and it will be wonderful to fill it with lots of greenery come the summer. There is a little chill in the air, the sun not having come around to warm this part of the house yet. The garden would need a bit of work but at least all of their builders crap was gone, hopefully removed and not buried!

-And that tap, the outside tap?- I venture, not expecting it to have been done at all despite asking many times. But the door from the conservatory was opened, a slight creak, which I ignored, I can fix that. Then he, as if a glamorous hostess from a 1980's game show...

-Ta dah!- and shows me the handiwork. All he can see is a brass tap which he turns on to show actual water coming out and then, as if equally miraculous, when the tap is closed the water stops. What I see is a brass tap, retrofitted onto a wall. The drilling has chipped parts of the brick where the pipe has come out of the wall. The tap is not in the place where I asked it to be but no doubt if I wanted it where I actually asked for it to be placed, I mean I'm only bloody paying for it, I would hear yet another story about pipes having to be moved, expense, this is where most outside taps go all of that stuff but there is at least a tap on the outside wall. Despite me seeing these issues I say nothing. I just want them gone from my house and from my life.

I know that builders, most builders, try to outrun the law of diminishing returns.

They dig, they build, they plaster, they put in pipes for electric and water and when the job is almost done, 95%, it's just the little bits of snagging usually caused by the fact they didn't do something properly in the first place, which might mean undoing something or bodging something else, snagging generally. If only they could do it to a slightly higher standard in the first place but most builders know that if they complete a job to 97% or 98% and the customer knows that will just take ages to complete they just want the builders out of their hair and will pay just to make them go away.

This is what I am doing. I can see the handles in the kitchen have not been put on as I would like them. Yes, I should ask him to do them again but he will moan like a baby, go off for a week in search of parts whilst doing another job concurrently, and it will never be done.

There is another series of grunts from upstairs either indicating pain or huge amounts of lifting and shifting and for a bathroom that is essentially being handed over today it fills me with trepidation and not the smallest amount of suspicion. Is this another bodge?

-Look, I don't mean to be rude but, I've got things to do and really I just want to see the bathroom and….- and then I hear the shower run in the bathroom, the boiler kicks in proving that whatever was being fixed or re fixed is now complete. I hear footsteps clumping down the bare wooden stairs and exiting the door. I see not two but three people.

The first man out, tall, same work boots as the builder but with a barely fitting boiler suit. Do they all go to the same store? Central casting for dodgy builders perhaps? The second plumber was a lot shorter, trousers rolled up a little to reveal, well, clear plastic spiked heels and painted toenails. Certainly not health and safety compliant. She turned around, hair up in a bun, a full face of makeup and, if I was not mistaken a little sweat on her top lip and she gives a little wink not to me but at the builder behind me before stopping outside and then into the waiting Transit van. The heavy man clumping down the stairs behind her was more your typical plumber. Dirty boiler suit, baseball cap worn backwards but all smudged with dirt carrying a big plastic box of tools.

-You're all done mate?- asks 'Andy, mate'.

-Oh yeah, all sorted. Everything flushed out and cleared- said the plumber. He boomed - Just need to put the panel back on the bath OK?- And then a cursory look at me - Alright mate?- To which I just smiled. He disappeared out of the door.

I went up to the bathroom, a bit of water on the floor but I could see new pipes under the bath. All the tiles were on the wall. The tall slim radiator, chrome, up on the wall, almost in the place where I'd ask for it to be put. Hmm. It was OK and it was finished.

-Looks great- I said to them, back downstairs.

-Yep, not a bad job- and for the first time, he didn't call me mate.

There was a little, just a tiny discernible note of deference in his voice. Was he about to say 'sir'…of course not. He was just lingering by the door, toolbox in hand because he was waiting for his final cheque. Just money. I gave him the envelope that was in my pocket. It felt, as I handed it over, like racketeering. I had invited them into my life and now I wanted them gone. He simply crammed the envelope into his pocket and any notes of deference vaporised. I was again to be sneered at and mocked. But they closed the door. The house was quiet. They were gone. I sat back on the stair, put my head in my hands and sobbed as my stress was released.

So, the whole point of getting this house, the reason for me suffering the indignity of the mocking builders is that the house can be rented out, for a reasonable price. I'm not greedy but just enough to keep me ticking over. A little security, less reliance on any work I might have to do. But it's not finished. It needs painting. It needs carpet and all those finishing touches and, I know if I don't get on with it on, the house will stay empty and cold.

•

Another dispiriting shop is a hardware chain store. Yes, those two letters, we all know them. Our local store, one of those giant warehouses had rows and rows of the same thing. If you wanted 9 inch nails and they had them but only one type, which was fine but if you needed galvanised ones, they didn't have them.

-We can order them in- they would say but they were never ordered in.

If anything the place was too big yet somehow never having what you really wanted.

Anyway, paint.

Obviously they had a dizzying array of paint, stacked to the gunnels with paint, paint tottering above you, hemming you in with all sorts of colours, from bright uranium orange to all shades of pastels from seen old men's shirts. Matt, gloss, lustre, semi matte. Exterior, interior, undercoat, primers and hardeners, paints with elastic fibres in to cover those hairline cracks in new plaster. Every type of every colour except I didn't really know what colour I wanted.

Unless you bought those magazines then you didn't know what other people had in their houses. You go to a restaurant, you order what's fresh, what's popular and the waiter will tell you. Colours on walls? There were magazines, of course, 'Interiors Inc', 'On my Wall' to the more dignified 'Country Life' and people bought these magazines. I don't know who they were but they must do as they keep being published. And, even in the magazine sections of the weekend papers there will be two or three pages, spreads of interiors where there will be a theme, I don't know, fruits, say.

And here we have Thomasina and Archibald poring over their magazines, stroking dogs and wearing clothes straight out of the 'Toast' catalogue, posing in their massive kitchen with an island, and Aga range. There will be a 'feature wall' of a tangerine colour with neighbouring walls being grey or taupe. On other walls a framed picture of an advert for grapes which was found in a Parisian flea market from the 1950's. There will be the obligatory black Labradors and their names will be in the accompanying article, possibly called Toby and Willoughby. The next page, Thomasina reclining on their enormous Chesterfield sofa whilst Archibald pours black coffee from a Mokka pot, the photographer catching the movement of the coffee, whilst in front of the huge log burner which flickers away. On the walls in the first drawing room, one wall is damson purple, a colour like a five day old black eye, and on that wall an original Warhol banana, with bruises, which featured on the Velvet Underground album cover.

It is just a newspaper article, on the surface, of trends of colours on people's walls. I mean it is just paint, but also it is this lifestyle pornography where we, the poor peeping Tom are allowed rarefied access into the world of our betters and they are our betters because they are richer. And the whole article is topped by Thomasina, (39) telling us all how she sourced the pieces (meaning bought the shit that was hanging on the walls)

-Well, Archie and I were in one of those charming flea markets on our way down to Biarritz for the skiing and I saw it and I just had to have it. Didn't I Archie?-

Archie, by the way he stands, by his sneer at all below him, is clearly a banker or some sort of investor as he just lets Thomasina get on with the decorating in their tiny eight bedroom Georgian manor house in Richmond.

These trends magazines don't sell themselves you know!

Are they merely taking pictures and reflecting what trends are or as I suspect, are they setting the trends? This season, apparently, it is earthy colours of biscuits and terracotta and next season why not freshen up your walls with the new trend of citrus colours, lemons, limes and tangerines. People will buy, maybe not the paint but certainly the magazines and newspapers.

I do not subscribe to any sort of magazine or trend and merely wanted paint with which to cover my walls. I approached the young lady in the paint section. She had on orange dungarees and to most men and indeed women this attire would scream angry feminist lesbian. For certain men of a certain age who stayed up very late in their formative years to watch Betty Blue, a woman in dungarees means something very different. It's either her or Felicity Kendall in 'The Good Life'. Indeed.

I looked at her name badge which said, in computer printed handwriting, Faye.

-Hello there, I'm just looking for some paint-

I say this whilst being in the kingdom of paint and bless her for not just looking around and saying, -well, you've come to the right place - -but I've no idea what to get. I tried very hard to ignore the fact that when Faye started talking it was with that slightly patronising tone that very young people use towards 'older people'. Faye, in her dungarees, multiple ear piercings, strands of hair being purple and green and tattoos on her hand, her hand! That must hurt! And I try desperately hard not to think about what the other tattoos maybe and where they might be... Oh, Betty Blue how you shaped a young boy's mind.

Focus man, focus!

She cocks her head to one side and she looks at what I'm wearing (yes, OK, a grey cardigan does not help my case) but her tone is just one step away from asking whether or not I needed to go to the toilet! She goes through every iteration of paint and also where I want to put the paint.

- Oh, well, if it is fresh plaster then you do need to put on at least one coat of watered down white emulsion. That plaster just sucks up the paint-

-Yes, OK, I knew that, yes...-

I didn't know this at all but as a man of a certain age there is an expectation of me knowing that.

-And colours?- she said.

-Um-

I hadn't given it a thought. It's a normal sized house to be rented out. Surely only needs Magnolia. Magnolia? People who read the interior section of the paper and then take on tangerine... well, in the drawing room of a large Georgian house in Richmond, that could take a little colour, for a tiny front room in a terraced house in Portsmouth where the room is already stuffed full with a 68 inch plasma screen to watch a constant feed of 'Love island' or 'Celebrity swearing' on ITV7 or 'Lobster men' on E4 (which sadly is about men who go out on a boat and catch lobsters not men who are crustaceans and have massive claws and who were then boiled alive and eaten with butter), sadly and a three piece sofa set that looked good on the advert but that was advertised in a large room not a tiny room and the floor space is all but taken up by over large furniture. A tangerine feature wall in this room would be frightening.

It would resemble a reception area in a tanning salon.

But then there is the grey trend. Again, who sets these trends?

In Southsea, maybe ten years ago, there was a new independent café. The owners clearly having been to London and London being the midwife surely to all of these trends. This café had oblong, chamfered white glossy tiles but any bare wall space was painted with battleship grey. Wooden benches, metal chairs and a coffee machine that looked like it was the control panel for the Death star what with all of its noise, theatre and snarling steam. A huge blackboard with different types of coffee but not just coffee but also the provenance of the single origin bean, the tasting notes of the coffee, Ethiopian bean with chocolate and brooding berry notes and this gave them a licence to take FOREVER to make the coffee and be charged at least 25% more than any other café. And, of course, people flooded in, mainly the hipster scene....all bad tattoos, eccentric bicycles, often vegan with no visible means of income but able to pay an hour's wages for one coffee and then talk *ad nauseam* about how the system is broken but mainly being narked about how they can't get a foot on the housing ladder, then how they wouldn't want to because, yeah, all property is theft man!

But it was the grey of course.

There was a rash of cafes, rising like a foam topped pox across the city and they were all grey and there seemed to be a time when all the warships in the dockyard would have to be painted tangerine such was the use of battleship grey in the city's multitude of new cafes. And then grey migrated into people's homes, as if their lives weren't drab enough. However, given that I make a point of wearing grey, I could... possibly...

-You could actually have any colour- suggested Faye.

-Any colour?-

-Well, if you bring in something, could be a piece of fabric or a fruit or well, anything, we can scan it in and make the paint from that colour.

I go a bit dizzy at this point about paint. This is the ultimate choice. I'm not very good at choosing between two things. Choosing between any infinite number of things....

-Have you got any samples of just ordinary paint?- Perhaps bringing the choice down to the mere hundreds might help.

She swivelled around and leaned over to access a cupboard which no doubt had many, many little books of colour. Now, I couldn't help but look. I am a man but all men's brains wired like that of our 16 year old selves. I did not overtly stare nor did I lean over the counter and yet I did not avert my gaze. As she leant over to open the drawer, the hem of her T-shirt at the back rode up ever so slightly and exposed the very small of her back. And there is something very alluring about the small of a woman's back. There is the very delicate undulation of where both sides of the waist gently cinch and then dip down together to join up. There is that flat plateau, this ridge this is often the most hidden part of a woman, never revered yet never revealed. In a dance with a woman you might just touch the small of her back placing the flat of your palm there, yet even the woman herself can never see it with her own eyes. And this particular small, delicate lozenge of skin revealed a small tattoo. A tattoo in plain view. A pink lobster, one claw open and raised.

After grabbing the tester cards she spun around, slightly flushed by the exertion and presented me with little books of colour and despite the colours being visible on the page they still had quite ridiculous names as if the names would be what swayed you to buy and not the colour... although... Dragon's Blood, Mermaid Net....Salty Tear!

-Did you say that you could do any colour? -I thought just for one single solitary moment of the colour of that hidden lobster upon the small of her back. I wondered just how many had seen this decapod crustacean, how many had gone diving beneath the surface. I could feel my own cheeks colour, (Old man Guilt) so I quickly grabbed the booklets and shuffled away before I embarrassed myself even further. Oh, Betty Blue what do you do?

•

I watched Annabel write out her 10 minute piece of writing. The seconds ticked by on the stopwatch. She's left-handed and her hand is like an anteater's claw around her pen, with her hand trying not to smudge anything she is writing. Her handwriting is a blur. She is wondering just why her handwriting is so effortful and almost illegible. Her whole body is contorted over the page. She looks not unlike someone trying hard to grab something from under a sofa but not quite able to reach. I scribbled these observations onto my report but my mind is not completely on my job.

What does one wear to a date? It's been so long. And, is it a date? I'm thinking it is a date. A day was given along with the time but, well, it was all a bit hurried. I didn't need a written invitation but, well, maybe that's how it's done nowadays, just all very casual. I mean, maybe that's how she wanted to play it, just casual. Anything more and it becomes... a thing. A real thing. OK so, yes, it's a date but...

-OK stop writing please. Pen down-

Annabelle shakes out her hand from the effort and sits back in her chair.

I ask her a question.

-So, Annabelle, do you go on dates?-

I hear the stopwatch tick on, the only noise in the room.

-Er...Is this part of the test?- she wondered, perhaps now senses heightened, looking for exits.

-Goodness no, I just wondered if people still go out on dates, if that, indeed was still a thing?-

Five or six seconds audibly ticked by.

-Are you asking me out on a date? I'm only 17... -And she turned in her chair to look at me, zeroing the stopwatch.

-Oh no no no, gosh, NO!-

A million child protection alarms go off in my head.

-No, absolutely not, sorry I'll explain myself. You see I have been asked out on a date but I didn't know what... young people... did-

The look she gave me was hard to describe. A good third of it was pity, maybe a little more was disgust at the thought of someone like me, elderly to her, approaching the age of 100, having any sort of romantic ideas when I should remain as some greying fossil. But a small slice of the look she gave, after kindly suppressing her gag reflex, was of kindness. Most of the older teens I assess, and you do spend quite an intense 2 hours with them, are kind and considerate.

-Well, if you must know, we just sort of 'hang out'-

-Hang out? Doing what, exactly-

I needed details.

-Just hang out, chat, but not really doing anything-

This sounded frightening. I needed instructions, I needed advice. I wasn't going to get any of that from this benevolent teenager.

I was on my own.

•

There are shades of grey and shades of black. My wardrobe is monochrome and this is merely for the task of disappearing. I try to merge into the background, a grey penumbral shadow, seen only at the very periphery of anyone's vision and if you focus....I'm gone. Black socks, white shirt, tie. Do people wear ties to dates? Do people wear ties at all? Okay, just a black tie. Jacket, coat.

I think about getting the scrofula bus but instead decide to walk. Anywhere to anywhere in Portsmouth is about half an hour's walk, slightly longer if driving. Glasses yes, wallet, yes. A quick look at the twinkling sky tells me that my umbrella is needed. Keys keys keys in hand; how many times have I lost my keys! Off I go.

Albert Road, for those that don't know it in Portsmouth is a long old road stretching from Elm Grove, with elms no longer, all the way east to Highland Rd, the cemetery and then Eastney. It's a road considered by many to be the heart of Southsea, stuffed full of independent shops, little boutiques, coffee shops alongside the old pubs, barber shops, bric a brac and tattoo parlours. And there is even a festival every year in the summer celebrating this street and all that goes on and yet, and yet, there is a paradox. If I talk to people about Albert Road, this great streak of independence railing against the mighty corporate dollar, people always lament....

-Oh yes- they'd say - I remember that lovely shop that did all the patisseries, charcuteries, yes, that's gone-

It has gone and nothing has replaced it except boards covered with 'trendy' graffiti.

And the old style tea rooms and coffee shops, such a high turnover of those probably because of the sky high rents again. So, like everywhere else, shops boarded up or worse, filled with vape shops, more Turkish barbers (I mean how many people need their hair cutting?!) and the shops with so much rubbish piled outside that it is a chore to pick your way past it, not least because of the number of homeless living under that same cardboard. I'm sure, when it is all cleaned up in 20 years time and it is wall to wall Starbucks and Amazon shops, people will look back to now and reminisce of how wonderfully gritty everything was, perhaps also lamenting the loss of the shop that sold rose tinted backwards facing spectacles.

OK OK. So I'm here. There are bouncers at the door of the pub. Why are there bouncers at the door of a pub? It's a pub not a nightclub. No one can afford enough drinks to get drunk anyway! I'll go in, have a quick scan round, if I can't find her then I'll go and no harm done. It wasn't really a date anyway.

It's a Sunday night, winter, but the pub is pretty full. I'm here early, of course, wouldn't do to be late. Is something happening? Oh god, not a live band, anything but a live band. Especially not a folk band! No, luckily it isn't a band but... there is a microphone set up. Christ, it's not one of those open comedy nights or a hundred times worse an open poetry mic night. Why would she invite me to that? Maybe she likes poetry. I mean, I like poetry but I don't want it read at me like a machine gun.

There is a whistle. A proper whistle, one of those which requires fingers in the mouth and I'm responding like a sheepdog responds to a shepherd. I look just past the bar to the source of the whistle. Everything and everyone else seemed to blur and slow down as if I'm looking through a telescope and then the object of my attention is at the end of that long tunnel. Different hair, very different clothes and yet all the features are in the same place.

It is her.

She cocks her head to reel me in and then pats the seat of a stool she has next to her. I can do nothing but obey my whirling Charybdis.

I spent but a few moments looking for a coat peg before realising there were none and neatly folded my coat to sit upon it. I'll iron out the creases later on. Still, I'm here and she's actually here. But she is also here with a group of other people. She clearly knows everybody at the same small table, everybody already having half drunken pints. Was this a date still? Did 'other people' cancel out the 'date'?

-You're cutting it a bit fine- she said.

We were now sitting so close that she had to arch her body away so she could look at my face and talk. I didn't overly mind the situation although, was it getting hot in here? Was it hot?

-You did say for nine though and- I patted my watch -it's now five to nine-

My goodness, her face was so, so close. My own face isn't that close when I shave. I can see she is wearing just the tiniest smear of makeup as her cheeks appear a little possibly flushed from what she's been drinking. There was lipstick but not overly red. It was the hair that was so different. With Minnie the Minx it was orange and in bunches and now it was dark, past shoulder length but in sort of wet ringlets. Her eyes were bigger than I remembered. Mascara? And she had on a sort of billowing Elizabethan blouse with a leather jerkin, buttons tantalisingly undone down to half-way. Facing me fully now she puckered up her lips, she puts both arms to one side in the air as if miming finding the edge of an invisible box. I know what this is. It also seems that everyone else on the table leans forward in anticipation of this moment, as if this moment and what I say next will change the axis of the earth. In my mediocre life anyway.

-Kate Bush? The image on the back of the 'Hounds of Love' album?-

Her face, at my words, does not break into a smile or a frown. Her lips stay puckered but her eyes, part Lillian and part Kate Bush do their best to penetrate my very soul. She smacks a kiss on my cheek and I can smell her floral perfume waft around me, the makeup she has on and yet there is something else. I feel as if my head belongs to my 10 year old self and I had plunged into the deep end of the swimming pool. Without breaking the surface of the water I can hear muffled voices but also the movement of everything else. And then I rise to the surface, my ears pop and every noise is as new.

-That- she says, her face just a beer mat's width from mine (why do I not feel scared or intimidated) -is a correct answer- -And that- now also addressing the rest of her friends on the table who suddenly come into sharp focus for me -is your successful audition to be in our quiz team. Are you getting a drink or not? Quiz starts in two minutes- and suddenly all of her attention turns from me to writing down the team name onto the piece of paper in front of her. The hounds of love in my soul bay and bark whilst I am waiting for my eye watering expensively G&T at the bar.

After the first round of questions, metals, and not just nerdy scientific questions about highest melting point of metal, tungsten. It was also how many times does Shirley Bassey say the word 'gold' in singing 'Goldfinger' (eight times apparently).

There was just time for a quick introduction instigated by Lillian.

-Frog, Tilly, Helen…this is Henry. Henry, this is Frog, Tilly and Helen…- and very quickly we all said our polite hellos, the polite people we are.

-So- I say, forcing myself into politeness but I am hardly one for chit or indeed chat, -how do you all know each other?-

-No! No no no – shouts Lillian -at quiz night we have no polite chit chat, nothing anodyne or dull or work related. If you want to do lists that's fine but polite chit… and chat are out- That was Lillian's final word….

…and then she acquiesced with a teenage worthy huff - This is all terribly dull and the week is dull enough BUT If you absolutely must know, Helen works at the university doing something very important… I couldn't say I know what, but a big cog.

Helen broke into a tired smile at this… -but we are not defined by our jobs… continued Lillian.

Tilly works in Drama and English at the university and she is very good friends with Alice who is not here and Alice is… what do we say… live in lover? Partner? Common law wife? To Frog here- and Lillian had her arms outstretched again, now accidentally being Kate Bush.

-Sorry, Frog?- it was loud in the pub, not quite rowdy but it was a natural gap between quiz rounds -I swear she said your name was Frog?

-Yes, it is Frog – said Frog - a nickname and there is a reason but it is far too dull a reason for Lillian here to allow us to talk about it. Some other time perhaps?-

I smiled back. It was clearly Lillian along with her ego who was head of the team and head of the friends. I can imagine just by how she is sitting, directing chat, that Lillian is the one who does the cajoling, the phone calls, the organising of everyone at the right time and I suspect she enjoys doing it. Polite bullying.

-Lists? You said lists?- I say, perhaps just for the need to say something. I'm sure Lillian could keep talking but I at least wanted my presence to be measured in some way. I turned up!

-You've never played lists? Everyone does lists. It's a work thing- said Lillian as if everyone know about playing lists.

-OK, so, you have a dull moment. Suddenly, through an e-mail or a note or something ghastly on the computer, unlikely to be work related but it is usually a name. Let's say you look on a form and you have a student called Terry... but no-one is called Terry anymore so, what do you do? You throw it out to the room. No matter how busy people say they are, everyone stops for lists. It's the glue that holds places together. Terry? And you just list how many Terrys you can think of. But I warn you, depending on which ones you pick can say a lot about you. Just jump in- said Lillian.

-'Wogan'- chimed in Helen, straight away whilst also having a peek at messages on her phone.

-'Christian'?- asks Frog -now then, stuff and nonsense- he says in a perfectly flat whining Mancunian much like Terry Christian.

-'Rattigan'? – says Tilly, her voice far posher but less confident than the others.

-Hmmm, That's a Terrence but still, I'll accept it- says Lillian, somehow obviously the adjudicator in these situations.

-and if we're going for Terrences I'll go for Stamp- continued Lillian.

-Oh, Terry meets Julie, Waterloo station, those blue eyes- says Helen, putting her phone away under the hawk-like teacher's eyes of Lillian. Frog listened, non plussed.

-Actor, 60's, Terence Stamp and Julie Christie – filled in Lillian. Frog smiled but was clearly none the wiser... he knew it was wiser just to smile and go with a force of nature that was Lillian. And then in a lull, I was enjoying the game but also the fact that they're all playing, it was a thing for them, you just did it. But the lull was suddenly there because I was expected to play along. I was not allowed to be a casual observer. I felt, just for a second, that the whole pub was silenced and this solipsistic world would not continue until I had said my line.

-Erm…(don't cock this up, you idiot!) 'Thomas', 'Scott', 'Nutkins'- were my offerings.

-Oh Yes, Nutkins. Mullet and finger bitten off by an otter. Nutkins, good one Henry- said Helen, who's obscure knowledge I was enjoying more and more.

-And what about 'Dactyl'!- I said, my confidence rising now.

-'Dactyl'?- snorted Lillian -You can't have that!-

-Actually- said Frog -he can as I assume Henry is talking about Terry Dactyl and the Dinosaurs. Early 70's band. Jonah Louie who was…- and Frog looked across at me to finish off…

-You will always find him in the kitchen at parties- We shared a smile.

-Well then, Mr Green, or are you both Jacob and Elwood this evening? Asked Lillian a little cruelly. Four Terry's. You'd better pull some magic out of the bag second-half of the quiz. We're second overall but second only to our mortal enemies… 'Einstein's Toenails' over there. Lillian, without pointing, looked in the general direction of a bigger table by the window. Four beery blokes all seemingly having a whale of a time and hardly looked like hardened quizzers.

-Well, I only know what I know- I said.

As I looked at the others though it seemed that they had been in this brow-beaten situation a number of times. It appeared, by the cowed eyes of everyone, apart from Lillian, that Lillian took her quiz very seriously and if they didn't win then there would be hell to pay.

-Right, I'm just going to powder my nose- Lillian announced, as she slung her wet-look hair over her shoulder. -I'm sure I've got 5 minutes. Drink anyone?- she offered but everyone said no.

So, here it is, the awkward little silence in a room full of people. They all seem to know Lillian well and I'm dying to ask them about her, but how does one start a conversation like that.

Fortunately I didn't need to.

-So, Henry, it is Henry isn't it?- said frog -Lillian didn't actually say. How do you know Lillian?

-Oh, well, I only really met her on Monday, I think it was, at her school. Apparently she'd seen me before.

All three of them nodded as if to say this was normal behaviour.

-She was dressed as Minnie the Minx-

-Yes- said Helen -she does that, she always seems to be in costume. First time I met her over 20 years ago she was dressed as Bowie but in full 'Ashes to Ashes' Pierrot clown Bowie. Just to come to lectures.

-Wow- I said, genuinely impressed by such a bold spirit.

-But- she continued -it always worries me that we never get to see the real Lillian.

-Hmmm- They nodded in unison once more.

-Also, she stole my lunch- I said - Well, I say stole. I did offer it up but...-

-Was it a very nice lunch?- asked Tilly. I bet it was cheese, olives, sourdough. You strike me as a man who does a good lunch-

-Do you know, yes, it did have sourdough. And a little tart with a glazed strawberry-

-And let me guess- said Helen -you just felt okay with it and you'd have given her more if you'd had it? Am I right?-

-Yes- I said -exactly right, but I'm not entirely sure why-

-Well, that's Lillian for you- said Helen -We've all fallen in love with her in one way or another. So, be warned, if you're not up to the challenge you should get out now. It will save heartache later-

-Erm- but I could say no more as Lillian jostled back onto her chair. It suddenly got very hot again. Is it hot in here? Absolutely nothing to do with Lillian's short skirt which, I think the proximity of it, is impairing my quizzing ability.

-Right gang- said Lillian, taking a hefty swig from her pint of bitter shandy- (looks like a man's drink but only you and the barman know it's mostly lemonade) -I've got a good feeling about this second-half. Henry, do you have any specialist subjects?

On the spot again.

-Um, Carry On films? Life and works of Steven Morrissey? Er...-

I received an increasingly disappointed look from Lillian.

-FA Cup winners since 1872?- I continued, my confidence plummeting.

-Oh splendid, yes, we don't really have sport as any of our specialist subjects, Oh well done Henry, our sports expert!-

-Well, no, not sports *per se* just FA Cup final winners since 1872-

-All the same, sport- And again I was dismissed and shushed by those pale lips as the really quite tedious question master came back to the microphone. I looked over at 'Einstein's toenails'. Suddenly they were the very model of concentration.

-And what is our team name, sorry?- I asked, probably at the wrong time as it seemed to halt Lillian's concentration.

-The Mice at the Mouse Organ- said Frog, as seriously as he could. I smiled.

So, this very serious woman is in a very serious team named after stop go animation characters from 'Bagpuss'. I kept these thoughts to myself until at least after the quiz, win or lose.

There were three rounds left. We, as a team, were only two points behind the leaders and miles in front of everyone else. But it all seemed to depend on the esoteric subjects that the quiz master picked. First one was all about satellites.

I mean, satellites, a good idea. So, obviously, 'Telstar' and Joe Meek! Skylab, Mir, Sputnik, 1957 but then also, gosh darn it, natural satellites like the Galilean moons of Jupiter, names of Shakespeare characters which now orbit Saturn and also the Greek classics of Charon, Phobos and Deimos. Despite being a non scientist on the table I think I did pretty well with my contributions, now believed by Lillian and not always having to be cross checked by the others, which I found quite insulting, especially for a first date. The next round was Disney princesses so I was out but thank goodness we had Tilly who seemed positively animated by this round. There was grumbling from Einstein's table. Not all the questions were directly about Disney princesses but about which characters were princesses, who voiced which character and also my favourite question of the night,
'What are the very first words spoken by Snow White?'

The second this question was asked, Lillian moves in very close to my ear. I feel her breath in my heart. Her voice barely a whisper above a whisper. It was getting very hot in this pub. They really need to do something about the ventilation!

-Would you like to know a secret?- she said.

Is this it? Is she finally coming out of character? Is she going to say that she loves me?

-Yes- I just about mumble.

-Thought so- she says and writes it down.

I mean, I knew that. I knew that's what she meant, just checking the answer with me.

The Disney Princess round was totted up. We were doing well. We were just behind 'Einstein's toenails' but by one singular point. What did impress me was four old blokes, nursing their beer and they clearly knew more than they were letting on about Disney princesses. A little knowledge is an embarrassing thing to paraphrase Mr Pope.

-And, ladies and gentlemen- the quiz master said and despite clearly doing this quiz every week his mouth was still far too close to the microphone and, all his popping sounds his T's and his P's just hammered tiny little copper nails into my head. Just move away a fraction of an inch please... -this is the last round and Portsmouth football club are still in the FA Cup, so it's a round all on the FA Cup final!-

Everyone on my table stopped what they were doing, either supping their drinks or doom scrolling or in Lillian's case writing down one to ten on the sheet and they very slowly but all simultaneously as if it were previously choreographed, looked at me with their mouths open and then their eyes flicking to each other.

Let's just stop for a moment. Everyone on pause. It must be, what, thirty years ago? I was at college doing 'A' levels. Was I particularly studious? No. Did I just do enough to not get into trouble? Yes. With an absent mother and a father just plodding on himself I was pretty much left to my own devices. If I wanted something of my own I realised that I would need to get my own money. If you asked Dad for money he might do a cursory lecture as to why I wanted the money, was it to be used to buy rubbish etc. He thought everything I bought was rubbish of course, but I felt that if I just had the money from Mum or Dad, and they were usually quite happy to give it, whatever I bought with the money didn't feel like it was mine, it was just borrowed.

Oh, what a Catholic upbringing does to you.

So, if I wanted money that was truly mine I would have to earn it.

I got a paper round.

It wasn't a normal paper round, one where you get up ridiculously early. Go to nearby paper shop, collect papers and deliver them on a bike before the crack of dawn. Did I mention, I'm not a morning person. I wasn't then either. No, this was delivering a local paper, a free paper to everyone once a week. I would have to go to a distribution depot which was essentially the old lady's garage and collect 500 newspapers and also any inserts that would have to be delivered with the paper. I had to pull a little cart to collect the papers which was another reason for merciless bullying. Cart boy. I ask you.

And I had a round not far from where I lived and you had to put a free newspaper into everyone's letterbox. Whether they wanted it or not.

Usually not.

It did rather open my eyes to how other people lived though. There is me in my fairly well to do house living my fairly well to do life but delivering these papers to people in tiny flats whose doors were all buckled and peeling. I could smell awful food being cooked behind these doors. Some people took great care over their tiny little living spaces whereas others were content to have a twenty year old Ford Escort Mk I in their small front garden, the rust in the door so thin and fragile like a frilled edge of a dying butterfly's wing. I assumed everyone lived as I did. I was wrong.

There was one man, as I remember, always came to the door as I was delivering the paper. The hinge on his letterbox needed the strength of Hercules just to open it with both hands. I wanted to open it with just one and simply feed through the paper but I just didn't have the strength in my hand to do that so I opened it as far as I could with one hand, slipped in just a corner of the paper in through the letterbox and then sort of stopped it coming back out with my knees. I could then open the letterbox with both hands and push it through with my knees although having to do this a number of times meant that on the other side the paper would exhibit a sort of crimped concertinaed effect. I was then very careful to close the letterbox as if I let go quickly, the thought of it snapping on my fingers was just a thought beyond the pale and made me quite ill. I also tried to close it slowly so the earth shattering noise of its snapping shut wouldn't activate the resident inside. Sometimes, if it was wet, with slippery hands, it was hard to keep the letterbox open. I would see the blurred outline of the man through the frosted and as I tried to put the paper through he would pull it from the other side which then led to a shredded paper. He'd open the door, the paper hanging out of the letter box like a Springer spaniel's tongue. He had to jerk the door open

186

as the wood was split and swollen at the bottom but finally open it he did.

-Whas' all this crap you're forcing through my door?- he said.

I was 14, maybe 15 and not equipped to answer any questions especially with adults I didn't know. I had yet to discover rhetoric or even Rhett Butler.

-Erm- I answered.

-Look, I don't want any of this free crap through my letterbox, I'm just not interested! I've not got the time!-

My father went to the University every day to work. He wore a suit and a tie. He shaved everyday. His shoes were polished, his hair was combed. His shirt was pressed. The man at the door, in front of me, was different. He was about the same height as me. He wore a maroon cardigan with buttons that seemed to be made of little squares of dark leather. His collarless shirt was crumpled and the first three buttons on the shirt were undone and showed a small hemisphere of a grey vest, half camouflaged by greying chest hair. The buttons of the cardigan strained at his generous midriff and the bottom button was missing. His trousers were of a suit but long past. The fly was done up as far as could be managed and the trousers were pocked with stains and hues of dubious provenance. On one of his blue corduroy slippers that he was wearing, he had a number of turns of grey gaffer tape that itself was worn to the fabric. But the man's face looked so old. His hair held a sort of product or else it was just matted and greasy and his skin was grey, almost as grey as his chest hair, like over boiled beef. The lines of his face moved as he spoke, as dark as they were, and this seemed to be the place where all of his smoke settled. His tongue was worryingly red when he often poked it out either rescuing a strand of loose tobacco from his lips or probing and exploring for undigested morsels around his pickle-chasing teeth.

I was utterly fascinated.

I stared past him to see the curtains closed, despite it being bright outside. The horse racing was blaring on the TV and was almost as loud as the pattern on the carpet in the hall. This man, for me, was from another world and this was when I started realising that other people do not necessarily live the same life as you yourself do. Although he always claimed he didn't want this 'crap' shoved through his letter box he always took the paper as if he was doing me a favour. Then he'd question me about what I was doing, generally, and then I'd say it had to get on, crap papers didn't deliver themselves and this little sketch happened every week. Until one week when it didn't.

The spring was just as strong in the letterbox, the TV was on just as loud yet I never saw that threadbare man looming large at the glass ever again. More than likely he was still sitting in his armchair, decomposing and found after three years when he hadn't paid his TV licence. And with the TV still on and constantly for so long, you'd think the TV manufacturers would use that in their advertising. But they never do.

Anyway, the part of all this is just me plodding on, naïve old me, just doing what I thought was the only thing I could do. Then I went to college. You meet people outside of the confines of school. You are allowed to explore the world and no one is telling you what the rules are. You see others do things differently. Your eyes are opened and everything you thought impossible is now obvious. You wonder why you didn't do it before.

It's like a piece of paper has two sides but you never even thought of turning it over until you saw someone else do that and the other side is amazing. But it isn't about the other side of the paper... it was having the curiosity to turn it over in the first place.

I met Hugh and Shoe at college. Hugh (real name) and Shoe (not real name) but everyone called him 'Shoe' so... I was in one class with Shoe and one class with Hugh but they weren't in my classes together and yet they were best of friends. I think I fell in with them mainly because I lived nearby and one of them, Shoe, had a car, a green

Volkswagen Beetle. He hated it. It was his mother's but it was better than getting the train or bus to college.

Sitting about, one day, eating our big sandwiches and that was the thing to eat, sandwiches with increasingly terrifying fillings. My standard, and I will stick to it, was Marmite, raw onion and Coronation chicken. It just works. Try it!

I mentioned my money problem to them. The fact is that I was still slogging away delivering crappy, and it was a crappy paper all about lost dogs, fruit and veg shows and 99% advertising. Actually It was skating on very thin ice actually calling it a newspaper such was the dearth of actual news inside it.

Anyway, these two didn't seem to have any issues with money at all. I put this down to neither of them having any scruples and being able to see opportunities.

For example....

Just before Christmas the refectory at the college stopped selling little 'Freddo' bars, the cheapest bar of chocolate on the rack so the refectory managers could get in more expensive chocolate to sell before Christmas. I moaned and groaned like everyone else. I even signed a petition. This was sent to the Principal to demand the reinstatement of the 'Freddo' bars. A very polite studenty action, all above board, following the rules and procedures of legal complaint and practice and when I saw that I had exhausted all avenues of complaint apparently the Principal had barely looked at the signatures placed on his vast mahogany desk.

Hugh and Shoe had taken a different approach to the problem. Where I had followed in the footsteps of Marx, (Karl thank you, not Groucho!) they had followed Capone. Hugh's father ran a business. He had a wholesale card. Hugh borrowed some money and bought two thousand 'Freddo' bars.

In the car park at lunchtime the mouth of the green Beetle was wide open, not unlike that of the cartoon frog on the packaging of the 'Freddo' bar. Hugh and Shoe were doing a roaring trade. And it wasn't just the foresightedness of buying the chocolates and selling them, no, they had an impromptu advertising campaign which went viral long before the days of social media. All they did, the day before, was produced a few, very bad quality photocopies, featuring a 'Freddo' bar with a gun to its head, with a strap line 'Save Fred oh!'. Within hours there were thousands of copies of copies pasted up and pinned on boards all over the college. On the first day of trading, the two of them sold out of 'Freddo' bars, not making a huge markup but certainly making sure that any extra money that the canteen thought they would be squeezing out of students before Christmas would disappear. The master stroke for both of them was to tell everyone to take their 'Freddo' wrappers, sit in the canteen, and then leave the wrappers on the table. Just to send a message. Hugh and Shoe didn't care about the message themselves but if people saw their sales as a political action then suddenly they were heroes and were swaggering around college like modern day Che Guevaras. This action continued for a week until the Principal realised that the profits for the refectory were being hit very hard and he swiftly put a stop to it citing Health and Safety, trading without a licence, breaching sanitation laws and closed everything down.

Hugh and Shoe were heralded as martyrs for the cause but really they had just taken advantage of a situation and made some money. And what had I done? I had merely signed a piece of paper. Those two had turned the paper over and looked at the other side. My eyes, whilst not fully open, were at least letting in more light.

Part of our revision technique before exams involved going to the local snooker hall. Again, on my own, I would have stayed on campus but those two were eager for the outside world.

During the day the place was dead, only a few of the twenty or so snooker tables were lit and they were taken up mainly by the perpetually unemployed. A perpetual pall of smoke hung over the tables thanks to a lack of any sort of windows or ventilation in the place. The balls clicked; the little clack of a potted ball and the hushed murmur of nefarious deals being done in the dark, smoky corners.

The place sold chips, of which we ate a lot. They were cheap, the price being displayed only in black ink on a pink fluorescent star; 45p per basket of chips. The baskets were plastic.

There was a relatively large television at the back where we often sat, ate chips, threw chips and whiled away the hours breathing in all the second-hand smoke. On Tuesdays, only Tuesdays, there was a bit more of a crowd. There was a separate room, "a sports annexe" said Fat Tony, (The owner was called Tony, a Scot, and he was fat so not overly imaginative of us) and every Tuesday there was a quiz. To my eyes it seemed to be for very old people from the local area and perhaps others, bussed in for the afternoon from the surrounding care homes in lieu of any sort of help in the community (thank you very much Margaret Thatcher). As we sat there watching bizarre sports on the television from all around the world but mainly darts from Frimley Green, Lakeside, the others got annoyed at the noise from the big crowd.

The highlight of the morning, of course, was the quiz. A gentle quizmaster and most participants were hard of hearing so amplification was necessary. There was feedback through the speakers, squealing from all the hearing aids and also the sibilant hiss from the question master's dodgy dentures every time he said Surrey, Santander, or Saracens. Whilst the other two squabbled over chips I saw an opportunity; not turning over the paper entirely but at least peeking at the other side. Every Tuesday there were four quiz rounds. The rounds though were usually quite similar. There was a current affairs round which was so simple that a cursory look at the paper in the morning would provide all the answers. The rest of the rounds were sport. And they weren't obscure facts but just normal facts. And so every week I listened in to the questions.

'Who won the Grand National in 1980', 'Who won the Derby in 1934', 'Who won the inaugural FA Cup' and so on. Over the weeks I realised that over 80% of the questions were just remembering who won what and when. The Derby, the Grand National, the Football League and the FA Cup and the World Cup. Everyone in their team paid one pound and the winners would get ten pounds. But there were loads of them there so I wondered, where did the rest of the money go?

I befriended one of the old boys who always wanted to chat. He was well over eighty but he was always suited and booted.

-Always dress like a gentleman, young man, as you never know when a nice young lady will pass by! You young 'uns with your tracksuits and sneakers and hair gel. In my day...- et cetera et cetera. Anyway, I asked him about the money and he said that the money was put in the pot. It paid for the room and the question master but if you got 90% of the questions correct then you won the pot. Sometimes they advertise it to get more people to come along.

Cogs whirred.

-How much is it up to now?- I asked, as innocently as I could.

-Oh goodness me, must be hundreds, maybe even a grand?-

-OK boys, this is the plan-

Oh how I felt like a gangster, coming across a real opportunity, it was delicious! It was a very simple plan. We were going to go along for the quiz, for a few weeks and we were going to lose. Play well, join in, but lose. But whilst we're losing, over the next few weeks we're going to memorise as many facts in lists about dates of winners of horse races, football and then in week three sting them for the big payout. We have to do it properly as I think if we get close but don't win then we'll be barred-

They didn't say they'd agreed but we had little else in the way of things to occupy our time apart from revising for our up and coming exams. We split up the list between us and you've guessed it, I got World Cup football and FA Cup finals since 1872.

On the third week the quiz master begrudgingly paid out £1232 into our hot little hands. He only did this because of pressure from the old people who I'd befriended. When we'd won with 100% of our questions being correct and explained to the quiz master that we'd simply memorised every final and every race he said we'd been cheating and yet the elderly thought that what we done was very clever and seeing as we paid in our money then we should be allowed to have the winnings.

We were barred from the snooker club for life, of course, but actually Spring was coming and it really was just a place to keep warm. I started going to the library a bit more, to keep warm but also to study. Hugh and Shoe, well they dropped a few more subjects between them, looked for more opportunities. Goodness knows what they're doing now. CEO's of global companies or doing a twenty stretch in Parkhurst. It's a fine line.

OK so, no pressure then, let's see if my memories from thirty years ago are still there. Goodness, wouldn't I be in Lillian's good books!?

I plonked the drinks, the free drinks, down onto our tiny table.

-Well- said Frog -I thought that the 'Einstein's toenails' coming over and accusing us of cheating was just outrageous. Sour grapes!- he said, loud enough for them to hear it as they glowered over the dregs of their pints, -but really, well done sir, well done-

I can't remember the last time I was part of any group that I wasn't forced into or born into and it being a good experience.

-10 out of 10! I mean, 10 out of 10!- Lillian seemed to be in shock, staring at her drink instead of drinking it.

-Who knew that Blackburn Rovers had won it four times in a row! Blackburn!- she continued.

-2000 holes in Blackburn, Lancashire- I say to no one in particular. Lillian smiles a secret smile but it draws a blank from the others.

Sunday night, annoyingly, is a school night and it is a night cut short. We were all parting our ways but I didn't want the night to just end. So, I say to Lillian as she was getting a coat on,

-Whereabouts do you live?-

-My goodness- she said -that's very presumptuous of you! Coming by to pounce on me are you?-

I freeze, for a second, she's teasing, she's surely teasing and she wanted me to flap like a goose.

-Well, I just wondered if you had far to go, that's all. I'm walking back, in a post quiz euphoria and was just interested-

-Actually, I have a house, well I live in a house nearby, Collingwood Road. A tiny place and the rent reflects the location and not the size of the house. I've been served notice. Been there for over five years. I love the little garden at the back but I think he just wants to sell up-

-Oh- was all I could say.

-So I'd love to stay in Southsea, I would, but living on my own, rents, I could get one of those ratty little flats but I'm single and despite having a "proper job" and she did the air quotes, I just can't afford it-

-Oh- I say again for lack of anything else to say. I thought she was going to cry. We were outside in the cold raw air and I saw her change back from Kate Bush to Lillian. Please don't cry. I'm not sure how I deal with it. But I just say -oh-. Does she want me to say something? Should I say something? Oh... This is where love is won or lost. The moment for a kiss, I think is gone. That would seem a little creepy now... But I can't just go. I have to say something, if only for the sake of saying something.

-Erm-

-Don't say 'erm', nothing started with 'erm' was ever considered important-

My goodness, what a profound thing to say!

-I was just going to say, when do you need to be out... because I might be in a position to help...-

•

Most of Monday had been spent writing up my assessments. I had to go in on Tuesday for another batch so they needed to be squared away. Just the laptop on the table. Should have been simple. For some reason though, I couldn't concentrate.

Most of the writing up is cut and paste but there is a little scope for writing with a flourish, putting your own little stamp on things but whenever I get around to writing these little paragraphs my mind would drift away to last night.

Just one night. A date but not actually a date and so, what was it? Did she just see in me a kindred spirit? Someone who paid attention to the details, someone, dare I say it, interesting? I found her fascinating and scary all at the same time. I had written off any hope of any romance in my life let alone....the L word and was quite happy to dress in grey and age. What else is there to do? But she would be maddening! I have my routine. I have my life. I like my life and I like it as it is. And yet...

Why did I say I would help her out? Why did I say she could stay in the house next door when it was ready? Why would I do that? It's complicated. I don't do complicated. And if it was just a simple thing of her coming in, just as a stopgap, why am I constantly thinking about it? I have met her twice. First time she stole my lunch and then second time? She just wanted my quizzing knowledge. Christ. And this morning there is another seagull in the bin! Not the same one, that must have been taken, no, it's another one! A fresh bird! It's a campaign, that's what it is. It must have gone in there on Sunday night, whilst I was at the quiz. I have to get to the bottom of this. And there was an answer phone message last night. Oh, Dad, -'just phoning up, seeing how you are- and (also, real reason), -how are you fixed for a quick shave on Monday, it's just that I'm going out to Bridge in the evening. Dad'- How am I supposed to get on and work with so many interruptions!

The house was quiet. No builders next door and just the tweet of the birds in the leafless Acer in the garden, all clamouring for randomly provided seed. God! Even the bloody birds won't shut up!

Should I get biscuits in? Special coffee? God, I should just get on with this work but maybe if I got biscuits or coffee she'll think it's more than it is. Perhaps I should just be a bit aloof, just let it happen and that's that, distance, the house, not forming any sort of relationship. 'Coming over at five' she said and it's, what now, five past ten in the morning. Perhaps I could get my work done and then get some biscuits in. And coffee.

The doorbell went at just a few minutes to five. I did my absolute best to wait at least for a heartbeat before I answered the door.
-Oh, hi, yes of course, you said you were coming at five- I said, oozing nonchalance.
-Oh if it's not a good time I could…- said Lillian turning to go.
-Oh no, it's absolutely fine. Come in come in-
I gave her a quick look up and down on my step. A white satin blouse under her coat, her waist cinched in with a black belt that was almost a dress. The two pigtails pinned up in circles at the side of her head.
-Princess Leia? Your Highness?- I asked.

Again there was that delightful bite of her bottom lip in recognition of my spotting Princess Leia. Too easy I thought. My house was clean, super clean and I had spent at least four hours getting it into this shape. Bathroom and toilets scrubbed. Everything dusted and hoovered. Even the oven was sparkling.

-Let me take your coat, your Highness!- I say, playing along and ushered her into the back room. An unplunged cafetiere was on the table, single origin beans, freshly ground. Triple chocolate cookies arranged on a plate, a little lemon tart with two plates and two cake forks on the freshly pressed linen tablecloth.

-Oh my goodness, you've gone to so much trouble. I just thought that...-

-All this? It's nothing, just coffee, few biscuits just pulled out the cupboard. That's all-

-Hmm- she said not really believing me. I didn't really believe it myself.

-Coffee?-

-Seeing as you've gone to so much trouble of making it, and milk?-

-Warmed? Steamed? Cold?-

-Oh, erm...- surprised at the choice.

-Don't say 'erm', that'll get you nowhere! Let me plunge and pour -which I did. I was in my house and in control. Cups

and saucers, three types of sugar. I sat opposite her at the table. I had put Classic FM on in the background, barely audible, just the tinkling of a piano occasionally. As she drank she looked around the room. I could see what she was thinking. Is this your house? Do you live here all by yourself? But she merely supped her coffee. The birds tweeted on the acers, the sun just dipping down below the houses opposite.

-Good day?- I said busy?-I asked.

-What? Teaching maths to year 11 who really hate maths? Walk in the park for me- she said, somewhat ironically.

-And what did they make of Princess Leia?-

-They didn't care. To be honest I don't think they even noticed. They don't notice anything if it's not on their news scroll or Tik Tok, it's just not real, ironically. You busy?-

-Well, just doing a few bits and bobs, bit of writing up, a bit of shopping...-

-Sugar, coffee, biscuits?- she asked.

-Maybe. Maybe- I smiled and supped.

After a few biscuits were laid to waste "it'll spoil my tea!" I got down to business, (not that!) Do you want to go next door?-

She put her cup into the saucer with a delightful ceramic clink and followed me.

-So- she said, her voice echoing around the hall, the bare floorboards and the lack of anything at all in the house. -This is also your house?-

She couldn't help herself.

Her index fingers twirling around, a mime for a helicopter if ever there was one, meaning the whole house in her question.

-Yes. Technically-

Why did I say technically? It is my house, legally and in every other sense. I am clearly trying to downplay the fact that I have not just one house, to myself, but another one, to myself. One house may be considered selfish but two houses is positively gluttonous. This is clearly what she is thinking. I braced myself for questions of entitlement, or privilege. I'm aware of how lucky I am but also...

-Okay, right. Well I can see it's finished- looking at the now dry pinks and terracottas of the freshly plastered walls -but not finished-

-So why can't I move into your 'other' finished house, the one where you live alone?- she says, just as matter of factly as she seems to ask every question. My mind is now scrambling hard to try and find a reason why she can't. She's seen that I am a single man, how can I possibly justify having three bedrooms to myself. One might level this accusation at the King. Does he need all those bedrooms himself? Couldn't people who need a roof just move into Buckingham Palace? And yes, I might argue with the Guardian where people with spare space should share and then there would be no housing crisis or any homeless. In principle I agree...of course...but I like my space. And this means in practice, distance from other people. Or does she move very quickly. After two dates, neither of which were dates, she is looking to move in. Is that what she thinks? Have I given off the wrong signals and somehow I am contractually obliged to let her move in?

-I'm joking. Stop panicking. I joke. It's a thing- She is pointing at me. -You need to calm down. So, what's the deal?- Oh thank god, she's joking...but why would she do that. But yes, I need to calm down.

-The deal?- I hadn't even thought of any details let alone a deal!

-Well, here's a house. It's empty. It needs painting, furnishing and I need to be out of my house by the end of the month-

-Erm-

-Again, with the 'erm', look I could even move in as a stopgap for a few months whilst I look for something more permanent. If you need a hand doing some decorating, I'm in. I mean, let me know how much the rent would be. I wouldn't stay forever.

-You wouldn't stay? Why not?- I found myself asking out loud, almost outraged that she thought of it and couldn't possibly countenance the idea of staying.

-Well, it's so far from everywhere- she said.

-Far from where, exactly?- I was sticking up for my area. I felt affronted.

-From Albert Road, from where everything happens. From pubs, from artisanal bakeries, two minutes from a handmade custard slice-

-This isn't the other side of the moon you know! We are less than two miles from there. Two miles! I walked there, and back, last night and felt all the better for both the exercise and the distance created. I live here because there is only one pub, no artisan bakeries and therefore no pointless troupes of hipsters queuing for artisanal bread at, no doubt, artisanal prices. It's bread. If I want artisanal bread I'll make it myself!-

It was a mini rant. Did I go too far? I went too far. Surely…

-I'll get a bike then…- she said.

I felt that had her housing situation not being so precarious she would have fought a rear-guard action much more strongly.

-…and you can make the bread!- she added cheekily.

-Oh, can I indeed!- And I found myself smiling. What was happening to me? If I get on my high horse, ranting away, I will moan to anyone who listens and my anger will last a day or more but now my rage was quickly extinguished, like a hot pan quenched in water.

-Well, actually, I'm ordering some paint and then carpet and if you are happy to help then, well, I couldn't possibly charge any rent until it was properly ready to rent-

What happened next took me somewhat by surprise. In that instant, that fraction of a fraction of a second, when I said she could move in, her arms were flung around my neck and her lips, red, were smooched onto my cheek. For that moment I was frozen. Physically, of course, as I thought I was being attacked such was the grip around my neck, the proximity of her face and I could smell not only her makeup, the waxy lipstick but also the shampoo she used, macadamia nut oil and hibiscus. But also, again, I could smell her, take away everything else, the secret cigarettes, the sweat from a day's hard work, that smell would still be there and I was smothered by it. Her womanly body, goodness, an actual real live woman with all the different shapes and planes and flesh and it was all I could do to not be completely overwhelmed.

For most of my life I have, I suppose voluntarily, given up touching any other person. My mother hugged me as if she was trying to hold on to me, crushing hugs, stopping me from growing up, crystallising everything, which is what she sort of did with her photographs, crystallising time itself. But she died and Dad, well Dad's not really a hugger. Happy to shake hands even with his young son who is aching for any sort of physical contact. And then, of course, if you don't get any contact you can go one of two ways. You can either withdraw yourself from being tactile or just hug everyone and everything. Both ends of that particular rainbow bring problems. Mine is that I will avoid any situations where there might be hugging or personal contact. I have built my hard carapace and I sit, at a distance, in my shell. The over huggers, in my distant eyes anyway, reek of desperation, reek of the need to love and be loved. So much effort required, just dizzying. Give me a polite handshake and a meal for one any day. But now? In this nanosecond? I freeze. I am frozen.

As she releases her grasp, a little flicker in her eyes, she realises that she might have overstepped or over hugged some sort of boundary. Does she think me a cold fish? Does this explain my need to live on my own? Swiftly she trails a number of stray hairs back over her ear, which really is the most endearing action I have seen anyone do.

-This is just fabulous. I mean, for someone who has been on their own for five years in one place I really don't have much stuff. When can I move in?-

-Erm- going from brain scramble, being emotionally attached to the forming of some sort of coherent answer, I blurted something out.

-Next weekend?- Which was completely ridiculous. I would need months to get everything sorted out, putting on the gas, electricity, the garden...

-That's great. Look I hope you don't mind but I better get off now, start sorting everything out. I'll keep in touch and see you, this Saturday?- and with that she walked back out, not even having looked at the rest of the house and disappeared out of the gate. I watched her as she went.

-I'm off to the allotment, she shouted back -not technically mine.... yes I noticed the use of the word 'technically' used back on me, cheeky....-it belongs to a friend and actually it's not far from here-

-So, not everything in a galaxy is so far far away?-

-Suppose not- and then she opened up my green bin from the other side of the wall and peered in. -Is that the same seagull?- She said this as if it was everyday she saw sea birds in people's domestic rubbish.

-Actually, no, it's a new one. Well, an old one, but a new one compared to the one from last week-

-I see, so someone is putting seagulls in your bin?-

-It appears so. Any information gratefully received!- I smiled. I wanted to say something to keep the conversation going, to keep her here but she put the lid down, gently, perhaps in respect for the deceased but it did tell me she wasn't a bin slammer. She simply wiggled her fingers and was then off, may as well be off to a galaxy far far away.

In the house next door, I'd heard my own phone ring, through the wall. I knew who it was. It was the right time. I suppose I should phone back.

●

-You don't seem very talkative? Something on your mind?- said Dad, looking up at me from the chair through the mirror.

-I thought it was the barber who was supposed to make inane chat, keep the client or relaxed and amenable, keep the client...pliant- I said.

-Hmm, you're finding rhymes. That can't be good. You're up to something. Are you up to something? Is that it?-

I ignore him of course, the old bloodhound. -Just here to shave, that's all-

Dad had already put the accoutrements out next to the sink. Laid out in order as if for an operation or a post mortem.

-I'm sure the razor will be better this time, eh Dad?- First time, yes, razor sharp but just too sharp. If the razor dulls just a little, you can have a few scrapes grace without cutting into bone. Anyway, price of these blades, I'm not putting a new one on for each shave!-

He was all lathered up and now, hot bowl of water, I felt just a little twinge of confidence. There was Dad, skin hung a little loose on his bones. But as long as there was hot water, plenty of lather I could just hold the skin and draw the blade. Don't get me wrong, it's still a strange experience shaving someone else's face. You are doing the actions that are natural but you don't get the feedback that you would normally get from the skin on your own face and so all your senses are heightened. The tips of your fingers feeling the tension of the skin you are pulling and the single stroke of the blade, listening for the hairs cut across the skin. Then the dunking and rinsing of the razor in the sink before repositioning your fingers, pulling in a slightly different direction, the skin may react differently. How strange to feel the warp and weft in his skin. You'd think skin would be unidirectional in its weaving but it seems to have different levels of elasticity at different points of the face. The jowls that hang like Victorian curtains stretch the most whereas the already stretched skin across the cheeks leave little room for pulling about. I also realise this is another face that I have been in very close proximity to in the last 24 hours.

As Dad is no longer flinching at every swipe of the razor it is easier for him to relax, making it easier and faster for me to shave him. I'm not quite there but there is definitely a flow to my work. Dad looks stoically forward into the mirror, still looking at my progress but at one remove. I'm nearly someone shaving him, not his son shaving him. He doesn't say anything because he is letting me get on with things. I say nothing as I am concentrating. But, in moments where I rinse out the razor, I get to look at his pink appearing face.

His hair, still mainly there, always a large bushel of hair, always being managed by the ever present comb plucked from the back pocket, has to be just so. The hair is mainly white and certainly thinning.

Skin is certainly testament to time orbiting the sun. His temples have little red and white spots, some raised, some not. But all across the plains of skin little lacunae, blood tributaries of red and blue rivers. Blood that still pulsed but now with the machinery of his skin laid bare. His cheeks, not sunken but sallow as if the material of the skin itself was thinning as if to belie what lies beneath, like the knees on a toddler's trousers, thinned to oblivion. But the eyes, sharp, tangy blue. The whites not as white as they used to be but they spoke of the intent within. He was looking, as he normally does, at the cards, photos and little bits of tat that peeped out from their tucked places behind the mirror. The overhead light cast yellow-grey shadows on the faces in the photographs from the cards above them.

-Why don't you frame those things- I say, looking at my next patch of skin to attack whilst rinsing the blade -I mean they're always there but I worry, in the bathroom, they'll just curl up as they keep getting damp-

-Hmm- he says again -everything curls up and falls off in the end. At my age it's more likely to be me than the pictures.

-But still- ignoring the morose comment -it would be a shame-

-A shame for who?- he said, suddenly getting animated and almost turning around until I was prodding a finger in his temple to keep him still -I put them there because I want to see them when I'm at the mirror. If I put them in a frame, well, it becomes art, it becomes permanent and it doesn't get looked at. A frame means a picture is viewed at one remove....like looking in the mirror.

I said nothing. It was never worth arguing and now was not an exception.

-Okay, so why are these pictures there then- pointing at the photograph of Dad, my sister and I as kids on a beach somewhere.

It is a caught action photograph. Dad is acting like some angry monster, launching himself out of the sand, carrying my sister and I, one of us under each arm. My face and that of my sister are facing towards the camera, squealing with delight whereas Dad, wearing a cardigan at the beach, had a stretched face like that of King Kong, threatening to throw us both into the sea. The glossy black and white had a simple white background around the square photo and everything is slightly blurred except for my sister's and my faces, such delight, such innocence.

-That one, for instance. I've seen it before but I can't remember where it was taken or of all the other family photos you just have that one to look at- I ask.

He just sat and contemplated for a while. I thought maybe he hadn't heard me or maybe he just didn't want to talk about it. I simply carried on with my task and was surprised when he just started talking.

-Swanage. Not that you can tell from the photo but it was definitely Swanage. You must be ten or something like that so you can tell how long ago it was. Just sand and the tranquil sea. You can just make out a fishing boat there, bobbing along. Such a beautiful day and nobody on the beach at all. I'm sure it was a school day. Your mother's idea, of course. There's my deck chair and actually I had things to do and so being attacked by two small children digging holes and flicking sand, I was bound to react!-

-Whoa, hang on a minute, this is a school day? But you would never let us take time off school, even if we were near death, burning with fever, we would still need to go in. "Oh run it off" you would say or "once you see your friends you'll be fine" and obviously we both had to have 100% attendance as some sort of badge of honour... and yet...-

-Well, check the date on the back if you don't believe me- he said.

I did.

I dried my hands mid shave and then gently pulled the photo out from behind the mirror. I flipped it over.

18 – 5 – 84 written in black biro, Dad's writing. I went to get my phone from the sitting room and punched in the date. I stared. A Friday.

It was a Friday. This was a small shock because we always, always had to go to school. Dad, as an academic and school was priority one, two and three.

-So how on earth did you, why, go to a beach on a Friday, on a school day? I asked him.

-Your mother, as I said, she having been to see the doctor the day before. She'd not been well and had had tests. I thought she was just being hysterical, doing too much, always travelling for work and those results, well... it wasn't hopeful. She didn't want the treatment, she didn't want to be cut up and so any time, she had left she wanted to enjoy-

-And there's you being grumpy by the seaside- I say, slightly jokingly.

-I was having to come to terms with the fact that my wife, your mother, was not going to be around for very long. Yes, of course, she was fine, snapping away, capturing your joy at an impromptu day off but I wanted to keep her. I wanted her to have her treatment and yet I knew if I kept on and on at her to take the drugs, cut the disease out then any time left would simply sour the sweet taste of what came before and so I pushed these thoughts down. Deep down.

-I think, in this photo, she was ready with the camera and she was secretly goading you two to flick sand all over my work and what could I do, tell you off? Shout? It was your Mother's Day and I had to be strong, to lift you two up. Physically and emotionally.

She must have developed the photo that day and gave it to me. I don't remember-

I looked at his eyes in the mirror. I could see that he did remember.

-But anyway, the picture, 'crystallizing time' as she always said. Time in the past. Anyway, anyway, have you finished yet, I've got to get to backgammon, got to look my best, eh lad?-

Suddenly it was as if that little slice of the past had disappeared and he was back in the present and if I asked him now about the photo, he wouldn't remember. I could look up his hard drive and it would say 'file corrupted-data lost-press Y to continue'.

I washed out the blade and the sink and wiped his face of the little melting blobs of cream. I let him do his own aftershave as I found my mind going back to that same day. What Dad had said about that day was the truth but it was his truth. All I remember, if anything, was having a new spade and a castle-shaped bucket, sand between my toes which often I didn't like but the sand was so soft then feeling the heat of the sand and Mum, just a vague memory now, a huge flapping straw sun hat and the camera always in front of her and the sparkling sea and Dad in his deck chair. It must have been that day and I can only remember being happy, splashing in the water but now, now I revisited that memory it is now tagged with Dad's own memories and I was there enjoying myself, being a child and there was mum so so happy and no doubt crying behind the lens and those big dark glasses. Now I feel guilt, guilt that I knew nothing of this. Annoyed at Mum by keeping us in the dark...but she just wanted to protect us. Annoyed at Dad for having told that story and muddying the memories of that day and then guilty as he had certainly said nothing about that day, the circumstances of it, until now.

And I did ask him to tell me. Maybe that's why he hesitated for so long, not sure whether to tell me at all, but it was the truth and maybe, now because he told me the story, played the file in his head if you like, he has erased it and now only I hold the actual truth. I carry the burden. It is a beautiful picture, a snapshot of unalloyed joy. I tuck the photo back in, underneath the edge of the mirror.

●

Why is it so utterly joyous to clean out one's ears with a cotton bud. We all know it's dangerous to stick anything in if you can't get it out but, oh, the joy. The nerve endings. If you get the cotton bud ever so slightly in your ear then run it around the edge of your earhole, just dipped in, like tickling yourself, a smooth itch to a scratch or a scratch to an itch.

I've had a postcard.

Hand delivered.

-I will be at B&Q. Paint enquiry desk at exactly 5:00 PM. Be there or be unpainted. L-

She has drawn her own stamp. A grumpy queen. The picture on the reverse is of HMS Belfast. I believe the angle of the big guns on HMS Belfast are so angled that if they were fired they would destroy Watford Gap service station. There's a fact for you. But she has given me the opportunity to meet up, possibly buy paint although I didn't know paint buying and paint choosing was going to be a joint venture but, is this a date? I will definitely have to get to the bottom of what a date consists of.

I had high hopes of seeing Faye and the hidden lobster tattoo. I bustled in at exactly five o'clock to see Lillian scanning along the shelves for paint.

Note to self: she always turns up early.

The word 'Breton' would cover what she is wearing this afternoon. Black and white stripy top, red neckerchief, short red skirt, very thick woollen black tights and bright red shoes with a little heel. Was this fancy dress? People do wear it but is it a character? I sidle up to her in the varnish section, feeling the need, the pressure, to come up with a line. I have to keep up with her.

-So, what are the chances of meeting you in this section?- Picking up a small tin of yacht varnish and pretending to be a spy.

-Varnishingly small- she says without missing a beat. I don't think I can keep up.

Everything that was pleasing about Faye, wearing her loose orange canvas dungarees and her tight T-shirt and the brief appearance of a shy lobster was displeasing when presented with Derek wearing a very similar uniform. The T-shirt was tight but in all the wrong places and I tried hard not to think about the image of him bending over and just revealing a clump of coarse hair at the small of his back. Still, Derek knew his paint which was fortunate as Lillian was in full interrogation mode. I told her that I'd already got test cards but apparently this was not enough. From Derek, Lillian had already garnered which colours people had been buying recently as well as any discounts or money off for multiple purchases. Lillian had a small black notebook and almost every word that Derek said was scribbled down in a furious hand, leading Derek to say....

-I mean, don't quote me on that, but that is our policy at the moment- as if he were a junior minister squirming under the lights, skewered by a Paxmanesque interlocutor. As quickly as she started, she stopped, snapping her book shut.

-Right, Derek we'll be back- she said with slight menace that it seemed Derek wanted to know when she would be back so he wouldn't be there.

-What is that?- said Lillian, pointing with her red painted nails towards my red wheeled shopping trolley.

We ambled our way to the emulsion paints but Lillian was still in interrogation mode. Was this a date? Did this happen on dates? Interrogation? Am I being too emulsional?

-Is it yours? Or are you just borrowing it? Does this action of admitting being an out and proud user of a shopping trolley delineate the... -she hesitated for the right word-... moment you crossed the Rubicon between young and old?-

I stopped walking.

-This is my trusty two rubber-wheeled steel handled shopping bag with a 47 litre capacity on its stand and a max of Thirty Kg payload- she did slightly snort at the use of the word 'payload' -OK it isn't a Humvee or a Chinook helicopter- and she did stifle the snort when she saw I was being ever so slightly serious. -Look, I live on my own and this trolley can carry one week's shopping. I don't have a car. If I had a car I would travel further and pay more for the privilege. Most people are sold on the fact that further is better whereas I am convinced further just means further-

This is turning into a rant...

-Most people who go to the supermarket, in a car, live less than a mile away and often buy what they could put in one, carryable shopping bag. Most of the people could do with the exercise. The planet could do with less car journeys. I have observed the habits of the old. They are wise and we ignore their habits at our peril. And, furthermore-

I had entered my 'I came to bury Caesar not to praise him' stage as I had my audience in front of me. -what if everyone had a little shopping trolley? People would be closer to their food. They would choose fresh food every two to three days. Streets would be quieter. You might even envisage local green grocers, bakers, fishmongers rising from the dead and claiming back the coffee houses. Streets would be quieter, people would be fitter and I, young lady, I'm ahead of the curve and...

-OK Winston, you can get off the soap box and put it back on the shelf! I'll get one. I'm convinced, but my pension needs collecting at some point-

I was left, mid speech, in the adhesive aisle.

Lillian grabbed rollers, brushes and a big tub of white emulsion in the time I would have been just pondering over the type of bristles on a brush. I paid and it all fitted into the trolley.

-Dereks?- She said as I was pulling the shopping along across the car park, looking for dropped kerbs.

-Oh, er... Guyler, Warwick, Bristow, Jarman?- I panicked.

-Jarman, yes, good one, wonderful... But you did say Bristow before Jarman so, not at the forefront...

-Well you come up with one then. Derek is hard- I said -it's old fashioned.

She thought hard. She was younger than me.

-Domino?- She said but her heart wasn't in it.

-Wrong, for all sorts of reasons. Griffiths, Bentley, or even Beatty! He used to present 'Mr and Mrs' on Tyne Tees TV!

-....Shun?- She said.

Shun?! I don't get.......oh, very funny(!)- That's for Terry Dactyl isn't it, hum-

We walked along, not quite arm in arm but we could have done. Was it only two weeks ago where she stole my lunch? What is this? Or should I stop trying to clarify and identify everything lest the action of identifying makes it disappear, as if pulling apart a butterfly to see why it it was so beautiful. I then ask her-

-Oh, I didn't say anything about your... costume. Is it a costume?-

-Well, nice of you to notice but, well, sort of sub-costume, more traditional dress of Breton. But no onions. No, tonight I'm meeting up with the girls, for French night.

She said this so definitely as if simply everyone would know what French night is. She saw my quizzical face.

-Oh well, quite a few years ago a lot of us girls got the ferry out to Saint Malo and we all dressed with berets and stripey tops and had a very nice time and so, if we meet up we tend to do French things, such as dressing up, but also as I am now off to that French restaurant in Southsea, the one with the golden snail, and act French.

Of course, of course, why wouldn't you do that. I don't ask about how many people you see with shopping trolleys in France but it is many.

She is utterly charming. She looks at her watch.

-Oh my goodness, I'm late. I did have a lovely time though. Still OK for Saturday?-

-I smiled to say 'yes' and then a very French depart on both cheeks and she was off in her Frenchness down the road. I trundled back home. Put my keys next to the phone which had a little flashing light.

·

-Hi Dad, everything OK? You said on your message you had news. What's up?-

I was assuming it was about his latest Backgammon win or more likely his losses.

-It's your uncle, Jim-

-Right?- I really should have been concentrating properly but I was looking through my briefcase for a form I thought I'd lost.

-He's dead-

I slowly put down my briefcase on the floor- your brother, Jim? Oh Dad I'm sorry. Do you want me to come over?-

-You can if you want, but I thought I'd let you know, your only uncle-

I heard him breathe on the phone, a little raspy but definitely still there.

-I mean how did he die?-

-His heart gave out. I mean, he'd been ill, you know that but, big old heart attack.-

-Oh- I said. Not really knowing what to say.

-Your cousin phoned up, let me know. She'll let me know about the funeral, the arrangements-

….which then means he'll let me know about the funeral.

-You'll want to go I imagine? Are you well enough to go?- I said.

To give him his due he did at least hesitate for a second.

-Yes, yes I should go- That wasn't really what I asked, I thought, but I let it go.

-OK, I'll be round later-

Life does seem to undulate. I go along, beige as you like and now, up up up with 'dates' choosing paint and then, down with thoughts of funerals. I stood awhile in the quiet of the hall. My keys were still in my hand.

A few cars zoom down the road and I see their red lights streak by through the glass in the door. I place the phone back into its cradle.

•

Ah, Saturday, that Peer Gynt moment, of gentle flutes, muted bassoons, all the woodwind giving the impression of walking barefoot through a spring glade, the grass, daisies, crocuses all moistened with dew and then with the stretching and reaching tendrils of the sun banishing the night sky, that crescendo as I lay in that perfect netherworld between sleep and awake. The pillow is warm, the central heating still burbling and the duvet is an all consuming womb.

During the week a radio alarm is set, some ghastly local station stuffed with mindless chatter about some benign news item. Constant twittering about a burst water main in Bursledon, traffic already backing up on the Fareham turn off and the music, either tedious 80's or tedious 90's pop or modern music which just sounds like a box full of angry tsetse flies and a woman with a modified and strangulated warble shouting about her boyfriend and how he 'done her wrong' and now she was a 'strong independent woman' until the next ghastly man comes along. All of this has the effect of switching the radio off and getting up, suitably angry. I used to wake up to Radio 4. This has the delightful bonus of not having inane music. However, the BBC spends an awful lot of time advertising itself and all of its services when I am actually listening to it. I mean why are you advertising it!

I'm listening already. I'm doing it, but if some ghastly politician comes on or some dreadful rent-a-mouth spouting something that is clearly said to either mask what they're actually being questioned about but also something controversial....I will switch it off and become suitably angry for the rest of the day. More often than not, the talking just becomes a burble and it fails to wake me up at all.

But Saturdays, after a night of shouting at the television, after a wine glass in the sink with a splash of water in it, (wouldn't want it to stain now), after a bottle opened and a vain hope of just having the one and then putting the empty bottle in the recycling bin at 1 am, after putting a glass of water at the side of the bed which, through habit must have been drunk at night.....after all of that, Saturday morning is bliss. The moment before all the thoughts of funerals, of shopping, of work make it into your mind and you can just lie listening to the relative calm of life near the pond.

-EEK EEK WARNING THIS VEHICLE IS REVERSING – EEK-

Oh God, I mean, whatever happened to vehicles reversing without a warning! Yes, people probably got knocked down but that would be good old evolution at work. If you see something large reversing...just move away! Surely the number of lives saved by this voice (and isn't it the voice of

eye, that it was Frog parking the screeching van and ably assisting Lillian. I said to them both that I'd be ready as soon as possible and I'll bring in coffee. 'Coffee for all' I said 'coffee cures all ills'.

Now, if I'd had the energy to climb back up the stairs I would have re entered the womb and slept for a thousand years. I simply schlepped to the kitchen to neck some paracetamol.

-Hi there. Everything okay?- I said, as brightly as I could peeping through the door. It was well past nine and I'd procrastinated long enough. At least I could open my eyes.

-Henry! We're in the conservatory!- shouted Lillian, right the way through the house, excitement in her voice. I trudged through the house, avoiding the upturned nails of the carpet gripper rod.

I remember as a child when we had the carpets up for any reason, my Dad would always point them out. 'Don't step on them', but also 'they were what trainee fakirs would use, starter kits to build up to a bed of nails'. He said it every time and so every time I see them I smile in spite of myself.

-Oh Henry, you didn't say there was a conservatory! I've got all the plants out here on the tiles. Will that be ok?-

-Erm, yes?- I said, but not sure what question I was answering. There were tiles so the water from the plants was fine. Would these sensitive little plants survive the cold nights under the glass. Of that I was less sure.

She hadn't waited for any answer anyway as she was in the backroom now.

-I've put everything in the middle of the rooms as I know the walls and skirting boards need doing...-

And I followed her voice into the backroom but by the time I'd gotten in there she was in the kitchen.

-And I do love the kitchen. Lovely oven- (noise of looking in the oven and I heard her voice gain a little echo)- what was she expecting to see in the oven, the Mormon Tabernacle Choir? Even with the numbing of the paracetamol, my head was still thumping. Is this what it's like to be married, I wondered? Waves of pain and nausea leading to agreement for the sake of a quiet life both aurally and metaphorically.

I could see she had lots of tupperwares, boxes of food, tea bags, jars of spices which were all on the side in the kitchen.

-It's just the big bits now- she said – I think, a bed, mattress, although the bed is in bits....

Emotionally or physically I thought.

....and cupboards, tv and a few suitcases-

-Do you need a hand with it? Hmm?- asking Frog obviously as he seems keen, able to lift and surely doesn't need me to help.

-Oh yes, great, many hands et cetera- said Lillian, directing me as if in charge of a tank battalion across the Sahara. It wouldn't surprise me if she had a list or a tick sheet somewhere.

Then it suddenly clicked.

She had on a blue set of overalls and her hair up in a spotted scarf. She was 'Rosie the Riveter'. Of course she was, sleeves up, work being done. Feminist icon.

As I walked over to the van I tried, without it being too obvious, to warm up. Just a few bends, a calf stretch, a touch of the toes (knees, who am I kidding here). I knew if I just lifted a box, a heavy box then that would be it, muscle strain and deep heat for a week. With age comes wisdom and also chronic muscular atrophy.

Frog jumped effortlessly, well of course he did, into the back of the Transit, curse him and his young supple limbs and also bless him as he spent a few moments looking at me and then around the van to see if there was a box suitable for me to carry. This choice of his was based on my clearly advanced age and my pathetic middle-aged frame.

It put me in mind of a long past Christmas. It must have been when Mum took us two to a department store Father Christmas. There was my sister, as cute as a button and she jumps up on his knee and Father Christmas, without even looking at what he was doing, pulls a present out of his red velvet sack and gives it to my sister who squeals with delight. Then its my turn, led onto the dais by a helper elf and before Father Christmas, old Saint Nick himself lifts me up onto his knee I see there is a poorly hidden look of revulsion behind his acrylic beard. You see I was still in recovery from chicken pox so no doubt covered in crusty scabs. I also had a huge fabric plaster over one lens of my glasses. I looked like a survivor from a plague from a previous century. I saw Father Christmas look in a different bag, much smaller, and this, I surmised, was a sack of toys for special children, those with life limiting illnesses. It was that look of pity that I now saw in Frog's eyes as I was clearly no help and he would rather do it himself. He picked out the smallest box of books with so few books inside that I could count them all at a glance.

-Will you be OK with that?- He said, innocently patronising so I took a much larger box which was near the door of the van, clearly far too heavy but it was too late now, I had started to lift it up.

I could feel every muscle in my arms and back crying out in pain as I lifted it but all pain was overruled by stubbornness. I just about made it into the house with the box, navigating the various steps and thresholds and once Frog could no longer see me I dropped the box in the hall and contemplated whether or not I should have a heart attack. No, not for now, but maybe later. I went back out to the van and also took the small box. A point had been made. I don't know what that point was, but it was made.

-If you don't mind me asking, where did you get those chairs from- as I eased myself back into one of the most comfortable chairs I'd ever sat. The move was complete and Lillian and I were allowing ourselves a sit down, contemplating what to do next.

-Well, both of these ones were salvaged- she said, sitting back in its twin. -Beautiful wood and actually the 1930's style fits the style of the house, don't you think?-

-Oh absolutely- I said. My body, my legs my back all seemed to be at the right angle. The long armrests, beautifully smooth wood, all rounded everywhere with not a sharp corner in sight. Why didn't I have a chair like this? I could also see that Lillian had an awful lot of art to go up on the walls. All of it was turned into the walls so I could say little about the art. The bare light bulb in the middle of the room did little for the mood but it did help me to focus on what I needed to say. Lillian, equally tired in her chair may be in a more receptive mood.

-So, erm- I said.

-Hey Henry, there's an 'erm', I sense we are sailing towards an island of indecision?- she said.

-Sorry. But, I've just been thinking that, well, things have been a little rushed-

-Things?- she said -what things?

-She knew what I was talking about but, and I watched her eyes close in the chair. She is making me do all the running.

-It was only a few weeks ago when we first met and you stole my lunch...

-Actually you offered me your lunch, at least a share, which is definitely not stealing...

-...Okay, so 'shared' a lunch- I patronisingly emphasised the word shared -and, correct me if I'm wrong, but I think there was a spark there-

-A spark you say?-

-Yes, I think so- Don't backtrack, say what you believe, say there was a spark, don't water it down with I 'think' there was a spark,... There was a spark.

- Hmm....go on- she murmured, eyes still closed.

-And then we went on a date...-

-A date? Did we? When was that?- she said, sounding genuinely surprised.

-Well, you know, the pub, the quiz.-

-That wasn't a date!- she opened one eye -that was a quiz. How can it be a date if three other people are there?-

I knew it, I knew it couldn't have be a date!

-But there are always other people on dates, aren't there?-

-Yes, if you mean that other people exist in the world, but they don't have a date at the same table.-

-OK, but then you wanted to meet up again. Just the two of us.-

-When was that?!-

Two eyes open now. This conversation was going in the opposite direction to my intention.

-You know, the paint-

-The paint? You mean, meeting up in a shop to buy paint?-

-Yes, just you and me...-

 -And Derek...-

-And Derek but, if you had a date wouldn't there be a Maitre'd or a waiter? Someone there in an official capacity, surely?-

-Shush! Shush Shush!- She shushed me, alert as if she'd heard a tiny sound. Was it those blasted mice in the walls. She sat bolt upright.

-What is it? Now finding myself quite concerned-

-Oh, sorry, I just thought I heard someone clutching at very tiny straws! Ha!- and she sat back in her chair laughing like a drain.

-Yes, very funny. Mock me if you will but we have gone from two non-dates to you moving into my home, well not my home... well, a home that belongs to me so, technically my home and... for me... it is all a bit fast. If I'm honest I get very stressed if my normal brand of washing up liquid isn't in the shops and I have to go through weeks of looking for it and then, consider another brand. It's traumatic. So, this....-

I very carefully, very properly didn't want to label this because as we know labelling things leads to things not existing.

-This? Do you mean by 'this' a relationship?-

-Well, I wouldn't put 'this' in that sort of bracket or pigeon hole but maybe, if there is a spark, then we could possibly have a date and then see where we go from there?-

Lillian blinked, leaning back in her chair but then having to shield her eyes from the bulb.

-Are you asking me out on a date?-

I took a deep breath. -Erm- But then she instantly growled at me, eyebrows furrowed -no not erm but, yes... ostensibly... I am asking you out on a date-

-Ha! Ostensibly!? Come on, be honest, when was the last time you went out on a date, 1896?-

I'd never seen someone laugh so hard. I thought she was in pain. I'm glad I was a source of amusement for her. But after the waves of laughter had subsided she stood up, dusted herself down and grabbed her jacket that was on the back of the chair.

-OK then, let's go out on a date… where are you taking me?- she said in a most serious tone.

It wasn't the same panic as this morning but it was very close. I stopped myself saying 'erm'.

-What, you mean now? It was more of a general question, possibly like children in the playground who say 'will you go out with me' and then just sort of go out in a sort of hanging out not actually think, organise, go out at all-

But it's as if she wasn't listening.

-I'll book an Uber as you don't strike me as an Uber guy. We'll go to Gunwarf and you can pay. You've got 5 minutes! Go!

•

-I can't say that I like this sort of dining- I said.

We're on opposite sides of a table, sat on benches, very long benches, on which other people (other people, again I am right there with Sartre), in a sort of quasi Korean, Japanese, 'can't-really-make-its-mind-up' Asian fusion but never any borscht, no Mongolian Yak drink I note. It's all pork balls and noodles, squid with chilli and that sort of thing. But eating, cheek by jowl with others of, shall we say those more used to eating from a trough, and could they not close their mouths when they eat? This slopping noise of moist mouths, masticating, it's all I can bear, it really is.

-Is this OK for you?- Lillian asked.

-Oh, yes, fine perfect- I say. I'm often found here eating directly from a bucket.

-And you're happy here?- she says -Comfortable? This being a- she ran up to the word- DATE!-

-Okay okay perhaps I was being a little nervous before, but I just wanted to know where I stood. So OK this is a date and...-

-Oh, please don't tell me you want an itinerary? At 8:05 we'll order and then you'll ask me 'ooh, what's that, I might have that'. Then 8:15 you ask me what my favourite colour is and then at 8:16 I slap you around the face and walk out because you asked such an inane question!-

-OK-No- but, and you might have picked up on this.... I am not Mr Spontaneity so your commanding, teetering-almost-on-bullying-me into a date tonight, well they might well have called the name of the restaurant- 'out of my comfort zone' serving meals such as- 'Irish Stew served with kimchi and a side order of barium meal' or 'a bare garlic bulb served on a bed of rice in the shape of a spunking penis.'-

She snorted, trying to hide her laughter behind the giant menu which seemed to be covered by a sticky residue of grease from previous diners. The word 'penis' was unnecessary and quite childish.

-At least I can make you laugh- I say

-Oh you do that alright, you really do. I assure you-

I said nothing. I didn't tell her about notes that I'd made previously for such occasions.

If you were making a speech, it's important. You make notes. You have one chance. You don't want to cock it up. First date, one chance only, you take notes with you. You use notes… and then you're damned for a lack of spontaneity. Give me enough time for planning and I can be as spontaneous as you like!

-Okay, so, do you want to order?- she asks.

I try and take control of the situation. I think it is in danger of becoming a situation.

-No, You order for me, what you think I would like to eat, but I will have an Asahi beer. A very expensive beer which tastes much like every other beer but I know it is better as I have paid more for it. That's how beer works, certainly after the first pint-

She gave me the beady eye, daring me.

-You sure? I like it spicy- she said.

-I'm sure you do!- I countered. Boom, first double entendre of the evening. Yeah, I can do this, I can talk to women. I can function on a 'date'.

-Oh, welcome Frankie Howerd. Okay then I shall order for two and that will be that.-

She placed her menu on the table and we both waited for the waitress who seemed rushed off her feet.

-So, come on then, we're on a date. What do we talk about?- She leant across the bench, her forearms flat on the bench, her hands palm down. Her face much, much closer to mine. The pressure was back on. Think man, think! Honesty or bluff- two directions and only one way leads to hell.

-Okay, so I'm going to be honest here, if you'll permit me- I say.

-I permit- she said, not unlike a judge giving sentence.

-Well, you are certainly one of the most, (this next word was important, not quite make or break but skating close to it), unusual-

She raised her eyebrows but she didn't move away.

-... People I have met. And I do mean that in a very positive way...-

-Go on...-

-Well, everyone I meet is usually so predictable and therefore so dull. I almost always know what someone is going to say before they say it and that makes life... predictable. Now, don't get me wrong, I like predictable, I like to know what is going to happen. I don't like shocks. And yet...-

-And yet?-

-Well, you are the most shocking and unpredictable person I have come across in a long time and, I'll admit, I'm a little scared, but scared in a good way. Maybe, just maybe it's good to be just a little scared-

-Wow. Most men, if I'm honest, ask my favourite colour and which costumes I like to wear in bed. First dates and also last dates.

I breathed an inaudible imperceptible sigh of relief. I am still in the game.

-Well, favourite colour and night time costume attire was second and third questions- and she smiled, and a more long lasting smile this time.

-And...as you are so unusual, so extraordinary in the truest sense of the word, what on earth would you see in me, this fusty old crustacean of a man, straight from the end of the 19th Century railing against all progress since the death of George the 5th! Apart from my exquisite taste in lunches of course...

-Well, yes, apart from the exquisite taste in lunch, I don't know but you do intrigue me like no one else does-

-Intrigue?- It was my time to lean forward on the bench, our faces dangerously close to one another, the clash and clamour in the kitchen and the mawkish chewing of food suddenly distant from my ears.

-Well, I can see that with what you wear, you dress from the 1930's, braces, shirt, jumper, jackets and ties all in splendid monochrome and yet you stand out because of this. Your shoes are buffed and polished and always you hide behind the paper but no one reads broadsheets any more and so, ironically, you stand out by hiding. I wear all sorts of costumes and no one notices me let alone notices that I'm wearing a costume, except you. You noticed. Which means you must notice other things. And I can tell that you are clever. I like clever. And not only with your job but, well not just clever but smart as if you've worked out the system but haven't told anyone else. 'Let them work it out.' But I can't say that I've worked you out completely, not nearly. But that's a good thing. Who wants a game they solve so early?

-A game am I?-

-Well yes, of course. An enigma. A puzzle.

-Hmm- I hmmm'd -OK so one last thing before we start our date...am I able to have an indication as to when you are joking and when you are serious. My little brain is working overtime here and I'm just about hanging on and I just need a wink or a nod to tell me if you're joking-

-Really?- she said, now leaning back out on her bench, also spying the waitress coming down the aisle. -But isn't that the point of the game?- And she winked. But did that wink mean she was serious or it was part of the game? AARGH! I don't know the rules, or maybe I do know the rules but I don't know what the game is...

Can I take your order? said the smiling waitress, an oasis of calm ready to stab our orders into her little electronic device.

-OK then, so if this is a date...- she says.

-Oh, is the jury still out then? I thought this was, definitely a date.

-Okay, a date- Lillian said, spearing a piece of crispy chilli squid into the fiery crimson lava sauce. I stayed far away from such foul liquid. My beer was just enough to quench any heat from the chilli infused pork dumplings -so (was she tutoring me on how a date works? teachers just can't help themselves), we could do some quick fire rounds, just to see what we like and dislike. Full disclosure but, if it's off limits it's off limits. I'll go first.

-Of course you will- I say, with a wink.

-So, favourite film- she says.

-No no no, you can't just reduce loves and tastes and culture into one thing. They have these lists in the paper and seemingly everything, like stock, has to be reduced and I want no part of it.

-Amelie- she said.

-Ah, well actually that is a wonderful film, sweet and life affirming- I tried not to show my annoyance at how good her choice was.

-So go on, your favourite film?- she said, again, leaning forward.

-Oh this is just not fair, I say. Whatever I say I'll be judged forever-

-Well, in that case, you just have to get over it. You're being judged right now by acting like a Sissy Mary refusing to pick a film-

-Alright, but I have the right to change my mind at anytime- often called the 'Female' principle-

-I'll ignore that- as she poked out her little tongue... -come on, stop stalling-

-Look, if I say 'Citizen Kane' you'll say, "too obvious", if I say, anything from Andrei Tarkovsky you'll say too pretentious and trying too hard-

-Oh my God! Just say it! If you don't tell me in 10 seconds you'll get a default and your favourite film will be erm, 'Pee Wee Herman's Big Top Adventure', or 'Carry on Girls!-

Okay okay pressure.

-'Les Vacances de Monsieur Hulot'. My favourite film-

-Never heard of it. Tell me about it- as she speared yet another fearsome piece of squid into her mouth by way of the lava.

-Erm-

-No 'erm'-

-Jacques Tati as Monsieur Hulot. Almost a silent film and it is just a piece of comic genius. There is love, there is humour and there are depths of despair and everything in between-

-And the story?- she asked.

-Well, Monsieur Hulot goes on holiday and that's it-

-OK- and then she pulled out her phone and started searching for it, I presumed.

-Oh no...you can't search for it. Don't diminish it. You have to just watch it- and I reached forward and put my hand gently on top of her phone, just touching her fingers at the edges and she acquiesced. She folded her little case closed and put her phone away.

-Do you have the film?- she asked.

-Bien sur!

-OK, fine, second date sorted. You can dress up.....-

-Hmm-

....You dress as Hulot and I'll do my French outfit-

-D'accord- I say with a smile.

-See, that's not so bad, is it. Favourite film leads to Oh I don't know, conversation-

-Yes, OK- I say, trying not to be grumpy and have another slurp of my beer. It was all a little too spicy for me but, if I pace myself, one bite, one gulp, I'd make it through.

-My turn then- I say. -Favourite artist. Mine is Yayoi Kusama, a Japanese artist. Bonkers. Dots and circles but with no end. And, yes I do own something that she has done. It was a present-

-Wow, again. My goodness-

-And you, come on, someone who goes to such efforts everyday with costumes absolutely must have an artistic influence-

-OK so, goodness. I suppose it has to be about the artist, but also the art...

-Oh, sounds like a bit of stalling there. Just a simple question. If you don't say anything in 10 seconds, well will have to say that your favourite artist is Picasso or maybe Hitler?-

-No fair! Okay okay, so it has to be the photographer, Marnie Green. I have a picture of hers, you know, the one of Andy Warhol, famously with his hands out to stop the picture being taken but with his fingers spread out so we can see his eyes... so in that precise moment as he is wanting us to see him or is he trying to hide but in the hiding... he becomes all the more visible. Just like someone we know! She was so good at that, what was it, 'crystallizing the moment'?-

But despite my smile she could see something was up, something not quite right. She was perceptive, I'll give her that!

-What is it? You're smiling and yet you seem upset. Chunk of chilli burning in the pit of the stomach? Can't handle the heat? Or have I said something?-

-Oh nothing really. It's just that, Marnie Green... is my mother. Was.

The diners, the cutlery, the pinging of incessant social media that provides the background music to all of our lives was faded down and we're suddenly alone in the restaurant. When this has happened before, and it has, there are levels of response.

Firstly:-Disbelief

-No way! I mean, just no way. You're making it up! It's very good but not quite believable. She was a fierce and independent artist and....-

-....I'm not?-

-Well, no but... no, you're pulling my leg, surely-

She just doesn't believe me. And you can always see in their eyes they think I'm playing a joke. But it is the truth. And it does hurt me when they don't believe me. My mother is alive again for just a moment and I want to believe it as well but then I have to go through the grief once more.

I suppose this is always the case, family of the famous. You see the work, you see how they belong to other people, you have to share them. When they die, every time you see them on an old interview with them on the TV, hear their voice on the radio they are still there. Shadows of themselves, keeping them alive but only for others. She is alive then frozen again in time.

Especially an artist who dies before their time.

You see these old Hollywood stars dying at 90 or 95. Strangely their plastic faces stretched and warped so they barely recognise themselves in a mirror, certainly no-one else recognising them. They are old. They've lived their lives, their heyday long behind them and people barely remember them. The fact they have aged, makes them mortal. Yet those stars that died acutely, in one moment. Take James Dean for example. A young man, a few films under his belt, flawless good looks and then he slams his Porsche into a telegraph pole. Had he lived, what would have happened? A few more films, not quite as good as his first, a few scandals with women, becoming addled by drinking, drugs or divorce. But there he is, decades later, untouched by scandal or ageing, still on posters and an icon to all the teens for all time. And all he had to do was die young. Kurt Cobain, Jimi Hendrix, even Vincent van Gogh to a certain extent. My mother certainly wasn't in that sort of company but in her particular slice of history, the late 70's, the early 80's she just had a knack of capturing moments. Who knows, had she lived she might have been happy snapping landscapes or just not even taking pictures at all. She had become an artist who had a little bit of success and someone who helped to define a moment, a movement, NYC in the late 1970's, all those punk bands, Warhol, Blondie, Velvet Underground....

But Lillian, sitting in a humdrum chain restaurant serving substandard Asian fusion cuisine, does not believe that my mother is my mother. Of course I will have to prove that somehow to all the doubting Thomases.

-I have some of her pictures at home. I can show you later if you like-

And I think because I wasn't bragging about it or cashing in, she was more likely to believe me.

The next stage is realisation.

-But that's incredible. What was she like? Lillian leaning forward even more now, a small child on a reading mat waiting to be told a story. I knew what she wanted. She wants to recall what it was like working with Warhol, The Factory, all those punk bands. Bowie? Iggy Pop? But I have to answer the question the only way I know how.

-She was my mum. She was there, at home, but often she wasn't there. She was a woman, loving mother, completely disorganised and did many things on a whim, much to my father's genuine annoyance. I really didn't know what she did until after she died.

I'm still finding out what she did.

Lillian now realised that being related to someone who is famous is not all beans and sausages. I know that Scott and Shackleton strode off bravely to the South Pole, and everyone remembers what they did or did not do but I always wonder, at the docks, departing good old Blighty, did they look back over their shoulder and consider what they were leaving behind? Scott, he was 43, leaving young children, a young wife....all left behind. So, all very well leaving notes at your death saying people should be looked after but then, but then, if everyone stayed at home then nothing would get done.

-I'm sorry, of course- she said, suddenly finding herself in a situation more serious that she envisaged on a 'date'.

-But I'm glad you like what she did- I said. -It is good. Yes, favourite film, favourite artist, it does rather foster conversation-

Lillian continued with her pork dumplings and I merely prodded them around the bowl with my fork having had enough of the heat.

-...Maybe... Are you eating that dumpling?- She asked, eyeing my bowl. She stabbed the spare dumpling.

-Apparently not!-

-Pudding?- She asks but it didn't seem to be a question.

-How dare you- I say -I'm just carrying a few extra pounds. It's my slow metabolism!-

She smiled even though her cheek was swollen with my dumpling, like a kid with a gob stopper.

The waitress came over, seeing that our dishes were empty.

-Would you like to see the menu?- she said balancing the dishes in one big bowl.

-Yes Vicki, yes we would- I said, spying the young girl's name tag but trying very hard to make it not look as if I'm staring at her chest.

-Vickis? -said Lillian, more to me than her.

-Queen?-I say.

-OK, Derbyshire, radio-

-Principal. Dallas, before your time-

-Oh, OK, Coren-

-Yes, good – I say -Beckham!-

-Damn it, yes, er er er Pendleton! Lillian shouted it out so pleased she was with herself.

-Good....erm...so...?- said Vicki, not sure what she had walked into.

-Oh my, sorry, just wondering who you might be named after- I asked.

-My Gran.. so...- she said, backing away, -I'll just get those menus then-

-OK, perhaps if we do that again we don't get so excited?- I said.

-Maybe... but good Victorias though. Not many there at all-

Pudding came and went and the Uber dropped us back home. The stars above all blotted out by the street lights which illuminated both of us outside our respective neighbouring houses.

-So, said Lillian, a slight slurring after three Manhattans. I had wisely stuck to my beer -what did you think of our first date then?-

-It was, without doubt, the best first date I've been on....this year- smiling at my own delayed caveat -But, you know where I live. I've got your number... we might want to do this again some other time?- I said as I was fumbling, trying to get my keys out. -So, goodnight then- but Lillian stopped, no, slightly stumbled forward and gave me a little peck on the cheek over the little wall.

-That's for being a man but not being a shit-

And she tottered up to her own front door as I went towards mine, both of us separated by a wall 2 foot high. She leaned towards me, blew a delightful little kiss, so delicate, so feminine. She then crashed through the front door, tripping over the step that she'd forgotten was there.

-I'm alright, I'm alright- she shouted to me.... and to the rest of the street.

-OK- I said back in a stage whisper.

It might possibly be an actual fact that I am in some sort of relationship with an actual real life woman.

I slept well.

•

2:47 am

Oh God. I'm up I'm up. I'm sweating. Is the phone ringing? No. Did I set the alarm to the wrong time? No. My heart is, well, a little panicked. A strange feeling of fluttering. Doing it now. It's not altogether pleasant. Is it a heart attack?

No.

•

-I thought you went to church on Sundays, that's why you didn't want me coming around. Do you need me to take you to church?-

A delivery had come this morning, despite it being a Sunday, and I decided to pop round just to see how he was. Despite the early hour he was up, dressed in smart trousers, shirt, grey cardigan.

-Did you get yourself dressed?- I asked.

-I'm not an invalid you know. If I take my time I can do it. I know that Rochelle helps in the week but, she's so quick, so rough. I know she's busy but...-

I kept quiet. I certainly wasn't going to volunteer for dressing duties every morning.

-But you're not going to church. So what are you all dressed up for?-

-Can't I just get dressed up? Go out? Have a walk?-

-Not if there's clearly an ulterior motive. But you're not going to tell me what it is so I'll drop it. Can I turn that TV off though? I can feel my fillings rattling out of my head!- I press standby on the remote. The noise extinguished. I could finally think.

-I've got you a present-

-A what?-

-A present. For you. Well, sort of for you. Look...- I gave the padded envelope to him and he tipped the heavy block out into his hands.

-It's a sharpening block- I said -You know, for the razor. I've seen a few quick YouTube videos but you can show me how to do it, to sharpen it. We can do a proper shave if you like- Dad held the stone, feeling the heft of it. His facial expression showed some sort of approval.

So, I laid out the stone on a towel. I wet the stone and then gently pushed the blade forward over its surface. Gently gently. Oh God I didn't want to ding the blade or break it. It's one thing watching a video but actually, how much pressure do you use, what exact angle do you hold the blade at? All I got was Dad's beady eye watching everything that I was doing. That was pressure enough.

-Have you got enough water on the stone?- he asked.

-I think so-

-I can hear grating. Can you hear grating?-

-I'm surprised you can hear anything given the volume of that television-

-What?-

Exactly. I can't hear any grating. Then, according to the video, I had to get the leather strop out, rub some jewellers rouge, a waxy paste with a bit of grit inside it on to the leather. I attached one end of the strop to the doorknob and held it taught at the other end whilst I gently, so gently, pulled the blade along the leather this time with the sharp edge trailing.

Do the other side. The fact the leather was just being held in the air meant I couldn't put too much pressure on it. Although still nervous about the correct angle, the constant beady eye, there was a routine to it, a flow that I could get into, up and down, up and down, a very faint flip-flopping noise from the soft leather as the blade made its journey. Then the grit was washed off the leather. The leather, soft but dry and here I would strop the blade, 50 or so times up and down, trying to keep the same angle, the same pressure until I put the blade down onto the side. Without warning I plucked a hair from his head, just yanked it out.

-Ow!- He protested.

-Big baby. Come on, you've got to know whether it's sharp or not. You've got to do the hanging hair test-

I had the blade in my hand, the sharp edge facing the ceiling. Both of us moved in closer to see the blade. The light from the bathroom glinted off the steel. I held the blade still and let the hair fall onto it. The hair, spliced in two, both parts falling to the floor.

-Well then- I said, my face very close to my father's who'd seen the same thing, -do you want a real shave with a real razor?- I move the razor so the light glinted off the edge and into his eyes, dazzling him.

-Hmm, I suppose- was all he could say.

Holding a razor in your hand, not a safety razor but a long straight glinting blade, gives one quite a powerful feeling. I'm holding it between three fingers and my thumb. There is certainly a weight to it but it doesn't feel heavy. The handle's pulled back and I hold it like an old fashioned set square. I've given him the hot towel treatment, open up those pores and then the lather. A good going over with the brush. The only real issue is that he is just a bit too low for me. I can still shave him but I'm constantly leaning over and I can feel the muscles in my lower back starting to twitch and spasm. I think, just for a moment, about buying a barber's chair, one that can be pumped up by a big old pedal at the bottom, lift the customer up to your own height. Nice idea but ever so slightly unnecessary.

So, this is it. Blade in hand, looking in the mirror, the old man also looking in the mirror, his eyes scrutinising every move I make.

So, from a time of rummaging about in a cupboard through old cans of foam and brushes and safety razors to this moment holding aloft the razor sharp rectangle of metal and I am to pull the skin tight and see what happens.

With the first swipe I learn that it is not the pressure nor the angle of the blade nor how taut the skin is. No. It is all about confidence. If I went in, pussyfooting about, short little strokes then 1) it would take forever and 2) dad would wince every time I'd come near him with the blade. Not a million miles away from the feeling of driving for the first time, on your own, having just passed your test. Suddenly you're on your own and you have to make your own decisions. Any mistakes you make are also your own.

To stop myself concentrating too hard on what I was doing I went full barber.

-Did you hear anything about the funeral?- I asked him, my little tongue poking through my teeth, carefully watching what I was doing. Actually, having such a wide blade, my goodness you can shave such a large portion of skin in one go. That's a huge benefit. If only his face was flat enough to benefit from it. It's all squashy and angular. Still, asking the question was enough to snap him out of his laser beam eyes as he had to think of his answer. He relaxed and so did I. So, this is why barbers talk.

-Oh yes, I did actually, it's on Friday.

I stopped shaving, mid scrape -What, This Friday?-

-Yes, I think so. Is that okay?-

-Well I suppose so but, well, it's a bit soon isn't it?-

-They did tell me last week-

Oh.

Instead of shaking the blade in the sink I found it easier to wipe the blade on the towel around his neck. It shed all the foam and hair off in one stroke.

-And you still want to go?- I asked.

He thought for a moment. -Yes, I would. Would you be alright making the arrangements?-

-Yes, I suppose so.... of course. I might just need to rejig a bit of work but yes, we could stay at a hotel. Might be a bit easier....- I said, aware that I was lengthening my words. The tricky bit just under the nose, over the lips. Dad automatically pursed his lips to help but I was suddenly aware of how big the razor was, like parking a big fat Lamborghini in a side street. A tiny bit too much pressure here or at the wrong angle and a nick and then blood everywhere. I shaved as close as I dare and that was an end to it. I washed the blade, stropped it a few times and realised that I had been holding my breath for the rest of the time. Yes, breathing is important when holding a razor sharp blade.

-Not bad.....- said Dad, getting up out of the chair at the second attempt and peering hard into the mirror, -.....for a first go- and at least he smiled at the mirror as he said that.

•

-I mean, who is that at the door. It's Sunday afternoon for Christ's sake. I'm not expecting anyone, am I?-

-Good afternoon- said Lillian, a very tight top on- Eyes up! Eyes up! And dungarees! Oh my goodness. Paint in her hair, freckled onto her face and arms. An opposite dalmatian. Did I mention dungarees? Goodness!

-Oh hello- I take my familiar stance at the door, blocking the entrance to pedlars, tinkers and prospective knife sharpeners and sellers of double glazing, but she is none of these. Of course, you're living next door.

-Did our first date not mean anything to you?- and she comically flutters her eyelashes. I was wondering if you wanted to help out with the painting? I'm just putting on a diluted coat of emulsion onto the plaster but, lots of walls, lots of paint-

I mean, she's absolutely right, but I was hoping to do the walls... well, not on a specific date as such but at least two days hence. But it is not just me. Here is someone at the opposite end of my activity spectrum and already with the splashes of paint. I'm feeling guilty but not so guilty that I want to drop everything and when I mean everything I mean the crossword and maybe a nap. Is this how it's going to be? Me being dragged along like an angry sullen teenager before having to agree to do something I should have done anyway!

At least the painting has an endpoint. Once it's done, it's done. I can relax.

-Give me 5 minutes, I'll change into some old clothes and I'll be over. Okay?-

Her smile was worth my sacrifice.

I don't know exactly how long Michelangelo was on his back, painting the Sistine Chapel but, my goodness, did he not get bored? I have a roller in my hand, a roller with thin paint dribbling down my arm, and cold paint at that.

I've painted two bare walls and I am already bored. The plaster is absorbing the water, the paint is providing a base for later coats and all I can think about is how long this takes, every single squeeze of the roller and then the wall is going to have to be painted again, and probably again. But, sneaking a look out of the corner of my eye I watch Lillian as she bends over, rolls the roller in the paint, once, twice, three times always three times and taps the end of it twice, always twice and then stretches up to the point where she was last time. Long stretches, up and down. She's clearly concentrating on what she is doing yet it is exactly the same every time. As if she is in a flow, a mesmeric flow. The paint never dribbles down her arm so she must be using just the right amount of pressure. It's unfair, that's what it is, it's unfair. And she can talk to me at the same time as doing a much better job. I feel quite incompetent.

-Oh, by the way, I saw someone fiddling about with your bin today, it was very early on, certainly before 6:00 am.

I froze, mid stroke, a rivulet of paint again streaming down my arm.

-My bin? Putting something in?

-Well I couldn't really see but they definitely opened and closed the lid. Open and shut case if you ask me!! Ha!-

I'll bet there's a bloody seagull in there, I'll bet but, in front of others, I didn't want to just fly into a rage that was brewing.

-Ok, Ok I'll have a look later on- And how long do I leave it before I sneak a look. It's like a ping on a phone and resisting the urge to check. Oh, the ping!

-I mean, look – she said -you can see it must have just been thrown in. Its wings, its head. It's all very unnatural-

We both stared into the abyss of the bin, the lid completely flipped open. Inside was indeed yet another bird, still a sea bird but smaller than before, either a young bird or a different type of bird. Its bill was certainly yellow but much smaller, much finer.

-Yep, definitely a bird. Definitely dead- I say.

What we must have looked like, two ordinary people, one in a boiler suit, one in dungarees and both covered in white paint both staring into a green bin. I've seen worse win the Turner Prize. What would it be called? The Futility of Existence? Fallen Angel? Icarus? But it is an affront to my sensibilities.

-So you saw someone tampering with the bin-

 -Yes-

-But it was dark?-

-Yes-

-But definitely Sunday morning?-

-Yes. Three times yes- she said.

I feel a trap coming on, and I rub my hands together in glee, not entirely unlike a wicked Dickensian character plotting the downfall of their nemesis. I instantly stopped when I saw that Lillian didn't altogether approve of what I was thinking.

-You could just phone the council- she proposed.

-I could, yes, but they would, and I base this on previous communications with the council, do nothing-

I slammed the bin shut. I'd had enough of birds in my bin and quite frankly I'd had enough of painting.

-Do you want to do something later?- asked Lillian, still at the side of the bin.

Ah, of course, what did I want to do? I wanted to be miserable, I wanted to stew, I wanted to eat cheese and crackers but now I couldn't do that. Yes, she moved in next door. But did this mean, given her proximity, we would be doing things... together... all the time?

-Sunday night, we could watch that film you suggested but we don't have to, it's fine if you don't want to....-

Oh and now she had seen my anger, my sulking and she could see that just because she was near me it didn't mean I wanted to be with her twenty four hours a day. I took a breath. I didn't want to spoil things but I could see that she was lonely but I was just alone.

-Shall we say 7:00 o'clock?- I said.

And again, the smile is all I need. And there is that little pain in my heart again. OK, so afternoon stewing, tidying, dinner... did she want dinner? Do I have to provide dinner?

-I'm not expecting dinner but I'm certainly not going to complain if it's provided-

The cheek of it!

-Oh, it was just a few odd bits in the fridge, just thrown together, nothing really-

We were sat opposite each other at the dining table. 90% of a very agreeable Chilean Merlot laid to waste.

-What? Who has prosciutto ham, smoked chicken, fresh pasta just 'lying about' in the fridge?

-Hmm, well anyway I'm just glad you liked it-

And here's the thing, I cooked the meal I was just going to have myself but it actually felt good to cook for someone else. I don't know why but... doing something to make someone else happy... and there is that heart pain again. Most likely indigestion, eating too quickly.

I was able to look at her face. Her hair, quite possibly her real chestnut hair, off her face with clips and tricks that women use. There were still little spots of paint in her hair. She seemed to be wearing normal clothes, no costume. Perhaps Sunday was a rest day for the costumes? But the film?

-That was not what I was expecting- she said - If you said French, black and white, 1950's then I'd be expecting breathy actresses, Gauloises cigarettes, smouldering looks, suave men and then artistic crashing of the waves to pretend something else was happening.

-And Monsieur Hulot?...I ventured?

-Was genuinely touching. Just the sweetest, most innocent film with no irony, no knowingness just, so sweet- And then Lillian, to my absolute horror, started crying. Streams of silver tears running up and over her rounded cheeks, over her lips before she dabbed her eyes with one of my freshly laundered and pressed linen napkins.

-My goodness my dear, it's just a film- These little actions, the tiny incremental things we do will all have consequences. I got up out of my chair and I went around to Lillian who was now openly weeping. Goodness, perhaps we should have just seen 'Back to the Future' or Top Gun! And I didn't know what to do. I sort of put my arms on her shuddering shoulders. A sobbing woman! There's no manual for dealing with this.

I didn't know what to say.

But it appears I didn't need to say very much at all. At the very touch of my hands on her shoulders she turned to me, grabbed me around the waist and sobbed wet tears into my chest. I could feel the moisture of her tears through my shirt.

-It was *sob* just so *sob* beautiful and pure *sob*-

Well thank God it wasn't anything I'd done!

But she stood up out of her chair which then crashed to the floor.

-Oh my goodness, you're such a good, honest, real person- she said right into my face, her make up blurred.

-Erm, well....- I answered.

-Oh, don't say erm- and she grabbed hold of my face and kissed me possibly harder than I had ever been kissed before. I heard the cutlery clatter to the floor but, astonishingly I did not stoop to scoop it up. We staggered, clutching each other, backwards, nudging against the back of the sofa. Lillian clawed at my shirt, slipping her warm hands in and around my chest, through the buttons, then untucking my shirt completely. I fumbled around with what Lillian was wearing and tried to pull the jumper up and over her head. Our lips still clamped together, she was somehow fiddling around with my belt and everything was happening too fast, it was a blur but I didn't want to stop, I didn't want to stop at all.

Lillian seemed to wriggle out of her own clothes before both of us tipped over onto the sofa. The shared taste of Merlot and chicken pasta in our mouths, hands writhing around each other and I was frightened to death. I couldn't remember anything that was supposed to happen but it did appear that Lillian did and she was quite happy to straddle me on the sofa. I managed, for a brief moment, just to come up for air.

-Erm, Lillian look, I think I'm actually having some sort of heart attack-

But Lillian was oblivious and seemed in a world of our own. Who was I to get in the way of her happiness.

We lay there, still, entwined in each other's arms, on the sofa. Lillian snuggling in as much as she could, my arm around her shoulder.

-I'm sorry about that, I really am- she said, -I don't know what came over me, it must have been the wine or the food-

-Oh you're blaming me now are you, my food!-

I cuddled her in further.

-I just got a bit overwhelmed, the film, the wine, it was all just perfect. Sorry-

-Sorry? Nothing to be sorry for-

The night carried on without us.

•

-Ok so, keys- a tap on my pockets betrayed their location, wallet, money, ticket, a tap on my inside pocket, the bulge of organisation was enough to quell my nerves. -Right. I just hope he's ready-

I toddled off with my wheelie case down the road. We have plenty of time. Plenty of time.

-I can't believe he's not ready, Rochelle, really, we've got to get a taxi and then a train up to Manchester. Today-

I hadn't seen Rochelle for some time, her existence only made real by Dad's daily account of what she was wearing or not wearing, her hair, the colour of her nails or any other mythical detail that he might recall. But now, after some time, here she was.

-Look, can I 'elp it if he's just gonna stay in bed, gonna refuse 'is tablets and dat?-

Rochelle was a big girl and, I'll admit it, I was a bit frightened of her, If only for her nails, like a spectrum of scimitars, ready at an instant to slice open the bellies of anyone stupid enough to cross her. Her hands were on her hips which themselves were at an angle acute enough to communicate attitude.

Nothing was her fault.

Nothing.

Her thick black hair was beaded into cornrows showing acres of her white scalp and she was spoiling for a fight.

-Look, Rochelle, I'm sorry but it's just that today, we've got to get going. Can we just get him ready now. I know his suitcase is ready as I packed that. I just need to...-

And it was industrial, necessary and heart breaking all in one. Dad clearly didn't want to go and like a demanding toddler he had put his foot down in a tantrum. Rochelle seemed to manhandle him like a ragdoll, so impressive was her strength. I merely stood by, complicit, handing her clothes, socks, trousers and cardigans. The speed at which this was done was nigh on miraculous, especially with those nails but in the pulling on of sleeves and trousers with socks thrust onto his pale feet, his face was one of contorted pain, a passive victim in this melodrama, arms grabbed, twisted and thrust in and through material until there he sat, sunken, small, his hands on his lap like an understuffed ventriloquist's dummy, head on his chest.

There was a little bead of sweat on Rochelle's brow, the sleeves of her purple uniform rolled up, here forearm muscles twitching, crisscrossed as they were with blue tattoos.

-So, what time is you back. I'm only arxing cos I gotta let the food people know-

I was thrown by Rochelle's gear change from fearsome Street Fighter to purring pussy cat in a mere moment. -Hopefully we'll be back tomorrow night, but not to worry about food, we can get something ourselves, can't we Dad?- Trying to involve him in some decisions at least. Currently it felt like I was taking a parcel up to Manchester. He didn't answer and simply pulled at his zip on his cardigan which was already done up to the very top.

-OK OK and don't forget 'is tablets, yeah? I've left 'em all on the counter. They've got the times and that on the bottles-

-Thank you Rochelle, so much- I felt myself becoming obsequious.

-Yeah well, you have a good time man, yeah?- she said to my Dad, crouching down to speak to him, placing a hand on his knee. Dad didn't look up, still sulking. Rochelle quietly slipped out of the room.

273

I checked my watch. OK, still got time, not plenty but we can make it. I looked down at the diminished figure in the chair, a proud though child like form. I certainly felt like a parent now. Yes, we had to get somewhere in a certain amount of time and seemingly I was willing to overlook any brutality or ill-treatment to make that train. It's no good trying to be all nicey nicey after the fact, a handshake of friendship after shock and awe. This would not be any easy trip. I knelt down to look Dad in the eye, if he'd let me. We needed to go.

-Look, Dad, I'm sorry, I am, but if we want to get up to Manchester we have to get the connection at Euston which means we have to go to Fratton station soon. All the seats are reserved. We have plenty of time but we need to get going now-

Plenty of time, still plenty of time.

Without meeting my eye he eventually pushed himself up out of the chair, looked around for his stick which, when I handed it to him, snatched it off me. I left him to shuffle over to the door and grab his coat. I took his case and the bag of pills and we bundled out of the door. Off we went to Fratton in the taxi.

Once we are on the train which was actually clean and on time, I allowed myself a brief sigh of relief. We were in our correct seats, at a table. Cases stowed away and I'd almost forgotten the mercifully brief rant about too many migrants from our taxi driver whose driving style was not unlike that of Nikki Lauda. The smooth electric train pulled out of Fratton station, all painted Victorian columns crusted with bird shit looking like great candle sticks from a bygone age.

OK so, polite conversation, get the ball rolling, he can't stay miserable all the way.

-I didn't get any breakfast- was Dad's opening gambit, said whilst looking out at all the industrial units abutting the train line, great steel sheds of indeterminate use.

-Oh, well if- and I was going to say "well if you'd gotten up when you were supposed to…"- but that would not go down well so -but there were those croissants you could have had at the little shop, bacon and cheese…-

-I didn't want a croissant, not with cheese anyway, that's an abomination-

-You could have taken the cheese out…- I countered.

-What? And still pay for the cheese? Anyway you can still taste the cheese even if it's been taken out-

And still he sat, arms crossed. Havant station nearing.

-Well, I was paying for it all anyway- trying to stay calm. Long way to go.

-It's the principle though-

Sigh -Yes it is the principle- At least he's talking.

We left after rush hour but the train was still busy. Little sirens heralded the opening of the automatic doors, people bustle in and out. Huge ruck sacks attached to people. An old lady, folded onto a seat, a smart violet hat and a shiny handbag perched upon her lap, off to London no doubt. Buggies collapsed and sequestered and babies bounced on mother's knees as a distraction but mainly, mainly people staring at screens, scrolling scrolling scrolling. I peer out of the window, the sun risen but the mist still captured in valleys through the South Downs. Some deer nibble at saplings and merely look up as we pass, mere observers.

-I wanted porridge really. I normally have porridge for breakfast. Fills me up. Rochelle makes some nice porridge.

-This is the same Rochelle who crammed you into your clothes less than an hour ago, yes?-

He didn't answer. At least he was staring out of the window now. -I could have bought you some porridge at the station. They have it in small pots-

-That muck! No way, just full of additives and poison. No, give me proper porridge. Anyway I'm not eating on the train, it's not right!-

-Dad, look around, everyone eats on a train. A train is, nowadays, merely an extension of what happens on the streets or at home-

-Doesn't make it right- I mean, the buffet car yes, fine, but not at your seat!-

-Dad, did you last get on a train in the 1940's, perhaps filming 'Brief Encounter'?-

He turned away, his sulk not entirely sullen as before.

-So then, I hope you don't mind if I eat? I mean I did bring enough for you, but if you're going to be so adamant...- And I pulled out the food I'd brought with me, mini brioche, cheeses, grapes, orange juice with two sandwiches. One with cheese and one without. I ate a crisp grape as lavishly and as loudly as I could.

-I also got some newspapers, but I suppose it would be an abomination to read a newspaper on a train, hmm?-

-Hmph- was all he could say -maybe later-

So we sat there in silence until Woking station at least, me with the Telegraph, up like a main sail sheltering from the withering looks from my father. Very petty I know but I had to save some energy.

The paper was full of what papers are always full of. War, this one in Ukraine and opinion of who's right and who's wrong. Slings and arrows against the government and the general running down of the country. The sun was struggling to punch its way through the murk. Long shadows thrown across our little table. Winter was starting to take a grip, take advantage of the withering sun.

Outside, London started. Advertising hoardings, cranes, more trains at more junctions and still our train pierced through the busy suburbs. Victorian walls butted up to 21st century concrete, great slabs of grey, London encroaching, London calling, whilst the overall impression was that the sides got higher, taller and the train shrinks in comparison. I checked my watch. We were good for time.

Plenty of time.

We could get the tube. Or we could get a taxi.

Plenty of time

-You OK Dad? I looked across at Dad, drifting off a little. He kept staring out of the window but not focusing on anything in particular.

-Hmm?- He said -Oh yes, fine, just watching everything go by, all too fast for me, everyone in a car, or moving. Where are they all going?-

I wasn't sure, given the spaced out look on his face, whether he meant this literally or metaphorically. Indeed. Where are they all going?

Slowing down now and pulling into Waterloo. All those miles and then suddenly you're in London and not actually London of the suburbs but the London where you can see all those towers obscuring the view of Westminster, the big wheel, the big grey river that snakes through it all. This is what Americans call London, England in the same way they say Paris, France. I swept the food back into the bag, grabbed our cases, letting everyone else get off before I manoeuvred a very stiff father out of his seat into an upright position and out onto the platform.

There was a little nip in the air but we had made it this far. Dad had his stick and despite him moaning about how uncomfortable the chairs were, he seemed ready for a little walk. So I did my best to manhandle the cases and bags and instead of taking a taxi we used the tube. Dad's idea. He used to work in London for a time but the last time he'd been up was maybe 20 years ago. He wanted to see it all. I just wanted to get to Euston in the time we had left.

-OK so, sitting on the platform in Waterloo tube station, the train coming in 30 seconds and it is only now you are telling me that you need the toilet. So, not when I asked you less than 5 minutes ago on the train platform. Not when we were on the main concourse and I asked you if you wanted anything to eat or indeed go to the toilet, no. You chose this very moment when we are about to get onto the Tube-
-I'm sorry- he said.

And there we are. How can I get angry. He's an old man and, I realise I am shouting at an old man who merely wants to go to the toilet.

-OK. Can you hold on until we get to Euston? It's only going to be about 10 minutes-

Please hold on.

Plenty of time.

-Okay, yes, I'll wait and maybe we can get a bite to eat at Euston- he said.

And breathe, and breathe.

Plenty of time.

It's the middle of the day, why is it so busy?

The train whooshes into the station, the column of warm air pushed ahead of it like a ghostly warning, a portent. The screech of brakes and merely a heartbeat of time to get Dad in, sat down, cases and bags in before the abrupt slam of the doors and off we go. I feel a bead of sweat on my own brow now. Why didn't we take a taxi? We should have taken a taxi. Does dad look a bit peaky? Is it just the lights, the flickering lights. I can't remember the last time I saw him out of his flat. I could see his knuckles, white, grabbing onto the chair as the carriage swayed and shivered over the rails out and through the stations. The many announcements, the sudden shuddering stops. The others in the carriage, well used to the juddering journey. Headphones on, eyes burrowing into screens, avoiding all human contact.

I smiled at Dad even though he wasn't looking at me.

I wanted to reach out, just adjust his hair that was a little ruffled, out of place. I just wanted this journey to go well, to go smoothly and then we'd be fine.

Why didn't I hire a car? I could have driven. Why didn't I do that?

Euston tube station.

Again the doors urgently open. Dad struggles to get out of his chair. I get the cases and bags but hold the door with my foot. I feel the door trying to close on it as Dad makes it out and onto the platform. The train disappears and there is a slice of peace. We wait a few moments for the crowds to disperse before getting the lift up to the station.

Plenty of time. Plenty of time.

I didn't even think there was still a proper place to sit down at any terminus station anymore. What with everyone buzzing through, in and out at a hundred mph, who has time to sit down? Well, apparently, us.

We made it to Euston. We are fine. It's getting on for lunch hour but we find a table. I'm not saying it's not expensive but I'm not worrying about cost today. Dad, across the table from me, looks a little flustered. He's hooked his stick onto the edge of the table and settled in, scanning the menu.

-Well I don't want anything too big, just something light. A bit of soup maybe? A roll?-

-Really? You don't want anything else? Could do a nice steak and kidney pie on their specials board. You'd like that, or if not that what about some seafood, a salad?

-Oh no, can't have seafood anymore. Doesn't agree with me.

-Why? Arguing crabs? Debating lobsters?-

-What?- said Dad.

-Never mind- I say to myself -Okay, soup and I think I'll just have a ploughman's myself. It'll supplement what I've got in the bag-

The waiter came out with our orders and, still with one eye on the clock, we tucked in. Yes, a nice lunch, breaking up her journey up North, all very civilised. The restaurant was set up so you could look down onto the hustle and bustle of the concourse. People frantically lost, others hugging others after being apart, others just moving from A to B.

I hear my phone ping. A message, from Lillian.

-Hi H. loved last night. knocked on door this morn- no answer. U avoiding me already? L ☺ XX

I tried not to focus on the grammar and syntax of the message and thought mainly about the semantics.

This I didn't need. I still haven't got the manual through the post of how to interact with women and now she's knocking on the door. Bad enough but now she thinks I'm avoiding her. Should I have sent a text this morning? Is that what people do? Maybe flowers? No. But...

-Oh sorry Dad, how rude of me, What is it?- I say, realising I am now just flapping and completely absorbed with messages on a phone and the politics of them therein. Dad was saying something.

-I haven't got, you know, a... c.....c.....ch.... And he does a sort of mime, both his hands, a bowl, a handle, his mouth and I could see him getting more and more frustrated. Trying to get a word out. He could clearly see, in his mind, what he wanted to say but...

-Ch......ch.....ch.....sh.....sp......-

-Got it- spoon!-

-Yes- said Dad with clear relief, -bloody sssspoon. You've got your own lunch but my soup's going... You know...-

-Cold?-

-Yes. Cold. That's what I said-

I went to get a soup spoon so Dad could slurp away, and then dunk his hunk of bread in. I watched him eat.

Rochelle had told me in her 'ersatz patois' that he'd been losing words a lot more but I'd never seen it. I just assumed he couldn't get a word in edgeways with her and it was just more a case of stuttering. Maybe he had been doing it with me.... But I hadn't been listening.

I looked through the little pack of pills and worked out that Dad needed two to have with lunch, so he knocked them back with his water.

-Okay, so, toilet?- I asked, not wanting to take no for an answer.

-I don't really need...-

But I must have contorted my face somewhat as he suddenly changed his mind. Toilets in public mean steps, a turnstile to navigate and there was Dad fiddling with his buttons. I offered to help but he didn't want any fuss. The clock was ticking.

Plenty of time. Plenty of time.

But now I could see that going to the restaurant had been a bit of a trial for him. When did my father get so old? There was even a slight tremor in his left hand. I hadn't seen that before. Was Dad even aware of it himself? Seems worse now.

The train was delayed. Not overly long but it seems that this is the overarching trend of all trains. Strikes, discord, mismanagement of a private enterprise. A weary apology came over the tannoy on the train apologising for the delay but no reason was given. What had happened to this country in the last 10 or so years? People are still here, some people are so desperate to come here that they risk their lives to do so but the whole place seems moribund, so grey and soulless. Nothing seems to work properly anymore with every public institution seeming to be on its knees. From libraries to schools to healthcare. Basic fundamental services that used to be the envy of the world now just like withered fruit, all their former goodness gone, syphoned off. There are still civil wars trying to keep places running but the trend is ever downwards. There was this great world promised when I was younger, we were constantly moving towards it and yet the faster we move towards it, the further away it gets.

The paradox of progress.

And yet, staring out of the train coming out of Euston there does not appear to be any shortage of building projects. Thin, spindly cranes turning in leaden skies, huge diggers eating the earth, places populated with high vis and hard hats. A paradox.

I get the paper out again, fold once then twice until just the crossword is in front of me on our little table.

-Dad, do you want to have a look at the crossword?- I say, pushing the paper across the table with my silver Parker pen on top. Twenty or thirty years ago I would have heard, the fold of the paper, the click of the pen and it was mesmerising to see Dad just fill in the answers, just having a brief look at the clues but it took a matter of minutes to complete and then onto other things. For him, completing the cryptic crossword was a limbering up exercise for the day, a quick mental stretch before doing proper work but now....I can see him, tempted by it, the familiar black and white squares in their symmetrical grid and yet he pushes it back to me.

-No son, you fill it in....but we can do it together.- And so we do.

-OK, so, one across, "pointed remark that is ignored by Ken's partner" 4 letters-

I already have the answer in my head. -Dad?-

-Hmm?-

I read it again. Is he just not engaging or is it the fact that he can't do it and actively disengaging, saying he's tired or some other reason.

-OK Dad, right, you'll get this one. "measure the same both ways" hmm? three letters-

-Oh,er,erm....- At least it looks like he's trying.

-TOT!- I say.

-TOT? Oh, yes, measure. I didn't quite hear what you said-
he said -look, you do what you can do and any you can't do...
I'll finish off, okay? I'm just looking out at the countryside-
-OK Dad, no problem. No problem at all-
I watched him stare out of the window. Flat fields studded
with cows, electricity pylons straddling the countryside like
great colossal beings. Their sagging wires home to
murmuring birds.

It wasn't until we got to Birmingham, the cold air seeping
into the carriage that I realised Dad had nodded off. His
little puffs of shallow breath seemed relaxed. The medication
had its side effects. May cause drowsiness. Was he always
like this, dozing in the afternoons? Was the TV only on so
loud to keep him awake? Wasn't he just ebbing away?
With long, painful stops at Crewe and Preston it was dark
before we finally pulled into Manchester Piccadilly. Dad had
been dozing on and off since Crewe. I had wiped away a little
bit of spittle at the corner of his mouth. We bustled out, as
much as we could bustle into the very fresh drizzle and got a
taxi to the hotel.

•

Over a very disappointing dinner at the hotel restaurant (I had some sort of tagine with far too much apricot and rose petals and it felt like I was eating a potpourri. Dad merely picked at his roast chicken, mini roast potatoes and thin gravy).

-I prefer gravy with a bit more body, stuff you can cut into, not this... what is it, jus?! We simply ate our meals. Dad had woken up a little at least even to the extent of ordering a sticky toffee pudding but the custard, again was too thin for him.

-Cats piss!- He said, loud enough for almost everyone in the half empty restaurant to hear. I avoided a drink. I needed a clear head to cope. Actually we took the time to contemplate why we were here. The funeral of his brother.

-Will you be alright tomorrow Dad, you know, the funeral?-

I watched him move a few stodgy pieces of sponge around his bowl, desperately trying to absorb some of the anaemic custard.

-Part of life, son, I suppose. Can't say our paths crossed often but he was my older brother. Dad, my dad, said to him that he had to look after me, as I was younger I suppose. And he did-

He ate a little bit of his pudding.

-One time in the playground, there was someone roughing me up. I was only small. Well, he came over, pulled this bully off me and gave him a left hook and a black eye. He got the cane for that. And he took it. Proud to take it he was. Didn't cry. Almost made him harder. But he certainly wasn't the academic type, like me. No. He was always off, making money. Not sure all of it was strictly legal-

I laughed.

Dad continued, -but he was a kind man, your uncle, a kind-hearted man. Did you know, your mother and I's wedding....-

-....Didn't he buy you that dinner set?-

-He did, and it was awful, so garish with all the green, red and blue swirls on it. Of course, he knew it was awful and I think he gave it to us as a bit of a joke but your mother loved it so much that we used it almost everyday. But anyway, what your mother didn't realise that his real present was five thousand pounds in cash. I certainly didn't know where it came from and I'm not sure I wanted to know but that was an enormous amount of money back then. I was earning a pittance working at the university and that money paid for a lot of photography equipment for your mother and it made up a very large part of the deposit on the house-

I was agog. I knew nothing of this.

-Yes, you could say that we owe your Uncle Jim a great debt. He didn't always have money so that's when you might have seen him crash on our sofa but he bounced back, he always bounced back. But now he's gone.

Dad put his spoon down in the bowl. Not crying but certainly thinking hard. All the time he and his brother spent together as children that I couldn't possibly know about and, the sad thing is, those memories themselves are also slipping away from Dad and soon there will be no one there to remember and it will be as if none of it had happened at all.

-OK, so Dad, I suggest that if you want a shave I do it tonight, give us a bit of time tomorrow as it's an early start.

I'd not brought the whole cut throat kit but I did have the safety razor, brush and soap. Got to keep the old man ship shape.

So, in the bathroom, a mirror but far too high for dad to look at himself whilst sitting down. I wonder what happens if you are in a wheelchair in these hotels. Brush, foam, hot water but one of those annoying sinks where the plug doesn't really fit in the plug hole which I guess stops you filling up the sink and flooding the place. So, occasionally I had to use the water just to rinse the razor but the water, at least, was hot.

-So, what did Mum think of Uncle Jim?-
-Your mother? Ha! She loved him. Jim, a free spirit, never tied down and your mother could only marvel at his freedom.

You know she did a huge set of portraits with him. She went through a period of taking pictures of people and their place, well, you've seen them, pictures of cobblers hammering shoes or gardeners digging and she was trying to capture something of the person, their essence through the intensity of doing their job. Of course she tried this with Jim but Jim was a flighty soul and he didn't really belong anywhere and this is what fascinated your mother-

As Dad talked he was quite happy with my moving his foamed faced around, swiping away with the razor.

-So they went to the racecourses. There he was, brown fedora, chomping on a cigar with a race card in his hand cheering on a winner and she captured something about him but never all of him, not his essence. They went to bars, to scrapyards, boxing fights and she tried with all her might to piece him together but there was always something that she couldn't capture, something he always kept for himself. I mean they're all tremendous photographs but she never exhibited them or sold them because she wasn't satisfied with them-

- And how come this is the first time I've heard of these pictures?-

-Well, I suppose I've never really thought about it until now, or just assumed you knew, or your sister knew-

-Oh- was all I could say. I thought I knew about my life. I've been through all of Mum's pictures and I thought they were a singular thread through my life. But... pieces are missing. No, that's not right, pieces it seems were always missing but I've just found out that the pieces are missing. Is that the same? I found that I was automatically shaving Dad. I had reached mastery.

-So, where are all these photographs? I've never heard of them or seen them-

Dad said nothing.

-Do you know son, I'm a little tired. If it's all the same with you I'm going to retire early. Lovely shave though. Been a long day hasn't it, eh?-

-Yes, of course- and I took a towel and got rid of any extra foam that lingered around his face. I left him to do his teeth, take his tablets and change into his pyjamas which he wanted absolutely no help with. Stubborn old man.

-Dad- I spoke to him from the door to the room as he was just getting into bed, -I'm just going to pop down to the bar, just for a bit, finish the crossword, okay?- He murmured in the affirmative, already drifting off to sleep.

I sat up at the almost empty bar nursing a hugely expensive but hugely necessary G&T. The ice clinked as it melted. I had my phone open and I was idly scrolling through all of the photos that are in Mum's archive. Some of them were held by the Photography Museum in New York, certainly the Warhol collaborations. The more personal projects with all the large portraits and those of 'people at work' were at the V&A. There was also the privately held archive, all the negatives of which were in storage at various sites. Once one set of prints loaded up on the phone I flicked my finger and scrolled, barely looking at each image. Each image when created had been carefully considered, framed, lit and then produced. And there was me scrolling through the life's work of one person in but a moment, like sprinting through the National Gallery, centuries of work seen in a blur.

The phone struggled to keep up with my desire to see all of the pictures, everything that had been taken but there was nothing of Uncle Jim. They must be archived somewhere. It was part of my role for her estate to catalogue the prints, discuss with people who wanted to use them around the world, use them in magazines and there were these photographs that apparently existed that I had knew nothing about. Did K know anything about them?

I ping my sister a hurried message, as if the bones of those involved had an urgent need to know now. To my astonishment my sister, currently in Peru, pings back a message almost instantly.

-prints had gone. burnt in bin in garden. you must remember. negatives lost. good luck at funeral. Sorry. wont be there. K-

What? I remember Dad having fires in the garden, always burning garden waste, usually at night. K and I used to watch him out in the garden from our bedroom window. But why burn the prints?

-Ping- if you don't know why, look at all the work person photos. all of them-

If she knows something then why doesn't she come out and just tell me?

-Ping-

-What now?!-

-just knocked on door and your still not in. Everything OK? L-

It was Lillian. Was I supposed to have told her I was out? Did I have to? I texted back.

-All OK- sorry. At a funeral in Manchester- Put a kiss? No kiss? Love you? Where is that manual?

X

I don't hear back from either of them. I take my melting G&T and sit on one of the large sofas. A football match is in progress on the big screen. An overexcited commentator explains every single thing that happens and it may as well be on the radio. Absently I flick through all of the portraits in the 'work people' archive. Pictures of grimy steel workers, the blackened faces of coal miners all smiling to reveal white spidery wrinkles. Waiters tending tables. My eyeballs are tired and stinging. I've seen these photos so many times. I'm not quite sure what I'm looking....

There is a section of academics, scientists and the like. There's one of the chemist wearing large goggles but he is staring through a liquid filled round bottomed flask which completely distorts his face. A great bulging eye and contorted lips like Shirley Bassey crossed with a cod and yet she has captured the essence of the man behind the flask, the humour but the studiousness. The next photo is of a research academic, bent double over a desk which is awash with paper. Thick horn rimmed glasses perched upon his head staring intently at numbers on the scrap of paper in his hand.

It is Dad and Mum has completely captured him, an academic trying to find sense of the numbers. In just one picture she has managed to capture him. Is this what Dad didn't want to speak about, the fact that he was so easy to capture but his brother, so much more interesting, was not, which is why Mum spent so much time with him?

My sleep was restless and troubled. Had something happened?

I woke before the alarm went off, flung open the curtains upon a beautiful vista of an array of air conditioning units on top of what looked like the roof of a sports centre next door. The traffic throbbed by. The sky was slate grey and the drizzle beaded on the dirty window. I put on the TV news, see if the world had become a nicer place. It hadn't. The usual roll call of war, famine, stabbings and economics. It was only after my shower and getting dressed did I wake Dad who seemed quite at peace.

-Did you enjoy your drink last night?- asked dad, pushing the remnants of a grizzled looking old sausage around his plate. It was good to see him eat a whole plate of anything.
-It was OK- I said, deciding not to plunge straight in with questions, not when he was in such a good mood. -K sent her best, of course, sorry she couldn't come but still-
-Where is she then?-
-Peru. Not sure where in Peru but far enough away not to make a last dash to the funeral-
-Hmm-
I hack-sawed my way through an almost translucent piece of fried bread and then felt it lacerate my gums as I ate through it.
-So, come on- said Dad -something's on your mind I can tell-

Was this the moment to say something?

-Well, you know, it's just with this funeral and these photographs that I'd never even knew existed and then I find out they no longer exist, well K said that... they were burnt. In the garden-

I paused my attempt at cutting through the gristly rind of bacon. Dad took a long slurp of his black coffee, dabbed his mouth with a linen napkin and stared at the commuters trudging past the windows of the hotel dining room. There was only one other table occupied in the breakfast room, looking very much like a sales rep, a laptop open at his table no doubt in readiness for a busy day. I didn't think Dad had heard me so I went to speak again but he raised his hand slightly, to pause me.

-Huxley, beware of headstrong, flighty women. They float like butterflies at points of interest, give it their all, give everything but for them the moment then fades quickly and soon they float off again in search of interest elsewhere. It's their nature and they cannot help it. They are drawn to its call. Why on earth your mother stayed with me I shall never know but I was certainly mesmerised by her. What did she see in me, after that point of interest fades and fizzles out. Stability? A stable family as she'd never had herself?-

I'm not sure I wanted to hear any of this. Were these new revelations? Was this going to completely change the saintly perception of my mother?

I suddenly thought about Lillian, next door. She's a fluttery butterfly of a woman who has flipped life over for me like a pancake. But I felt nothing but love from Mum and then she died. Should I just stay on my own, although in comparison to now, my life was ash in the mouth. I could not go back. So I am propelled forward, uncharted waters where I have no control at the wheel. Just as frightening and impossible to contemplate. But I have to do something even if I do nothing. Do I fly to the sun, bask in the heat, risk my wax melting or do I remain a cold moon on the outskirts of space, trundling the same weary path. What is it with this 'better to have loved and lost' crap! Isn't there a middle way? Can I not forge my own path? Oh, right, that's what men do isn't it? Most men want their own cake and eat it while someone else is making the cake but not sharing the eggs that they put in one basket, to make their cake!

Oh goodness, I liked my life. I did good work! I actually helped people! I didn't sell arms to a poisonous dictator. I didn't traffic innocent people for profit but I don't know what is going to happen now and I don't like not knowing what is going to happen. And if I take a year to make a decision... it will likely be made for me by my own inertia.

I waited for Dad to continue, my knife and fork poised over my fried breakfast. But he'd stopped, either forgotten what he was saying or forgotten it all completely, file wiped.

With all the brushing up, taking tablets, finding the stick we only just got to the funeral.

A Catholic do.

The taxi pulls up and I can see that everyone has already gone in to the church. There was a different accent for the taxi driver but there was the same casual racism. We bustle in to the back of the church hoping that we'd find a seat. The door creaked open, the smell of furniture polish and wax and burning candles hits me, sends me back forty years or so being dragged to church on a Sunday morning. My finger pulling at my itchy tight collar, wet and flattened hair and polished shoes.

The church was all overly polished pews that looked ripe for sliding on and light painted saints looking benevolently down from the windows upon all these gathered here. I see at an instant that there is little concern about finding a seat. I count about ten or so souls inside the church. The door slams behind me and everyone turns around as I wince. The slam echoes around the cold interior. We walk up the aisle, dad a little unsteady on his feet today, grabbing hold of the end of each pew as he reaches them. Each alcove we pass, fenced with iron railings, held a stone carved statue. Martyred saints and horrific deaths to virginal figures in blue, eyes looking toward their beatific child. On the other side of the church a dark confessional box, curtains drawn and centuries of sins absorbed into the wood.

Each step on the dark parquet floor takes us closer to a slim pine box with brass handles lain upon two trestles. It's far enough, and Dad shuffles into the nearest pew and sits down. I pass him a hymn book from the end and an order of service. In the corner of the church, at the front, a tiny cardiganed woman with wild white hair, coughing for England. At the nod of the priest, she starts to play the introduction of the 'Lord is my Shepherd' on a wheezing old organ.

It's only at other people's funerals do you start to think about your own. Here we are at my Uncle Jim's funeral, a gregarious man by all accounts, seen and being seen with all manner of people throughout his life and yet, his funeral is sparsely attended to say the least. Does this mean, as is often proposed, that funerals, that last hurrah, is a reflection of a life lived? I heard tell recently of a friend of a friend who throughout their whole life did much for charities, worked in schools, with disabled people, your class one living saint but she died, dropped dead from a heart attack at the age of 66! Today that's no age at all. The cathedral was packed for her funeral mainly because she died whilst doing her good work, and there were plenty of people alive and willing to go to her funeral, to celebrate a good life but with her work still in the minds of many.

Here though lies Uncle Jim, closer to ninety than eighty and most people are astonished he lived so long given the speed at which he lived life. He was ill for a few years before he died and it's likely he outlived anyone who would ordinarily turn up at his funeral! And even now you still hear of people who stepped forward during the war, decorated hero and yet aged 95, stuck in the nursing home for twenty years, no family, no-one to remember them at all. Did Scrooge change his ways only to get more people to attend his own funeral as if an empty, pitiless funeral would embitter his soul? No. Funerals are there to remind the living of two things:-

1) We are all going to die

2) If you're going to do something, do it before you die.

With only ten or so mourners present I do my best to sing along to the hymn. If only for Uncle Jim. As I sing I notice there is a single red rose on top of the coffin and the rose is next to a framed photograph of about A4 size. It was, without question, Uncle Jim. In the shadow of his fedora brim, a close up of his face, the stub of a cigar champed between his jaws, his eyes wide and just the glimpse of a race card near his cheek but he had the biggest expression of joy I've ever seen on a face.

So, not all the prints were destroyed.

I saw the joy on his face and yet, yes, there was something deeper in his expression, something hidden that did not want to reveal itself. Don't you find that some people have a twinkle in their eye, something about them, usually rogues but lovable rogues. And yet, ten of us at his funeral and still the twinkle in the photograph.

The priest, a young Nigerian man, deadly serious in his role, rolling his r's with every opportunity he could and his powerful voice unnecessarily amplified and unfortunately every time he spoke into his little microphone there was a hiss and a pop and feedback from the ancient speakers high up on the columns.

A hush as the organ wheezed its last. The priest took to the lectern.

-Today we are mourning the passing of our Brrrrrrother James. I deed not know him and nor did I meet heem but here, in theeeeees communiteeee.....he was loved. He leaves behind his daughter, Penelope, who would now like to say a few words about her father, James-

302

The priest, with his crackly microphone, sat down, weary, as if he had addressed thousands. There was Cousin Penny, who I'd completely forgotten about, to my shame. A small, birdlike woman, a bit older than me and no doubt still struggling to make ends meet. She held onto the sides of the lectern for support. She slipped out a tight little ball of tissue from the cuff of her thin grey cardigan, rubbed it under her nose and then popped it back in. A practised action. She was unsure how close she should be to the microphone. She was hesitant as she spoke.

-Erm, I think the photograph says it all. That was Dad in his prime, screaming at the horses, a cigar in one hand and no doubt a pint in the other if not also a betting slip. He was always a free spirit, and free with other people's spirits, especially if they were buying...-

Dad chuckled.

-.... but he had a heart of gold. He was always the life and soul of any party and he'd always put a pound in your pocket if you needed it. He loved the horses but they didn't always love him back and so he turned his hand to all sorts of things. Driving taxis, road sweeper, scrap metal merchant to second-hand book dealer and there was always a hot dinner on the table and food in the cupboards. He was a man who lived life in the present and at full speed and... and... I shall miss him dearly- Again Penny took the damp ball of tissue from her sleeve and dabbed her eyes and then sat back down.

The priest rose slowly from his exhausted state, and took the lectern once more. It was the parable of the Prodigal Son. Penny had chosen it for the funeral I imagine and I watched her, sitting up at the front pew listening to each powerful, resonant word. I assumed she was a regular at the church, the way she instinctively knew when to sit, when to stand and when to kneel without being given a big steer by the priest. But the Prodigal Son? I've never understood it. I mean I know it, I know the story but why is it a parable? A lesson about what exactly, I don't know?

A father has a farm and the younger son, not wanting to wait for his father to die for his inheritance asks him for money. So, the father divides his wealth between the two sons. So, my first question is what does the father do for money now? What if he gets ill? Does he have a pension? How does he cope? What does his wife say about all of this? Does she have a say? Anyway, the younger brother, impetuous soul that he is, takes the money and leaves and essentially over a period of time, pisses it all up the wall, arguably because the father, despite having given him money hadn't educated his son with how to look after the money. So the younger brother is now destitute and has to take on degrading jobs and only then does he think, -hang on a mo, here's me grafting away while even the servants at my father's house are eating better than me and I'm the son!- So here he comes, skulking back home, and his father is straight out there, big hugs, fatted calf and all of that and if I was the older brother I would be mightily pissed off. And he is, and the father just says that he, the older brother has benefited from being at the farm all this time. Well, if I was the older brother I would have wanted to go and have a great time as well, pissing away the money and today it would all be about travelling around the world, backpacking, something monstrously middle class which helps no one apart from create more work for Outback police in Australia given all the people that go missing, to know I was coming back after spending the money, and have a job. I thought that the point of religion was to follow the rules, to not stray from the path. Honour thy mother and father which is what the older brother did and because he did that he's missed out on an opportunity to piss away a load of money! And as the older brother and father, having less money, are they expected to work harder because half of the money the father has earned has been pissed away? But the older brother has followed the rules, doing what he was told to do because he respected the fact that the person telling him what to do might be wiser, have more insight. I know it's supposed to show a merciful God, a God that will forgive wrongdoing as long as they come back. But here, now, I see the small frame of Penny, only child of the profligate Jim who had a twinkle in his eye, a life of Riley and always down the boozer or the betting shop. There might have been a hot meal on the table but perhaps there could have been more had most of it not gone into the pension funds of the landlord at the Dog and Duck and the shareholders at Ladbrokes.

Penny, her threadbare cardigan, her hair white at the roots no doubt from scrimping and saving. That's what happens when the Prodigal Son returns. The memories of the fatted calf a long time distant. Was my dad the 'older brother'? He went to school, did as he was told. But then, we all end up in a wooden box whichever path we take.

There is incense.
There is holy water, ritual upon ritual.
The coffin is carried out to a nearby freshly dug hole.

We shared a car with Penny who, despite all the friends of Jim, is on her own. We hug awkwardly. Not a deep hug. I've not seen her for maybe thirty years and yet I know her and she knows me. She hugs my dad, a more heartfelt hug.
Uncle George.
And we sit in silence in the car.

The low thrum of the car's engine moving steadily, impossibly slowly. There is no hurry. The priest walks ahead and we are there.

I am astonished at the view. On the outskirts of Manchester, on a hill. I look across, a valley with an old mill, a relic from an industrial age, and beyond, the moors full of patchwork browns, greens, purples and secrets. Back in time to a time before everything.

The sky still slate grey and there is now a bitter wind. I see patches of blue over the moors with low cloud scraping across them. Little pinpricks of rain fall upon the soft ground around us.

The hole before me is fresh, the soil is a rich ochre mash like milk chocolate ice cream. I didn't look right into the bottom for fear of falling in. The sides, the spoil, are covered with bright rectangles of artificial grass, and it is on this we stand. The priest at one end of the hole says a few words, the inevitable ashes to ashes, but a hole in the ground is certainly a more visceral reminder of your own mortality then merely thinking about your aches and pains. Cold, in a box, in the ground.

I stare around at the gravestones. Some black speckled slabs of granite, gold lettering of 'loved by' or 'greatly missed' from five, ten, fifteen years ago and where people would have been standing nearby watching other boxes lowered into their own holes. But off to another side and the headstones, not polished granite at all, chiselled into the hard stone are copperplate names eroded by time, beautiful blooms of lichen etched into the stone. Eighteen forties, seventeen nineties and families long gone would have wept at a graveside for those lowered into the ground.

We are all, at some time, the mourner and the mourned.

Crumbs of soil scatter on the lid of the coffin as it is lowered down. Penny's birdlike shoulders shake and it is Dad who leans in and hugs her and she wails loudly into his comfortable chest. There is no beam of light that appears through the cloud, no twittering robin that often people can take solace from and say 'ooh look, that beam of sun or the robin that's just appeared. It must be his spirit'. The clouds, holding back for so long have decided that enough is enough. Under hastily erected umbrellas everyone scattered like woodlice in light, just Dad and I left at the graveside. Penny thanked us for coming but she'd only been given the morning off from her work and had to get back. But at least we had made it to Jim's funeral.

Dad was clearly pondering some great thought, as I held the umbrella over his head. The rain splashed down onto the coffin lid. Perhaps he was thinking of the past, reminiscing about his brother and the times they had got on, the times they hadn't or perhaps when one gets to a certain age you attend more funerals than weddings and with each funeral attended it is one closer to your own.

-You'll look after me, won't you lad?- He said, still staring down into the hole.

-Course I'll look after you, I am looking after you now if you hadn't noticed- I said, pretending not to know what he was really talking about. I was hoping he'd leave it at that, some vague comment and we could go back to living our lives.

-You know what I mean. I'm lonely. I don't want to be on my own...-

-But you're not on your own are you? You've got all those people who live in your block and...- but he cut me off.

-You know what I mean. I don't want to die on my own. Okay?! There, I said it. It's a very selfish request I know but I don't want to die on my own. Some of those old codgers at the block, well you get to know them one week and then they're either dead the next week or gone gaga. Such a high turnover there it's hardly worth getting to know anyone. And I have to admit, staring down into this hole, does rather focus one's mind-

-Selfish?-

-Well, you've got your life haven't you, you do your work but also you might have put your life on pause to look after me and, I'm sorry about that. I am-

This was becoming a bit more emotional than I was prepared for.

-Dad, it's fine, it really is-

-And yet you've never married? Have you just put your life on hold?-

-No! Not at all-

How was it that this old man could read me like a book? I shifted my feet a little, the rain was coming in and, as emotional and heartfelt as this was, we were both getting soaked. The weather has no respect for feelings. We shuffled back to a covered bit of the church and sat down on a bench. It was dry at least but the rain tried hard to get to our feet. The wind and rain conspiring together.

We watched together as a grave digger, in a high vis waterproof, folded up the artificial grass and then with a mini digger started to fill the earth back into the hole. Initially I thought it was disrespectful, using a machine to fill the hole but then I wasn't the one out there filling in the hole in the rain. The dead themselves were surely not going to complain and all that is left is a filled hole.

The rain let up a little and we walked along the road a bit. There was a café, all steamed windows with the word 'café' in big red letters on the window. We went in and grabbed a table for two in the corner.

If I wasn't in the middle of some morose situation with my father I would cheerfully have taken some pictures of the café. We are in a café that no longer exists. Except it does. Dad seemed non-plussed with it all because he probably hadn't been in a café for twenty years but assumes they are all still like this. The place is filled with square tables, all duck egg blue chipped Formica. Each table has either two or four proper kitchen chairs with real cracked red leather pads on the seats. There is a counter, behind which squats a bubbling still of water, its lid clattering like a shivering cymbal. A brief menu board on the wall, spelt out in little plastic white letters on a black pin board. Just coffee. No espresso or latte or flat soya macchiato, just coffee, no doubt in white mugs, instant, with milk.

And tea.

I sat Dad down and ordered two teas and two bacon sandwiches. I was not even offered the option of no milk with the tea. The man behind the counter was actually wearing a vest under his apron and he appeared to be a permanent feature of the café. The lady, just as old, takes my order with a smile and says they will be over in a minute. On the walls were posters of George Best and Denis Law and I'm guessing by the dust and its thickness that the posters have been on the wall since Dennis and George were playing. I come back to my seat not sure if the café is a relic of the past, a living fossil or it is a post modern recreation of an old café. The ancient crust on the nozzle of the tomato shaped ketchup bottle gives me my answer. No one could recreate such details. This was the real deal.

It was the first time I had thought about Lillian for some time, the fact that she would love this place but like me, in an ironic way. I stop myself taking out my phone and concentrate on Dad and put the ketchup bottle down.

-Look, son, I think I just need to tell you…-

-Dad, come on, you're fine. You've got your tablets now. I'll be there for you. Don't worry. I'll look after you whatever-

But he reaches across, places his hand on mine, first patting it and then clasping it hard, not wanting to let go. His grip is strong and tight as if when he lets go he'll fall. I put my other hand on his but I do see the back of his hand is bruised. Why do I not notice these things before.

-Dad, why is your hand bruised? If it was that Rochelle I swear…-

-No no no no, he said, no, it's from the doctors, puncturing me with pins and needles, trying to get blood from me and replacing it with I don't know what-

I was worried now. What was he talking about?

Look, son, they've done some tests, found some cells and I had a scan at the hospital.

-Scans?! When did you have all that done?-

-Son, I'm a big boy….. I can get a taxi myself-

I found myself grabbing his hand now. I felt the hairs on the back of his hand, his soft clipped nails and the rough little patches of skin on his knuckles and his gold wedding ring, now rattling loose on his finger. I absently twisted it around and around.

-Anyway, it seems that I am riddled with this thing and they said "oh we can do this or that, zap it with something or other"-

I suddenly found a hard lump in my throat and I was finding it difficult to speak if I had indeed anything to say. I looked at Dad but he had started to go in and out of focus through the water in my eyes.

-But, Christ- he continued -all that effort and for what, a few extra months in pain. No thanks. Your Mum had the right idea after all.

The old lady came along with two mugs of very milky 'builder's' tea. My Dad thanked her as I couldn't speak. I was holding on to Dad as I wanted to hold on to him forever and never let go. I finally spat out some words.

-But why didn't you tell me? I have a right to know-

-Do you? Do you have a right? If I'd have told you, what would you have done? Gone to the hospital? Demand I be treated? Chemo? Radiotherapy? And for what? So you can look after me, keep your life on hold and I can go on just marking time? No. I'm being selfish but it's my life and I don't want it to end in a forest of tubes, clinging on to some pitiful existence as if clinging onto a life raft. I've seen too much of that in that block. Those old dears shuffling around with their drips, like zombies. Anyway, far too late now, riddled with the thing. It's in my bones and that's that-

I let go of his hand. I didn't know what to say. He had kept all of this from me. He didn't trust me and he'd dealt with all of this on his own, and so I wasn't really there for him at all. Our bacon sandwiches arrived, stodgy thick white bread and greasy bacon inside. Dad surgically opened his up straight away and gleefully tranfused in the ketchup. I'd lost my appetite.

The train journey back was mercifully uneventful. We splashed out on a taxi across London. Dad slept most of the way. I couldn't help looking at him as he slept on the hard train seats, his skin was thin, almost waxy. His hair, although combed was also long and straggly. Did I not see that he was ill or did I just choose not to see? We got back to Portsmouth on time. Nothing had changed. I made him a light supper, put his clothes in the wash and trundled home with my wheelie case. I sat in the front room, opened up a bottle of wine and wept.

There was a knock at the door.

I turned off the light.

There were no more knocks.

I knew I had an assessment this afternoon and so, despite my throbbing headache and jumbled thoughts I gathered myself to go out to work. There was a letter on the mat. It was still morning so it couldn't have been delivered by Royal Mail.

-Dear Henry, I fear I might be intruding on something and being in the way. I understand if you want some space. If you want me to leave then do let me know. I'm picking up all the wrong signals. L-

There was o-x-o drawn in bright red lipstick.

I folded up the letter and placed it in my pocket before leaving the house. There was the nasty weasley neighbour passing by. I didn't have the energy to deal with him. I didn't have the energy to deal with very much at all.

Fortunately my assessment was only a few streets away so I decided to walk just to clear my head. Around the pond the crows still skulked in the bare branches, ruffing up their murderous feathers. The dog walkers made their orbits around the calm waters, little stumbly old dogs in harnesses. The old homeless man sitting on the bench, blowing into hands, keeping warm, his ever present plastic bags by his feet. He waved out. I waved back.

I walked on.

I recognised the man immediately. Clive. A very talented carpenter that I had helped some years ago with his reading. Bless him, he had simply wanted to read his young son a bedtime story despite not being able to read a word himself.

He invited me into his cosy little house on Ebery Grove. Almost everything in the house was made of wood. It was like being inside a tree! There was a beautiful occasional table in the space under the stairs. All types of coloured woods, mahogany, oak, chestnuts and elms all in squares inlaid into its top. In his front room which was sparsely furnished there was a beautiful set of drawers, polished yellow oak with orange sunbursts and I can only assume he made the chairs as well. They're either fifties Ercol or very very good copies. This man who had magic in his fingers to create beautiful pieces of furniture out of almost any piece of wood can barely function in this so-called modern world.

He invited me into the back room, having cleared the most beautiful thick chunky dining table of paperwork and I was able to place all of my testing materials onto it. I almost didn't want to as the table looked as if it should be in a showroom. We chatted about what a coincidence it was and how things had been going for him since the last time we spoke. He told me about all the things he had made both big and small and as he did his eyes twinkled, his fingers twiddling with the need to move a saw and plane and yet when I talked to him about reading and words and writing, his head was downcast and his twinkle dimmed.

I knew that his wife had had to do all of his invoicing and paperwork, to send and proofread his emails. You see, two or three hundred years ago this man, Clive, would have been considered a master craftsman and he could have got on well in society with very little worry. Now? In such a word-based world where there is no choice for him apart from exams and more exams, Clive is still a master craftsman but he hardly feels valued because of his dyslexia. Anyway, now, because he has to take part in a course he needs help with his reading and writing. And in order to get that help he has to prove he has dyslexia and so that's where I come in. He is one of the most open and shut cases of dyslexia I have ever seen but still I have to test him. As he manfully battles through all the tests I give him I find myself still distracted.

I felt the letter in my pocket. I had failed, fallen at the first. She wouldn't want me, abject failure that I am. Can't deal with life and can't deal with death. In fact Dad seems more happy with life than I am. It just seems these past weeks had been a change. I don't like change. But then who chooses change when it is usually thrust upon you? I finish up with Clive, pack up my stuff but then we get to talking about his work.

-I'm lucky really- he said -I just sort of fell into it. I suppose it was because of my dyslexia, failed everything at school and couldn't wait to leave. A friend was doing carpentry and hating it and wondered if I'd like to do it. I never looked back. You've just got to find what makes you happy, you know. We're all a long time dead-

I pondered on what he said as he looked at the little pile of wood he'd set up in the corner of the room. Where I just saw a pile of wood he saw a marquetry top for a coffee table that he was about to start.

-I'd love to buy one of your tables. In fact I do probably need a bookcase of some sort-

I clearly didn't need one but everything he made was just so beautiful, so tactile that I could see why collectors became so obsessed by collecting. We all have our little obsessions.

-Oh yes?-

-I had a bit of building done, actually the house next door, but it could do with some very nice furniture.

-Oh right, building work you say? Here, you might like this, my chippy mate told me this builder around Portsmouth, making a fortune he is. He's doing the work but also he's using the space to make porn movies on the side!-

-You're joking!- I said -My goodness, some people are so gullible!-

-Straight up, if you pardon the pun look, there- and Clive whips his phone out.

-You're a broad minded gent. Wait one second...- as Clive stabs at the screen... -I mean you get to see all of the work he's done and it's all good work but...... -and suddenly I find myself in his hall watching a porn video on his phone.

-There, look, lovely bathroom. He's come in, boiler suit, she's there just coming out of the shower... lovely looking girl and... well... there we are. I mean you can see the bath can take the weight of both of them and look, lovely black and white tiles, beautiful shower head... mind you she's not using it there in a conventional manner. And if I scroll forward, lovely sink and, again, really takes the weight! Lovely splashback.

I felt quite sick.

-Right, yes, lovely...... but not really my thing Clive, sorry-

-Right oh, sorry- and Clive switched his phone off.

I managed to scramble a few words out, a good-bye and I left Clive at his door and after he closed the door and I was outside in the fresh air I really thought I was going to be sick.

Women plumbers? Unions he said! But she was wearing plastic high heels and makeup.

I am an idiot.

I bent over, hands on my knees, just catching my breath. As I look down though, directly in front of my puffing, blowing face, was a round red circle drawn in chalk. I managed to stand up straight. I turned left, towards the pond and maybe ten yards away there was another red circle, same size, in chalk. And so I walked along following the circles and when I got to the next one, ten yards further on another big red circle about the size of a saucer. A woman passed the circle with her dog. But she didn't see it. The dog did though and she had to pull his lead to come away from it. Then there was another and then another. Now I was at the end of the road. For just a moment I thought they'd stopped but after a car passed by, I saw there was another one on the other side of the road. Then, turning towards the pond, there was one fifty yards away. What was going on? Why is no one else noticing these red circles? Why am I following them, and yet I am. Despite the two cases I was carrying, and a heavy laptop in one of them, still I trundled along, following the dots. They went all the way down the road right up to the pond. The dots, closer together now, went down the ramp down to the pond, now ten yards apart before they got much closer together right up to the bench underneath the lamp post next to the weeping willow. On the bench there was a woman but she was dressed up as a small girl. A particular girl. I put my cases down in front of her.

So, light brown hair in a bob, a tight mustard roll neck jumper, pleated red knee-length skirt, mustard knee-high socks and Mary Jane shoes with red straps and thick square glasses.

She was provocatively licking at an ice cream, wrapping her tongue around it to avoid any drips. She said nothing but continued to swing her dangling leg, one crossed over the other.

-Okay Velma... Velma Dinkley... You got my attention-

She stopped licking her ice cream.

-Jinkies! You are good! You followed the dots. So that's all I need to do in the future!-

-Well no-one else even looked at them. And anyway, it's winter. Where do you get an ice cream from in winter?

She pointed at the direction of the house. -Ice cream van. I'd be quick if you want one-

-Just a '99' please- I say, rooting about for change in my pocket and finding that I hadn't got any.

-Hey- said Alice, -Lillian's already paid for it-

-Really?- I asked.

-Yes, really- and she handed me my ice cream speared with a flake. I notice the tall girl was wearing long stripy black and white stockings poking out from under her white overalls.

-I'm Alice by the way, a friend of Lillian- and she offered an enthusiastic hand, which I shook.

-You know- said Alice -Lillian is quite 'out there', some might say bonkers but she's been hurt many times. She's a real keeper. But if you mess her about...- and she reached across and pressed the little button which played the theme from 'The Godfather' in twinkly little bells.

-Well, a threat from an ice cream van. How can I refuse such a generous offer-

Alice smiled, and picked up from where she left off reading the enormous 'Infinite Jest'.

-Do you know everyone?- I asked, coming back to sit next to Velma.

-Not everyone but a few- said Lillian.

I licked my ice cream.

-I got your letter by the way. I'm sorry-

-Don't apologise- she said -Don't ever apologise-

-OK but, I was going to say I've been busy but I haven't really. In all honesty I'm a little scared-

-Scared? I knew it. I can be too much for people can't I? It's my problem, trying too hard to please-

-No no no, it's not that at all, it's just, well, change I suppose. Ironic that I didn't have any. I had this image of just going along, doing what I do, forever. But I met you which is lovely but you've kind of thrown me. I thought all of that time for romance was long gone. My Dad, who I thought I'd be looking after.... he's dying and who I was just a few weeks ago is not me today and for someone who doesn't like change, that's a lot of change. Although none in my pocket-

The ageing engine in the ice cream van fired up. A tinkling song played and it took a while to place it.

-Lily the Pink- said Lillian. -She always plays it if she's near my house-

I smiled.

We sat in silence for a moment, hearing the tune disappear down the road.

-I'm sorry about your Dad- she said.

-Thank you- I realised that Lillian was the first person I'd told. -So what was with the red dots?-

-You said you were a person who notices things. I just wanted to check-

-I see. Is this some sort of test?-

-Might be...- she said as she crunched the last of her cone. We both watched one of the big geese jump into the water from the bank with a resounding splash.

-So then- she ventured, looking at the goose sailing away, -what about us?-

-Us? As in...-

-As in you and me. Two pronouns become one pronoun but a collective pronoun. I need to be defined.

-Oh...Us. Isn't this a bit "Sex in the City" a bit "boyfriend and girlfriend in the playground" and I thought modern women didn't want to be defined by titles. I'm too old for all of that malarkey-

-OK. No us-

-I didn't say no. I just meant, perhaps we're attaching too much energy, too much symbolism. Maybe... and don't blow me out of the water here...we could pretend to get married. Not actually get married but try it on....like a costume. Hmm? See how it fits? I must have done something right if you're willing to draw red dots on the pavement and organise an ice cream van-

-Really? Henry? You mean it? Actually pretend marriage. Oh Henry, I could kiss you!-

-You don't have to pretend with that-

And Velma kissed me, grabbing my cheeks far too hard and smearing my ice cream onto my face.

-We could be like… I said-

-Sid and Nancy?…-

-Ended badly, no.

-Kurt and Courtney?- She said.

-Definitely not, ended very badly. No….

….Burton and Taylor? I said - Too tempestuous for you?-

-Yeah, but just think of the costumes- she said- but not the diamonds? Anyway, what about Lillian and Huxley?

-Who's Huxley?- she asked.

I smiled in response.

-You're Huxley? Not Henry?-

-Huxley means everyone asks questions. No one asks Henry anything-

-Hmm. Huxley Green. Huxley Green- She kept saying my name with different cadences, different stresses, different accents. -So why the change?- she asked, butterflying around the thoughts in her head.

-Erm… no not erm… it's just, life is passing me by. I know life is all these big moments that people inflate to gigantic proportions and yet life is also emptying the dishwasher, cooking beans, returning books to the library. I think, I really do think, that I was passing all of these mundane little episodes, just getting past them as quickly as possible to get to… to get to what I did not know. I still don't know but at least if I'm aware of what is passing by then maybe, just maybe I should start enjoying those little fragments of life that sew everything else together. It might be nice to share these moments with someone else!-

-And you might wear just a tiny bit of colour? A badge, a tie that isn't black? A coloured sock?-

-Whoa there, steady, one monochrome step at a time!-

Velma snuggled up next to me on the bench as I crunched down on the end of my own cone. A duck quacked on the island in the middle of the pond.

-Can we visit your Dad? Would that be OK?-

I hesitated. This is exactly what Dad had meant. Had I been holding back my own life? Had I now been released to live my own life?

-Yes, yes of course- I said, beaming.

-Great. I'll probably get changed out of this, have a quick shower....

-Oh, yes, about that- having a quick and nausea inducing flashback -I might just come in and give it an industrial scrub down-

-But it's all clean, it's brand new!- Lillian protested.

-Just let me do it. I'd feel better-

●

Next Sunday morning, early early.

Well before the dawn we were ready. A whole week of gleeful planning had gone into our ruse. All we had to do now was wait. A digital camera was recording. The scene was set. And there they were, footsteps, normal footsteps down the pavement. Nothing sneaky, no tiptoes or else that would have suggested furtiveness and nefarious activities. No, just normal clicky footsteps. The footsteps stopped directly outside the wall of my front garden. He looked left and right, surely a sign of guilt. There was no one else about. But someone was watching. Under his arm he was carrying something large but light, wrapped loosely in a newspaper. He reached over to my green bin, a little noise of straining as he reached for the lid. This swift action had seen him deposit a number of seagulls into my bin.

Not this time.

The moment he opened the bin, the lid sprung open and flipped right over with a crash. He lurched backwards in terror falling onto the car behind him on the street, setting off the car alarm. His eyes were still transfixed at what had exploded out of the bin.

-Hello there!- shouted Lillian, red dots on her cheeks on a powdered white face, a fool's cap with bells jangling on her head. -I am a Jack-in-the-Box! I'm here to stop naughty boys putting naughty things in other people's bins!-

By now, with Lillian shouting as a fully springing Jack-in-the-Box, all the surrounding neighbours (pre planned, who knew they were such nice people and had also had stuff put in their bins) had pulled apart their curtains, leaned out of their windows shouting "shame shame Boo!" Like a scalded cat, the very weasely man with his crooked nose and bitter heart who lived amongst us, scrambled to his feet. Another dead seagull slithered out of the newspaper onto the floor and in a cloud of embarrassment and expletives he ran off towards the darkness of the pond.

Lillian switched her phone off but not before posting the episode onto some corner of the internet. There was a light smattering of applause from the neighbours' bedrooms when she gracefully took her bow, still in character, pretending she was on a spring. As I watched through the darkness of my front room I found a little tear forming in my eye and the little pain in my heart was back. Perhaps instead of early angina it was a feeling that my neighbours were kind and caring people, perhaps it was the feeling of humiliating that weasley man, finally, or perhaps it was looking at Lillian, still wobbling about in my recycling bin at five am dressed as a Jack-in-the-Box and knowing she did that for me. Perhaps, just perhaps, it was love.

•

Time wore on, as it often does. Walls were painted all sorts of colours. Carpets were fitted and a forest of plants grew and grew and grew. I didn't see any reason to advertise for another tenant as Lillian or whoever she was seemed to be just about perfect. I did receive a pair of red socks which I wore and this did not seem the end of the world. I would be in the market for another pair of red socks which I might wear, occasionally.

•

The curtains were partly drawn and what little light there was in the day was fast disappearing. I sat on the edge of his bed, looking around the sparsely furnished room. The one wardrobe with all of his now oversized clothes. The chest of drawers, especially the top drawer that held most of his personal effects, photographs, memories; his whole life in one drawer, sat squat against the wall. The slanting light hitting the glossy surface, the sturdy turned handles, the smoky patterns in the polished wood.

On the bedside table a small squat brass lamp, with a functional lampshade, was on. The sharp white light illuminated the crisp white covers of the sheets, his crumpled pillow and his thin paper face. His blue eyes recently sunken, his cheeks hollows; shallow dips in a landscape, made more dramatic by the angle of the light. The dull thrum of traffic outside in the distance, audible now the TV was off. He was half sat up on three slumped pillows, tightly tucked in under the sheets, in his pyjamas. His breathing, at times, was like rustling paper, the rise and fall of his chest barely perceptible.

Next to the lamp, next to the plastic bottles and tubes of various drugs, some of which were set out ready to take at regimented times, next to the half glass of water, was an ornate silver picture frame. A photograph. Black and white, the face of an impossibly beautiful woman with two small children. The boy a little older than the girl, beaming as much as the woman. One of the very few photographs that my father had taken.

-You OK son? You doing alright?- he said, a barely audible whisper.

-Yeah, I'm fine Dad, just fine- I just managed to say through the lump in my throat.

He raises up a trembling hand just a little.

-What, what is it, water? tablet? Dad?-

But his hand reached up to stroke the fine white hairs that have grown on his face these last few days.

-Could do with a shave, eh son? Never know who I'm going to see. Always got to look your best!-

-I smiled.

-I'll get the stuff. We'll do it here okay?-

And with a strain of effort Dad's face broke into a smile by way of an answer.

I know what he's doing. Even in the state he's in, he's trying to put me at ease. It's men, isn't it. Women, I've seen it. All quite happy with small talk, chit chat, quite happy in each other's company for hours. Men? Ha! Can't sit and chat for five minutes without the awkward silences creeping in so they have to do things, play cards, dig allotments or watch the football. This is how they love.

I bring in a bowl of hot water and place it carefully on the chest of drawers. I lift up Dad, just a little, shocked at how light he has become, all hollowed out. He winces and grimaces and then relaxes into his pillows, propped up as much as I can. He closes his eyes and now taking care around his fragile skin, I wash him over with a damp flannel, around his face, under his chin, around his soft ears until I see the pinking of the skin, the blood rushing to the surface. I brushed the soap gently onto his fine white bristles, the skin moving as I did so, until a thin layer of creamy sandalwood soap remained. I could see his nostrils just flare slightly, breathing in the exotic fragrance.

I opened the blade.

I took my time because his skin seemed so fragile that I was afraid if I stretched it or pulled it or forced it then it would snap or tear. I pulled the blade from the tip of his Adam's apple to the point of his chin in one long gentle stroke. I took my time as I was unsure of when it would be the last time I would do this. I wanted to do it well. I wanted to remember.

Friends who have children always tell me about firsts and how firsts are celebrated. First tooth, first riding a bike without stabilisers, first kiss… but when do you read the last bedtime story, when do you put the bike away… when is the last kiss.

His eyes are closed but he is smiling. I pulled the blade, I feel his face move and twist to allow the skin to tighten instinctively. I hear the shearing of the blade, slicing the hairs. He pulls his top lip over his teeth. He anticipates the blade. One, two, three sweeps and I'm done. I wipe the blade on the towel. I rinse off his face with a towel and put a few dabs of moisturising cream onto his skin, wipe the little bits of sleepy dust out of the corner of his eyes as he comes back to me.

I closed the blade with a click and place it back on top of the drawers. He puts his trembling hand up to his face, his frail digits stroke the soft skin.

-That's a good job son, a good job-

I go to pick everything up, pour away the water but he whispers to me.

-Just come and sit on the bed a while. All that can wait-

He pats lightly on the bed and I sit up next to him. He closes his eyes and smiles. I look down at his face, trace my fingers over his hair, stroking it, curling it behind his ear. The light through the curtain almost gone as the night swallows the day.

All that can wait.

Printed in Great Britain
by Amazon

23339351R00189